the alpha centauri symbolism

by
John C. Wilson

WHITMORE PUBLISHING CO. • *Ardmore, Pennsylvania*

To all of those people in the world today who are suffering from Multiple Sclerosis who can and do think. And to Marilyn S. Wilson, John C. Wilson, Jr., and Connie Tschilds.

Contents

Prologue

ONE MUST BE ABLE to discern between the real and the unreal, between the plausible and the implausible, all things relative and those things impossible. Such is our lot, and we wonder about this. Science has made such advances, and yet the average individual is still plodding, still scratching to make ends meet and to hold himself away from the creditors who loom ever more pressingly at his doorstep. In this story the impossible becomes the probable. The time, as we know it, is today.

1

The Realization————————————————

BILL ANDERSON WAS A man who had devoted himself to his wife and child. Some five years ago he had contracted multiple sclerosis, and with that his dreams had toppled as a parent, husband, and vice-president of a rather successful business. His education was terminated with his completion of graduate work in Arizona, giving him two degrees and three languages. The only thing that MS had left him was a highly deductive mind; the rest of him was physically shot. His speech, walking, and general coordination were shot down the tubes. He became a ward of the state, which he appreciated, but it was not exactly what he had in mind. So, at the age of thirty-eight years, he had been kicked out of his business, his home, and had been divorced. All of his so-called friends had all but completely shunned him. He was a man alone, and he felt that he would be alone for the rest of his life. Money and the making of it through the only thing that was left open to him now became his prime concern.

What about Bill Anderson the man? He stood 5'10", weighed 155 lbs., was broad shouldered, had black hair, and could pass for thirty-four years of age. The business that he had been in was the electronics field. He had studied electronics since he was fourteen years old. He could read schematics like other people read road maps. The degrees that he had gotten were in languages and international commerce. He had a presence about him that seemed to command respect. With the mustache he had grown, he was considered rather handsome. He had many opportunities to command,

and the results had always been good. It was because of this that the company was also assigned to sell weather. Bill had gotten to know weather just as he knew the electronics field. If there was one thing that could be said of this individual, it was that he had an unswerving sense of what was right. Sometimes he appeared very dogmatic, and for that he was criticized.

Anderson liked to read extensively. Certainly he kept up with the daily business and political news, but what interested him most were the Mayan, Inca, Aztec, Egyptian, and Sumerian cultures. Also, he had a great interest in the galaxies and their movements, stars, quasars, and black holes.

Bill Anderson had been reduced to wearing glasses and using a cane to get around. But he also maintained an inner faith that this would be compensated for. He had been very athletic, and this illness had almost killed him. Three things that he had left were an excellant personality, extensive education, and a good upbringing.

In addition, he had become a guinea pig for all of the new drugs that had come out on the market as cure-alls for his illness. Nothing seemed to have the desired effect, and the researchers had just diagnosed the illness as a virus, but they were not sure as to what kind of virus it was. He had a lot to be thankful for, in that there was no pain associated with it. Also, he was thankful for the fact that the illness wasn't any more critical than it was. He would live and die with MS, but the prognosis had not been determined. For all practical purposes he would lead a normal life span. But he no longer had any ties. This began to interest him very much, because being a person with no ties might also work to his benefit.

In his estimation, his life had been a full one. He would have no complaints if he were to die at that very moment. Something told him that his life was far from over. He pondered for a while what he might do for society. There must be something he could do. One day while still pondering this very question, he came up with a solution. At the time, it didn't have anything complex associated with it. He would write to NASA, submit an application, and see what happened. He thought that he might be helpful, and this seemed to prove helpful to his whole outlook.

In the meantime, Col. Joseph Jafferies had received Bill Anderson's application and looked at it with a great deal of interest. This was something that he had been waiting for for some time. It could be a hoax though. He would have to check this person out with a fine-tooth comb. So he immediately had a surface check made on this fellow. He had people go to Anderson's undergraduate school as well as his graduate school, his high school, his past and present neighbors, his creditors, his last place of employment, his banks, and finally to his former wife. What had to be closely evaluated was his stint in the armed services.

Joseph Jafferies was a graduate of Kent State University. He was a quiet individual. He stood about 6' and weighed 180 lbs. He had gone through the astronaut program and had gone up into space three times. He was now very well suited for his job because of his thoroughness. If there was one thing that he wanted to do, it was to get back into space again. The application he had received from Bill Anderson might allow him to do this.

After Jafferies had gotten back the results on Bill Anderson, he took the voluminous package to Col. George Collins, who read and reread the information contained therein.

Two months had passed since the investigation had first started. Finally Collins directed Brig. Gen. Alvin Dodd to interview this individual thoroughly to find out how suitable he was for the project at hand.

Col. George Collins was a graduate of UCLA and had also been in the space program. He had played football for UCLA for three years as a tackle. In his fourth year he had to quit because of a knee injury. During his years at NASA he was enjoying a good job in the space program, then his bad knee came back to haunt him at high altitudes. He was canceled out of the space program and became an aide to Gen. Dodd. He was gregarious and liked talking to people.

One Monday evening, about 8:00 P.M., there was a knock at Bill Anderson's door. Brig. Gen. Alvin Dodd walked in. He watched the way Bill walked with his cane. Then he sat down and started asking Anderson some fairly direct questions.

Brig. Gen. Alvin Dodd was about 6'2". He was as broad as he was tall and must have weighed about 250 lbs. Dodd was a

3

graduate of Ohio State University, where he majored in political science and played four years of football as a tackle. He was very likable and knew the ins and outs of the American political structure.

Dodd took out a bulbous packet of papers from his pocket. He then laid the papers on the coffee table. He had already read them and was quite knowledgeable of their contents. He looked Anderson square in the eyes and commenced his interview.

"Mr. Anderson, this pile of paper represents you and the life you have led to the present time. It is also a report of your potentials, character, and abilities. I must admit that this is all very interesting. I realize that there has been a delay in time in replying to your application. I must, therefore, ask you if you are still serious in your request to become a part of the NASA team."

Bill Anderson's reply was affirmative.

"Then my aides, Col. Joseph Jafferies and Col. George Collins, believe you might be suited for a new mission that we at NASA have been toying with for some time now. Are you at all familiar with the words *Alpha Centauri?*"

"Alpha Centauri is regarded as our nearest star or group of stars in our galaxy. It is 4.4 light-years away or 26.4 trillion miles distant."

"Have you ever heard of the word *parsec,* and do you know to what this applies?"

"The word *parsec* has three meanings, but the best definition is that it is a unit of length equal to 19.2 trillion miles—unless you preferred it defined as a heliocentric parallax."

"I see that you are wearing glasses. How long have you been wearing them?"

"My wearing of glasses is directly related to my illness. Before I contracted MS, I had no need of them."

So ended the interview. In a parting comment Dodd said, "How long will you need to be ready to go to Houston?"

"Depending upon my acceptability, I will need at least two weeks to put my house in order."

"There will be someone who will contact you concerning the specifics." Dodd had not given Anderson any answer one way or the other.

Two weeks later Bill Anderson received a phone call from Col. George Collins, who said, "I have just arrived at the Air Force base and would like to know if I might see you within the next few minutes."

"That would be just fine. I am looking forward to meeting with you." Fifteen minutes later Bill met the colonel at his doorstep.

As soon as Collins was seated, he came right to the point. "Mr. Anderson, NASA has gone over your qualifications and has made the decision to accept you, based upon a rather thorough screening. We would like to have you join us in two weeks time, based upon what you have said to Brig. Gen. Alvin Dodd. However, this whole thing is top secret and must remain that way until you return from this mission."

"I'm glad that you have brought that up. What exactly is this 'mission' — as you have phrased it?"

"Before I get into that, do you accept our offer?"

"The only offer that I have heard so far is that you have decided to accept me into NASA. Oh, by the way, there is some fresh brewed coffee on the coffee table that should be hot enough for you. Why don't you pour yourself a cup? You'll find some cream and sugar there also. Now, what do I get out of this package? Suppose I don't return from this mission? I know that I should feel honored for being acceptable material, and I am. But the fact of the matter is that I want something more."

"There are risks — one hell of a lot of them. Thank you for the coffee. But monetary remuneration for you and a guaranteed scholastic fund will be established for your son. The name of this project is called Alpha Centauri. Need I say more?"

"Then the answer is yes. I will be ready in two weeks."

Collins got up and shook Bill's hand, saying, "Welcome to the crew. We will be picking you up in two weeks time. All you'll need is you. No suitcases of any kind. We'll even supply you with a toothbrush and shaving gear. Also, don't bring any money; you won't be needing it. Say, would you mind if I took some more coffee? This stuff is good."

"Help yourself. I'm all coffeed out or else I'd join you."

Brig. Gen. Alvin Dodd met Bill at the airport in Houston. He asked about Bill's trip and how he liked the ride on the new fighter plane.

Bill decided to break the ice that he saw was quickly forming, so he suggested that they get down to business.

Gen. Dodd's reply to this was that Bill had only passed the preliminaries in the way of questioning and that there was more—a lot more—in store for him before they could get down to brass tacks, as he had called it.

Bill then asked what the first thing on the agenda was.

Gen. Dodd advised Bill that the first thing that they were to do was to get Bill some clothes and some shaving gear. After they had done this, the next step was to go to Brig. Gen. Dodd's office. There a group of people awaited Dodd's arrival. Dodd indicated to his secretary that he would see Col. Abrams first. He and Bill walked into his office. Bill took a fast look around. Impressive but still military.

Dodd introduced Col. Abrams to Bill. "Bill," he said, "this is our meteorologist. We refer to him as 'that person with his head in the clouds.' "

Abrams smiled cordially and shook hands with Bill. Abrams stopped smiling and looked at Bill rather quizzically. He indicated that he was going to ask Bill what he considered the toughest of questions, so that Bill would either sink or swim with his answer.

Abrams was 6'2" and weighed about 190 lbs. He had balding light hair. He was in his mid-fifties. A graduate of Michigan State University with a B.S. in meteorology, he joined the Air Force and was assigned to the SAC base at San Marquis, Texas. Dodd had picked him up after news had gotten around about Abrams being able to predict fog conditions at the SAC base. Abrams now played tennis to keep himself fit.

"It says in your application form that you sold weather. Do you have any idea as to what you sold? What specifically are the contents of our atmosphere?"

6

"Do you want to know something? You sound to me like a typical meteorologist. In answer to your first question, yes, I sold weather and I liked doing it very much. There is a great need for someone who can accurately predict the weather. In answer to your second question, yes, I had an idea as to what I sold. The atmosphere that sustains our existence on earth, as we know it, is not exactly 100%, it is more like 104%. Its main constituent elements are as follows: Nitrogen, 78%; oxygen, 21%; argon, 1%; water vapor (oxygen and hydrogen), .01-4%; and carbon dioxide, .03%. The atmosphere as we know it measures some 600 miles high from Earth. The pressure exerted on the normal human life form is 2,016 lbs. per square foot. That is the long and short of it. Now, if you don't mind, I have some questions for you. Let's say, for all practical purposes, that you do have a spacecraft. Does this craft have its own gravitational force, or do its occupants flounder around in a state of weightlessness? Also, once the craft reaches its destination, is there a simple way to rejuvenate those elements which have been expended?"

To this the brigadier general only laughed.

Col. Abrams assumed a more somber appearance. "Yes," he said, "a gravitational field has been effected. There is also a way to effectively and easily rejuvenate the gasses that have already been expended. But it would require that you find a planet that has an atmosphere that is similar to ours. We also rejuvenate the CO_2 that you will be breathing out of your systems."

The brigadier general spoke into his intercom, "Andrea, would you please send in Aaron Rugen? Also, please bring coffee to us all, including one for Chris Spalding, who will be joining us presently. Thank you very much."

Aaron Rugen came in smiling from ear to ear. He looked at Abrams and said, "I see that Anderson is still here. His answers must have been goodies." He turned around and shook hands with Anderson, introducing himself and saying, "I really have a winner for you." He once again looked behind him and said, "Hi, Alvin."

Aaron Rugen was considered the top scientist for NASA. He weighed about 160 lbs. and was 5'9". But this was hard to say

7

because he walked around in a slouched position and never stood up straight. He wore a lab technician's smock and scuffed-up shoes. A graduate of Drexel University, he received a degree in electrical engineering. He had worked rather closely with Dr. Werner Von Braun on rocket fuel propellants. He was considered the top scientist of his day and had all the accolades and notoriety that went along with it. There was nothing military about him.

"Here is that winner I was telling you about. You'll notice that the parts are not marked and that the name of this gimmick has been deleted. All you have to do is tell us what it is."

"Thank you for the small favor." Bill started leafing through the small group of prints. These blueprints looked like something that was designed for thick film work. Anderson was very appreciative when the general's secretary came in with the coffee. Bill thanked her and then asked her what her name was.

At that moment Gen. Dodd interrupted, "Please excuse my lack of courtesy here. Bill, I would like to have you meet Captain Andrea Webster."

At that, Bill stood up.

Dodd continued, "I grabbed her right out of ROTC, and she has been my secretary ever since. Her ranking denotes her abilities with the job that she tackled when she came to work for me. She is in civilian garb because that is what she requested when she took this job."

Bill commented, "It certainly is a pleasure meeting you. You know, Andrea, I think that you are a very beautiful girl."

Aaron Rugen quipped, "Yes, sir, young lady, you can pull rank on me anytime. I agree with Bill—you are five feet six inches of gorgeous. Alvin, how come you never told me this?"

Andrea thanked both Bill and Aaron and walked out of the room blushing.

Anderson took a couple of sips of coffee and began to study the blueprints more closely. This was the third time he had been over them. Something didn't make any sense. Finally he said, "Aaron—I hope that I might call you by your first name. There are some questions I would like to ask before I stick my

8

foot into my mouth. Are these schematics for thick film work? What exactly is the imput voltage? Are the serpentine patterns that you make mention of exactly 20kv?"

"I like calling people by their first names, too. Bill, in answer to your questions, the imput voltage is 12 volts d.c. The prints are designed for thick film work. The serpentine patterns you mention are indeed 20 kv resistors."

"The tubes that these resistors are attached to couldn't by any chance be proton tubes, could they?"

"They are."

"I would like to congratulate you, Mr. Rugen. I guess that I have more questions than I have sense, but could you tell me how many ceramic cards you are using? What is the thickness of the material, and why is it that I don't see a converter-charging unit on page two of this packet?"

"There are five cards, 95 percent alumina, with a thickness of .025. You didn't see a charging unit because the system doesn't have one yet."

"There isn't a charging unit because the system isn't ready for one yet. You are getting two or three minutes of operation when one of the cards blows up on you. It isn't always the same card. You know, when I was selling thick film ink at Bergman Electronics, they found that they had to use what they called bathroom tiles because heat was being transmitted through the ceramic and not through the fins they were using for dissipation. Also, they increased the number of bathroom tiles, each connected by using 16 or 18 awg. wire. They found that they could get a clearer print that way. Would it be too much trouble for you to increase the number of cards you are using and to increase the thickness to approximately one-fourth of an inch? This is really a treat for me. I've never before seen a schematic of a force field. What does this thing give you in the way of coverage?"

"Thank you, Bill, I think that you've solved my problems. At any rate, I'll try it and tell you how I made out. As to the coverage, let's say it fills the entire laboratory. At the present time I have no idea."

Rugen then turned to the general and said, "Alvin, I don't know about you, but in my estimation Anderson is right for the job. He's right, 100 percent right. I do have blowouts in my circuitry, which has been explained in this meeting, but they have always given me headaches. I have known all along that the circuit was right, but I hadn't considered the whys and wherefores as to why I'd have so many problems. I think that I need someone like Anderson around."

Rugen looked at Abrams and said, "How did he fare by you?"

"If I ever leave NASA, I would be more than happy to have Anderson sell my goods."

Then Aaron said, "Alvin, this is the first person, short of Lt. Col. Chris Spalding, who can think, and, I might add, correctly so."

Brig. Gen. Dodd raised and lowered his head in affirmation. Then he spoke into the intercom once more. "Andrea, please show Chris into this office."

2

The Mission ───────────────────

IN A FEW SHORT MOMENTS, Andrea came in with Lt. Col. Chris Spalding. Immediately Bill got to his feet. Reluctantly the others followed.

Dodd introduced Bill to Chris. "Chris, this individual has passed all of the interrogation, and it looks like he will be your partner on your trip to Alpha Centauri, as soon as we work out a few bugs in your conveyance, which have been elucidated in our meeting here today. What do you think of him? Do you think that you can live with such an individual?"

Chris looked at Bill. Then she turned to Dodd and said, "Yes, I think that he will do quite nicely, based upon what I have read about him. Also, I want it made clear right here and now that he will be given the rank of commander of the star ship *Alpha Centauri*."

Dodd looked perplexed. "I thought we were to make you the first officer on this little jaunt. This comes to me a little bit of a shock. You mean that Anderson is more qualified than you are?"

"No, I think that we are equally qualified. However, Mr. Anderson has had more experience than I at commanding. You know as well as I do that one does not have to go through Astronaut School in order to be an astronaut."

"That is a point well taken. All right, he will be considered the commander of the star ship *Alpha Centauri*."

During this intercourse, Anderson had sat back in his chair—for the first time—and looked at Lt. Col. Chris Spalding very closely as she spoke. For some reason, he

11

thought that he knew this girl. She was, in Bill's estimation, a very beautiful woman, with long flowing hair, a fairly lithe form, and an excellent body. According to Aaron, she also had an excellent mind. A person would be out of his mind not to want to be with this girl. Bill appreciated the opportunity afforded to him by NASA to be with this beautiful person for such a time as it may take to get to Alpha Centauri and back. Bill appreciated this chance very much.

The lieutenant colonel was now looking at Bill and without breaking her smile or moving her lips she told Bill, 'Thank you very much. I admire you and your mind, and I have been awaiting your arrival for some time now.'

'Anderson, get hold of yourself,' thought Bill. He thought he had distinctly heard this girl speak. But that was impossible because he didn't see her lips move in speech at all.

Brig. Gen. Dodd said, "Gentlemen, you have all heard Lt. Col. Spalding's request. Are there any objections to this?" No one spoke up.

"All right, he is a commander. Mr. Anderson, I think it is about time now to get down to brass tacks. What we are offering you is twenty thousand dollars a year, tax free. You'll also retain your disability status with the government. In addition to this is a provision for your son. We will pay for four years of education at the college of his choice. Aside from that is now the rank of commander, which has already been bestowed upon you. What do you say to this offer?"

Bill said, "General, we have a deal."

"All right, I think that we can now call this meeting to a close. I think that you and the lieutenant colonel should get more acquainted. Welcome to NASA. Report here tomorrow morning at 0700 to begin your indoctrination into our realm."

Abrams, Rugen, and the general all left the room. At last Bill was seated alone with one of the most beautiful creatures he had seen, and for the first time he was at a loss for words.

Chris turned to look at him and smiled cordially. As she sat there smiling, Bill heard that voice again. 'Bill, I, too, think that this is a time for pleasantries, but we must leave this place right now. This place is bugged.'

12

Anderson looked a little shocked. He thought, 'All right, I think that I can hear you. Can you hear me? If you can, scratch your right ear with your left hand.'

Chris looked at him, raised her left hand to her right ear, and started to rub it.

'Chris, you must be fun at parties. If this place is bugged as you say it is, let's verbally take our leave.' "You know something? It seems to be very close in this room for me. It must have been because of those questions that were thrown at me by Abrams, Rugen, and Dodd. Now I find that I have a lot to ask you. Do you know of a park bench nearby where we can sit and absorb some sun?"

"I think that I know of just the spot where there is a bench and a big tree. You know that too much sun can also be uncomfortable. I believe that we should also be moderate."

Upon leaving Dodd's office, Bill thought, 'So this is thought transference. I never in my wildest dreams thought that such a thing was possible.' Here Bill was doing it. Upon passing the front desk, Bill said good-by to Andrea. Andrea looked up from a pile of papers that she was sorting out and smiled cordially. She said, "Good-by, Mr. Anderson. Welcome to NASA." Bill thanked her.

When they got outside, Chris, still smiling, thought, 'You know, that girl Andrea really has a mad crush on you.'

'You see? I told you that you must be smashing at parties.'

To this Chris laughed out loud.

Bill liked the way she laughed. It seemed that she put her whole heart and soul into it.

After a while, they found the park bench and the large oak tree that Chris had spoken of. They sat down, and mentally Chris came right to the point. 'You know, they really did a job on you with your walking. You were a hard one to bring down. For some time I have been following your progress with your past wife and your business. It was only after we worsened the effect of the illness that we were able to get through to you. Do you remember hearing a voice that told you that your life was far from over? Well, that voice you heard was mine. It came to you when you were really down on yourself.'

13

'Chris, you used the words *They* and *We*. The voice that you allude to as telling me that my life was far from over came to me days—in fact, weeks—before I made out an application to NASA. Also, are you telling me that there is a cure to the illness that I now find was induced?'

'We think of the Creator as the We and They that I allude to. Did you know that you and I are the only ones left on this planet of ours skilled in the ways of the great Elders?'

Bill pondered what Chris had said, and then he said silently, 'The last time I heard the great Elders mentioned was in David's time or even further back in time to the Pharoah. What happened to them? Where have they all gone to? How did we get here in this time and place? Chris, what you have said is very heavy, very heavy indeed.'

'The Elders were assimilated or absorbed into our different cultures. It is the only way that they found that they could escape. Now, every generation or so, a person pops up having the gifts that these Elders had. It isn't genetically feasible to say to whom or to which family this will occur. Or, for that matter, how much knowledge he or she will possess. I only know one thing, and that is that there are sixty people we must save and relocate from the planet Ohg in the Alpha Centauri system. It has been requested that we do this by something or someone who knows our every move. Through some great upheaval, these people have sent for help. I have no idea whether we will be too late or not, but we must try.'

'Chris, I'm with you 100 percent on this venture. Somehow you and I must travel 26.4 trillion miles to arrive at Alpha Centauri. I suppose that this has all been worked out. I'd like to see this craft. Also, I think that this trip is not going to be a bed of roses. Something tells me that there's someone up there who will try to block our way.'

'It is for this reason that you are here. You have been designated the commander. I follow you, you don't follow me. It is so ordained. Also, I'd like to have you come to my apartment to see the sketches and schematics I've made. They'll tell you how far this project has progressed. In getting back to your illness, I don't know how they might reverse this process or, for that matter, whether you will be cured. But it seems to me that you are fine just the way you are.'

'Thank you very much. I'm sure that answers will evolve in their own natural way. By the way, the word *ohg* is now an archaic term in our language, and it means earth. We might use it as a clue as to how to find this planet, knowing that earth is ninety-three million miles from the sun. Your invitation to go to your apartment was the nicest invitation to ecstasy that I have had all day. Certainly, I'll take you up on it.'

Chris hurriedly thought, 'That idea of ecstasy was not what I had in mind. I only meant that you could go over the drawings and schematics and study them before tomorrow. In fact, I want you to destroy them if possible.'

'That's a point well taken. All right, then, let's go to your apartment. Don't condemn a horny old man. You know, we could also wait a few minutes and get a ride from Andrea, who's been sent out to look for us.'

Just at that moment Andrea pulled up in a jeep. "Hello, you two. I've been looking all over for you. Gen. Dodd forgot to tell Bill where he was to be billeted. I've come to take him to his lodging."

Bill smiled and looked at Chris, thinking, 'You know that she's not telling the truth. A fine guy I'd make at a party now.'

Chris smiled at Bill, and then she verbally said to Andrea, "Andrea, I'm glad you came when you did. My business with Mr. Anderson is concluded. On your way, could you be a dear and drop us off at my apartment? I was just telling him that I was living in a hellhole. I would like to have him see my place firsthand so that he might make a comparison between his living quarters and mine. It'll take only a few minutes."

Andrea said, "Sure, I'd be more than happy to."

Chris and Bill climbed into the jeep, and the three of them started to roll toward Chris's apartment. On the way, Chris started to use her telepathy, 'Andrea, you don't want to come in. You want to stay here in the jeep. After all, you know that the apartment is bugged.' She repeated this three more times.

Bill said, "Gosh, this place is bigger than I imagined."

Andrea piped in, "Yes, this reservation encompasses some fifty square miles."

Suddenly they were at Chris's apartment. Andrea excused herself, saying she had better stay with the vehicle or else someone might give her a ticket.

Chris and Bill went inside. Bill mused, 'That was some job that you did on Andrea.'

'Ah, here is my palatial homestead. Over there is my bug in that potted plant.' Chris went over to the plant and put her hands through the leaves. Then she thought, 'Here is that bug I mentioned.' After replacing the bug in the plant, she went over to a very poor reproduction of a Goya painting and took it off the wall. She put her hand between the backing paper and the reproduction and came up with a load of prints and drawings. She also had a large amount of notes. She thought, 'We are lucky that those fatigues you were outfitted with could also hold a house in addition to you. Just make sure that you stash those papers first before you strip in front of Andrea.'

'What size bowl of milk would you like?'

'I am a bit catty. But did you hear what she has planned for you?'

Bill then turned his back to her and stuffed all the papers down his jockey shorts. 'If I were you, I wouldn't concern myself. After all, we are two of the greatest party smashers of all time. But I do appreciate your concern. That must mean that you care for me after all and don't think I am a bum.'

'One of these days, when we don't have pressing matters at hand, I'm going to take you up on that moment of ecstasy that you spoke of.'

Bill smiled, turned toward the potted plant, and said, "You know, Chris, I have been going around your apartment rather quietly. It seems to me that I haven't heard one baby crying. It's true that the furniture looks like it was gotten from some motel that went under. That picture is an unbelievably audacious imitation of art. But the apartment is spacious and roomy. You don't have that boxed-in effect that so many apartments have today. I can't see what you are grousing about."

"I guess you're right. But I wouldn't like to live here all my life."

"Well, I really must get going. Andrea is waiting for me outside. There is one thing that I would like to say to you. Thank you very much for being you. That is a funny statement to make, but I sincerely mean it. I think that you are a very beautiful girl, and I want to thank you for being with me. This afternoon was extremely enjoyable for me. I guess that I'll see you tomorrow."

"Thank you. I truly think that you are the right man for the job. I'll be seeing you tomorrow. I, too, had a very enjoyable afternoon with you, Bill."

"Thank you for your appraisal of me. That was good to hear."

Meanwhile, Andrea was becoming a little impatient. But that all changed when she saw Bill.

Bill climbed into the jeep and said, "How fast can you get me back to my apartment?"

"Almost immediately. But what's so urgent about getting there?"

"Because I have to go to the potty seat." Andrea laughed.

"I'm glad that someone finds it amusing. There is also something else. When I came here, I was wearing a summer suit. Do you think that I might find that suit in my room? You know, I think I prefer civilian clothes over this tent that I'm wearing. What I'd like to do is get changed into civilian garb and take you out to dinner. How does that sound?"

Andrea looked a little perplexed.

"I sense something's wrong. What is it? Is this a no-no? You know that I like you very much and, among other things, would like to have dinner with you."

"Well, I'm only pouting because you and I are in the service and we need a pass to get off this base. I, too, would like to have dinner with you, among other things, as you have so aptly put it. I think that the only thing we can do now is for me to drop you off at your apartment. I'll be by again at 6:00 A.M. We can have breakfast together and then I will take you to Dodd's office. In the meantime, I'll work on those passes."

"Andrea, I'm sorry. But as to the other things that you've mentioned, you have a deal. Good luck to you. I guess that I completely forgot where I was."

The jeep pulled up in front of a fairly large building and

Bill got out. He said, "I'll see you at six o'clock tomorrow morning. I'm sorry about this evening. I was really looking forward to it."

Bill left Andrea sitting in the jeep and walked into the building. He walked up to the main desk, got his room assignment, and went directly to his room.

When Bill got into his room, the first thing he did was look around. The room was exactly like Chris's, except that instead of a reproduction of a Goya, he had a very poor reproduction of a Rembrandt. There by the phone was that same funny-looking plant. He walked over to it and looked carefully. There, nestled in a plastic fern, was the bug. Bill smiled and thought he had better flush the toilet, to make sure that he was telling Andrea the truth. During that time he was unloading his jockey shorts of the prints, schematics, and notes that Chris had given to him. After he had finished, he went over to the Rembrandt, raised the paper backing, and stuffed all the papers into it. Then he placed the picture back on the wall, took two steps back from it, and thought, 'This picture really has a story to tell. I think that I like it.' Then he went over to the plastic plant and the phone that was sitting by it and picked up the receiver.

After a while a voice said, "Yes?"

"Front desk, please."

A few moments more and another voice said, "Front desk."

"This is Anderson in room 208. What time do you start serving dinner?"

"Oh, yes, Mr. Anderson. We have already started to serve dinner. I hope that you find our accommodations satisfactory."

"Yes, they are. Would it be all right if I ate dinner in fatigues?"

"Fatigues will be fine."

"Thank you, how much more time do I have?"

"Until nine o'clock, your time."

"Thank you for your help," Bill said and hung up the receiver.

Bill was looking at the Rembrandt, which seemed to be glowing. He looked at his watch, which read 5:30 P.M. He had

18

plenty of time to fill his stomach. What he really didn't have time for was this project, if it was to get off the ground.

He took the picture down and took out the schematics, notes, and drawings, and started to go over them. He found that he really couldn't believe his eyes. The spaceship was huge. It was shaped like a flying saucer the size of a football field, with three levels. The main control system was located on the first tier or level. There were a computer system on board, a propulsion system that he had never seen the likes of before, a heating system, and a control system that was fairly simple. All of these were located on the first tier. The second tier held the general sleeping quarters, a medical lab, and a hospital. The third tier had only one section to it; it held the nitrogen, oxygen, and argon bottles and the rejuvenation system. There were additional storage facilities for extra gas bottles. He saw that this rejuvenation equipment was portable and could be moved quite easily. Bill read and reread the notes that Chris had assembled. The schematics, prints, and notes made quite a deal of sense to him. In her notes, Chris made elaborate detail on the proton field, which was also operated from the control room on the first tier. Bill thought, 'Well, I've seen it, but I don't believe it.' He put all the papers into the bathtub. Then, while still looking at them, he thought, 'Disintegrate.' The papers went up in flames.

He watched the papers burn and was amazed.

It was now 8:30 P.M. Bill turned away from the tub and decided to go for some coffee and maybe a roll if they still had one. 'This night is going to be a long one,' he thought.

Once again he took a look at the bathtub. There wasn't even a shred of ash. The papers had completely disappeared. Bill then went down to the mess hall after he had replaced the picture on the wall. Very carefully he looked around the mess hall area. It was still filled with people who seemed to be dressed in different stages of uniform. But there was one person there who was sitting alone, dressed in a colonel's uniform, and who seemed very interested in Bill. Bill decided to tune into this person's wave patterns.

'There is Anderson. I wonder why it took three hours for him to make his appearance. After this guy gets some chow, I think that I will have a look at his room. I, Krakowski, don't really trust this guy. Those reports on him were just too good to be true. No, sir, this is one guy I'm really going to tag.'

Bill thought, 'This guy is really out for blood, my blood. It certainly is nice to know who the good guys are.'

By this time he had found a table and sat down. A waiter came around to the table and asked what he wanted. Bill said, "I want a pot of coffee, two sweet rolls, a cup, a saucer, and a pitcher of cream."

The waiter said, "I'll see what I can do." Then he left. Soon Bill had his sweet rolls and everything else that he had requested. He had all that he needed.

Bill said to himself, 'Now to get down to business. Those prints, schematics, and notes were great, but I think that we will need more. If there is someone up there that is hearing my voice, please acknowledge it.'

The voice came through loud and clear, 'Yes, Commander. We do hear you and every word that you are thinking. What is it that you want?'

Bill looked around nervously.

'No, Commander, only you can hear our thought patterns and what we are thinking.'

'I have been over the prints, schematics, and notes that Chris has given to me.'

'Yes, but didn't you just say that?'

'Is it true that someone is up there waiting, with the express purpose of confiscating the craft and killing all who might be on board?'

'Yes, it is true. There are three different races of people. At the present time there is a ship hovering over this base.'

'Then we will need some additional equipment from you that I didn't see in any of the drawings that I have gone over.'

'Finish your food first and then we will talk about this further in your room.'

'Also, please include Chris in our discussion.'

'She has already been listening and will continue to do so.'

Bill looked at his watch and saw it was now almost 9:00 P.M. Very quickly he devoured the rolls, had three cups of coffee, and left the mess hall area.

Bill went directly to his room and on his way he passed Col. Krakowski. He said, "Col. Krakowski, I hope that you found everything in order?" Krakowski only grumbled and went on his way, saying to himself, 'I don't know how, but this guy is onto me.'

Bill only smiled to himself as he walked into his apartment. What he had done should not have been done. He would have to watch himself more closely from now on. Bill walked over to the only armchair that the apartment had and sat down.

Almost immediately he heard that voice again. 'You are right, Commander. Your outburst to Col. Krakowski was not good. If you had not scolded yourself, we would have done so. Please be more careful in the future.'

'I'm sorry. It won't happen again. Sometimes I wonder why these precautions are put on people like Chris and me. At the time, I resented it. Is Chris listening to our conversation?'

'Yes, she is. Now what is it that you wanted to discuss?"

'Let's go through the prints as we all envision them. First, there is the hull. As I remember it, there is an inner and outer hull. Is there some way we can make an airtight ramp on the third tier? It would be for a reconnaissance craft, and also we could move the rejuvenation equipment out onto it. That rejuvenation equipment is extremely portable, but there isn't any place to move it to. There should also be airlocks between the ramp area, the personnel area, and the storage area, which will house the gas cylinders and the rejuvenation equipment. The airlocks, the doors, and the opening and closing of the ramp area should be controlled from the main control room on the first tier. Chris has said that there are sixty people to save and relocate from the planet Ohg. What I want are sixty foldaway beds, replete with pillows and blankets, to put in the middle section of the third tier. This is where I plan and envision these people will be during the entire time of their relocation. Also, in the prints I saw no lavatory facilities. This was true for the entirety of the ship. It may have been an oversight. But I think that these things are important down to the last item, which happens to be toilet paper. That means that we will also require a water system and septic tanks for the flushing of urine and fecal materials.

That material and other types will have to be emptied from the spacecraft. The controls for this must also be from the control room on the first tier. The ventilation system must also be per level per section on each tier and controlled from the control room on the first tier. Access to each level can be only by use of the elevator, which has already been included in the schematics.'

'I also want three robots. They are to look like huge tops, approximately 4'6". Their motion would work on an antigravitational principle. They could go as fast as they wish in any direction, levitate items that are extremely difficult to raise or move and carry them from one place to the other. They must be able to use all of the instruments in the control room from buttons to levers. They would also be equipped with stunning rays. Above all, they must owe their allegiance to either Chris or me.

'On the underside, the ship will have two disintegration rays. The front of the ship will be equipped with two laser guns. The disintegration rays and the laser rays will be capable of destroying anything within a one-mile radius. In addition, from the underside I want six individual tractor beams capable of making a ship powerless and incapable of using its engines, its weaponry, or its self-destruct mechanism. All of the rays are to be operated from the control room by one of the robots. The names of these robots will be Athos, Porthos, and Dante. They will hold themselves responsible only to the thought patterns of Chris or me. We will direct these robots by means of mental telepathy only. The robot Dante will be the only one that can lock onto a target and destroy anything it directs its disintegration rays at or, for that matter, lock onto a target with the laser beams. The tractor beams can be operated by anyone. The main thing is that this will be done by a robot and not us, although it will have been done under our direction and unerringly so. The robots will each have a built-in computer system which will contain the summation of all of our knowledge. This brings us to the main computer on the first tier in the control room. This computer is capable of remembering directions of the ship and can bring us into any course we desire. It can also track the direction in which a spacecraft has gone and follow the residual particles left by a spacecraft's engine. Both the robots and the computer will possess emotions.

'On the second tier is the medical laboratory and the hospital. It should have a direct tie-in to the main computer. All knowledge of medicine and diseases and their cures must be contained in the main computer banks that the laboratory will have access to.

'Now, going on to the first tier, there is no reference made to a television screen that can immediately show where we are going or where we have been. Since I am really not sure how fast we will be going, I want a projection that will automatically be adjusted to that speed in which we are traveling and a magnification up to and including six times that rate of speed. This screen is to be 4 ' x 4 '. That brings us to a two-way radio that is extremely powerful and can cover all frequencies. Both the viewing screen and the radio should have a computer tie-in. The computer can understand and evaluate any language being spoken and translate all communications into our tongue if we are receiving or their tongue if we are broadcasting. We therefore can use the communicator to communicate with the other people, whomever they are. This may be intership or for exterior communications. In addition to this, I want a dispenser installed which will be capable of giving us any food or beverage we might desire. Something has told me that we will relocate these people from Ohg, but that it will be impossible to exist on the planet Earth again. If this is true, then I want to live as comfortably as possible and I want to thwart any attempt by our newly found adversaries to conquer or take over this planet.

'Well, I guess this concludes all that I have to say, except that the changes that I have mentioned are to be accomplished by the robots.'

'Commander, that is not all that you have on your mind. If there is to be rapport between us, I want you to say all that you are thinking.'

'All right, then here it comes. In addition to those things I have already mentioned and requested, there are a few more

23

things that I would like to see. First, I would like to have an instrument located in the control room which can ascertain and evaluate any and all elements, including gasses, of any planet. Before we put the nose of this ship down into any atmosphere of any planet, I want to know what we are getting into. Secondly, it is my intent not to do battle with any foe. Therefore, I would like to make a request for an invisibility shield which would make this ship undiscernable by any tracking device or, for that matter, by the naked eye. The control for this device is to be located in the control room on the first tier.'

'Commander, you have just given me the idea as to how large you want the ramp area to be. It is to be big enough to accommodate one of the alien spacecraft.'

'I would also like Chris and me to be able to communicate with anyone or anything that we come into contact with, by mental telepathy or by use of the television screen or the communicator.'

'All right, Commander, we have heard your requests and think that they are all satisfactory. For the present, when they are not working, those robots will be stored in the third tier, in with the rejuvenation equipment. They will be in boxes marked Spare Parts Rejuvenation Equipment and will be coded A, P, and D, so that you both will know who they are. They will do their work when all of the humans are gone. All of your requests will be met. Is there anything else that you have thought about, Chris, as you, too, have been listening to the commander's long-winded conversation?'

'Yes, I have been listening to this whole conversation with a great deal of interest. First, Bill, thank you for getting rid of those papers. All right, we have a hospital with computer tie-in for any and all known diseases. I would like to go one better. I want that computer to also have detailed information on all of the known diseases in this galaxy that man does not know about and their cures. I want the computer to be able to tell us how to cure them. In addition to this, I want all of the medicines available and stored in the laboratory. I also want a portable and fixed geiger counter in this laboratory, which can detect the slightest amounts of radiation. Also, I want the entire ship to be lighted with indirect lighting that will never burn out or have to be replaced. It is only on the second tier, in the sleeping quarters, that I want dimmer switches installed. On the first level I want illumination for all of the dials, with the rays to be marked by red buttons. One thing more: welcome aboard, Commander. There is one more thing that has until now eluded me. I also want two very comfortable chairs in the control room for Bill and me.'

'Your requests will also be complied with. Now it is three o'clock in the morning. You both have a very busy day coming up. Could I suggest that you both get some sleep? There is one small detail of which I forgot to inform you. The spacecraft that I have made for you goes at a speed of seven parsecs per hour. No one who has been involved with this project has any idea of this fact.'

3

The Alien Starts to Rule the Minds of the Weak ─────────────

BILL SPENT A VERY restless two hours in bed. He kept thinking about the speed of this craft. Seven parsecs multiplied by 19.2 trillion miles meant that the ship was capable of 134.4 trillion miles per hour. This meant 2.24 trillion miles per second. Until now, he had thought of the speed of light, 186,281 miles per second, as the ultimate speed that anything could possibly go. But this certainly had that beaten. He was confused and a little numb. He really didn't know what to make of this new information. His main concern was, What if they overshot Alpha Centauri altogether? How could they decelerate this craft once they got it going? He had it fixed in his mind that he would try to use two parsecs to find out how the craft responded. That meant that it would take about forty-five minutes to get there.

Suddenly he was awakened by Chris. 'Come on, you big lumox, wake up. It's five o'clock in the morning. Don't you remember? You have to meet Andrea at six for breakfast.'

Bill bounced out of bed and thanked Chris because he had forgotten to notify the desk as to what time he was to be awakened. He thought, 'Chris, you are a lifesaver.'

'I like your idea of trying only two parsecs per hour to find out how the ship handles.'

'Thank you, but I am a little scared about going so fast.'

Bill had his shower and shaved. Then he went down to the mess hall to meet Andrea. As he looked around the mess hall, he spied Krakowski. This time Krakowski was with Andrea,

26

who waved at Bill and asked him to join them at their table. He was a little surprised to see that Andrea knew Krakowski and that they were seated together. He was also surprised about the time. It was some fifteen minutes before he was supposed to see her. He thought that she would be late rather than early. He sat down with them, and Andrea formally introduced the two men.

"Bill, this is Col. Krakowski, head of all of the incoming personnel at NASA."

"It's a pleasure to meet you. Is there anything that I could possibly do for you?"

"No, there isn't a thing that you can do for me. I just wanted to meet Bill Anderson. Now, after I have met you, I must take my leave."

Bill stood up to shake hands with Krakowski. Never before had he shaken hands with a clam. This accomplished, Krakowski was gone.

Andrea watched Bill rather strangely. Finally, when he had seated himself again, she said, "What exactly have you done to make Krakowski so mad, or should I say vengeful, at you?"

"I really don't know. But why do you ask?"

"Well, here is the long and short of it. Krakowski asked me to come here early so that he might put a plan into effect to trap you. I am supposed to tell you that you are to rendezvous with me at 8:00 P.M. this evening at that park bench with the big oak tree. Except you won't find me but, rather, an informer. In addition to that, there are to be six handpicked guards, who are to catch you and throw you into the brig."

Bill sat back in his chair and carefully looked at the place where Krakowski had been seated. Very casually he moved the napkin that Krakowski had thrown down before he left. There it was, another bug. He smiled as he replaced the napkin where it was.

Andrea was still looking at Bill, waiting for his answer.

Bill wiped his brow with his napkin and said, "Andrea, I think that I will meet you at the bench by the big oak tree at 8:00 P.M. this evening. Now, if you don't mind, I think that I would like to move to that table over there by the window, which has some sunlight shining through its curtains."

Andrea protested, but Bill only smiled and took her by the

27

hand. Soon they were seated at the table that Bill had pointed out.

Andrea looked a little dismayed, and Bill caught her by the hand again. He looked over the table, didn't look any farther, and said in a low, modulated voice, "Andrea, I think that it is safe to talk now. Whatever you and I said over there was being monitored. If what you've said is true, then you have just blown it. They—whoever they are—are completely cognizant that I know what their plans are."

"Bill, I am sorry."

"It's quite all right. I think that the best thing that we can do now is keep away from each other."

"That seems very final."

"Not so. It will only be until I find out what is going on."

Bill had been probing Andrea's mind and realized that she was telling the truth. He had also been probing Krakowski's mind and knew that the only change of plans now was to have twelve picked guards rather than the six he had originally planned for. Krakowski was not very happy with Andrea. In fact, he had decided to get even with her by implicating her with Bill.

"Andrea, something is wrong. I appreciate your concern and honesty. This all goes beyond Krakowski, and I had better find out about it fast. What I would like is to have breakfast with you every morning that I am here. Is that a deal?"

Andrea looked a little put out and reluctantly said, "Yes, I don't know why you are so concerned, but because of it I'm concerned also. I'll stop thinking about trying to get those passes until you tell me it's safe to do so."

"Thank you. What about some chow?" They placed their orders with the waiter. Then Bill sat back in his chair. He seemed deep in thought, and Andrea decided not to disturb him.

'Are you up there and can you hear me?'

'Yes, Commander, I am here. In answer to your question, yes, it is the alien that is causing this situation.'

'Can this alien pick up our conversation?'

'No, Commander, he cannot. We are on a different wave pattern. The alien can subjugate only weak minds. Until you

28

capture this craft, both your life and Chris's life will be in jeopardy.'

'Thank you for confirming this fact.' Suddenly he looked at Andrea and apologized for becoming absorbed in his own thoughts. Their food came and they ate it. Then Andrea took him to Dodd's office.

The first person they met was Aaron Rugen, who had the biggest smile on his face that Bill had ever seen.

"Bill, it works. It really works! It has been in operation now for six hours."

"What about the charging unit that is supposed to be a part of it?"

"That's been taken care of. That's why it has been in continuous operation for more than six hours."

"When can you install it on board the spacecraft?"

"It's being done now. They should be finished by 11:00 A.M. The main control will be from the control room."

"Thank you."

"Thank you? No, Bill, it is I who should be thanking you. You can't begin to imagine how much time you have saved us. This whole project hinged on the completion of that proton device. Now I think that you are ready to go to Alpha Centauri. This morning I went over the entire ship. I might say that it is truly a work of art. Did you know that they have cushioned lounging chairs for you and Chris in the main control room?"

"Aaron, I haven't seen the ship yet."

"Well, you'll have that opportunity today. I really must get going to make sure that the device is installed correctly. At any rate, thank you very much."

Chris and Dodd were waiting in Dodd's office when Andrea and Bill strolled in. Then Dodd opened fire at both of them. "It's about time that you came in. I was about ready to call the guards out after you."

"General, you know that we are early. My watch reads two minutes before seven."

"Well, damned your watch, Anderson! Mine reads five minutes past seven."

"I'll change my watch right now to correspond with yours."

"All right, let's not waste any more time. There is work to be done. I have assigned Capt. Bill Robinson to put you two through the ropes. Andrea, what are you standing around for? Get busy."

Just at that moment Robinson came in. "You wanted to see me, sir?"

"Yes, I did. I want you to put a crash course on Lt. Col. Chris Spalding and Comdr. Bill Anderson immediately."

Bill mentally scrutinized Robinson and found that he, too, had been bitten psychologically by the ideas of the alien. All that was on his mind was how to effectively get rid of Chris and Bill. He had made up his mind on how it was going to be done. He was going to use the centrifuge, which was meant to test their abilities under stress before they blacked out. He would make sure it was set to begin at a higher speed than the human body could stand.

Anderson asked, "When will it be possible to see the ship?"

"You will see it as soon as all the testing is accomplished."

Bill then turned and looked at Chris and thought 'You wouldn't by any chance know how to operate the controls of a centrifuge, would you?'

'No, but I have been following your thought patterns since you got up this morning. We are in real trouble, aren't we?'

'That's not half of it. I think that we are going to find this prevalent as we go through the day. We are going to have to watch out for each other as well as for ourselves. These people have become robots. All of their sense of purpose is to destroy us, thereby destroying or aborting this mission and making it easier for them to capture the ship.'

"Capt. Robinson, before there is any testing, I would like to see the astronomer on this base to go over some fine points with him."

"Sure, then we can go to the centrifuge to see what your reactions under stress will be."

They went to the astronomer, who described how to get to Alpha Centauri, saying that the constellation Centauri was in the southern hemisphere and that Alpha was the first star of three in that constellation that they would see. It would be one of the brighter stars. They believed that it was a double star

30

now, but they weren't sure. When asked whether this star was in fact extinguished, the astronomer said that he really didn't know, because what they were seeing happened about 4.4 years ago. He went on to state that all they could do on Earth was to see what was historically happening.

"That kind of puts us at a disadvantage, doesn't it?"

The astronomer said that he saw the predicament that Chris and Bill were in. There was nothing he could do about it, except to assume that these things were still in their places.

Bill looked at Robinson, who looked as if he hadn't absorbed any of this conversation, and said, "Let's go to that centrifuge you mentioned earlier." To Chris he silently said, 'Chris, here is the plan. I want you to zap Robinson the same way you got through to Andrea. We'll do it by the numbers. I want you to make Robinson think that the number one on the gauge is really twelve. That will be true all the way up the scale. The number eight will appear in Robinson's mind as the number twenty. Also, while you are in the centrifuge, I want you to be reciting the Lord's Prayer to yourself. Can you do this?'

'Bill, all I can do is try, which I will do. I also take it that you don't want me to respond to Robinson but to keep on reciting the Lord's Prayer to myself?'

'That's it, girl. I want him to believe that he has really gotten us. I'm going to be in there with you. When we walk out of there under our own power, Robinson will be so shocked he will be afraid to try anything more on us. After all, he knows that there'll be others who will probably succeed where he has failed. By the way, I am going to be saying the Lord's Prayer also.'

On the way in the jeep, Chris tried her darndest, 'Capt. Robinson, the dials on the panel for the centrifuge are something that you know quite a bit about. You have tested many astronauts in your time. But you want to kill these two. For some reason, the number one on the panel is really twelve. You know that this represents G forces on the human being. The number one on the panel is twelve Gs. You know this beyond a shadow of doubt. There is no doubt when you are in the military. The number one is really twelve, and you know

31

this. These two will surely die under your excellent knowledge. You have no doubt. For doubt is only for the weak people. One is twelve, and that is fact.' Chris repeated this three more times, and then she reached for Bill's hand.

They arrived at the testing facility, and Robinson led the way to the centrifuge. Chris and Bill got in at opposite ends. Robinson told the technician assigned there that he personally would be doing the test and that the technician could go and have some coffee. Robinson's face lit up with glee and a certain amount of satisfaction As he thought that he was doing this for his country and not himself. He immediately switched the centrifuge to what he believed to be twelve. Since he didn't want to watch, he decided to go to that coffee machine outside the testing area which he had seen when he came in. Just to be on the safe side, he thought that he had better check up on his two victims. "Chris and Bill, how are you two doing?" There was no response from either of them. Capt. Robinson smiled and went for that coffee.

Robinson had his coffee and decided he had better get back to the equipment and turn it off. He went back into the room and turned off the machine. Then he decided to see what the centrifuge had done to his two victims. He removed the protective covers and stood back in amazement as both Chris and Bill got out of the machine very slowly.

Bill tuned into Robinson's thought-wave pattern. Robinson thought, 'Somehow these people have survived. I know that the doctor will succeed where I have failed. I'd better take them over to the laboratory fast to get their shots.' Robinson smiled at this idea. 'Shots, indeed.'

'Chris, I could kiss you. That was a beautiful job. Now there is another challenge coming up. Apparently the doctor is also in on this. Can you make the doctor feel that he has given us our shots when he really hasn't?'

'That's going to be a toughy. I think that I had better try another approach. By the way, I'm going to keep a record on your promises to kiss me. Who knows? I might even hold you to it.'

Robinson then said, "Your next step in the procedure is to go to get your inoculations against this and that. As soon as you are finished, you will have your first chance to see the spacecraft."

At the infirmary they met Dr. Claud Kussman. They followed him into his office. Once again the doctor introduced himself and said that he needed more information and questions answered before the examination could begin.

Chris started in mentally to reach the doctor. 'Doctor, we all know how long you have worked and struggled through medical school. The years that you have spent and the sacrifices that you have made to get that degree must have been hard. Well, you have done it, and you should feel very proud of your achievement. Do you remember, when you embarked on your career of becoming a doctor, that you were all required to say an oath to yourself and to your colleagues who represented the profession you were embarking on? Do you remember that oath? It was called the Hippocratic oath. Do you remember it? In essence you were dedicating yourself to save lives wherever, whenever, and however you could. To this day, you cannot, you will not, willfully destroy or take a human life. You will try to save it above all costs.' Chris repeated this to him three more times.

The doctor looked at his watch and said that in his estimation two foolish people like Chris and Bill didn't really need a doctor but, rather, that a good psychologist would do quite nicely. He wished them both the best of luck. He had no idea what kind of shots to give to them, so if they would kindly and quietly leave, he could get some work done.

A very dismayed Capt. Robinson took them to the spacecraft. Bill was still tuned into Robinson's thought patterns. Robinson was thinking, 'I guess the only thing left to do is to completely confuse them. Then we will let them go on a trial flight. They will either crash or be shot down.' Robinson laughed to himself.

'Well, that's real cheery. By the way, Chris, why don't we lock our lips together and never stop doing it?'

'Here we are, going to get the bum's rash or the bum scoop, and you are wondering how long our kiss is going to be. Boy, a fine guy I got myself involved with.'

As they stepped up to the spacecraft and the loading ramp,

which was extended, who should pop his head out but Aaron Rugen. He said, "Well, it's about time you arrived. Here we are, all finished, and you two finally show up."

Bill excused himself from Chris and Robinson by saying that he wanted to check where they had put the force field on the outside of the ship. Chris and Robinson were to go to the control room and he would meet them there directly. Bill then walked up to Aaron and said, "You want to know something? You, sir, are a sight for sore eyes. What do you know about the control room and the operating of this ship?"

"Well, I guess that I know all about it, at least how to make it go. Why are you asking me this? Isn't Robinson supposed to brief you on this?"

"Let's put it this way: I don't trust him. What I would like to have you do is to stand around and listen to what he has to say. Don't correct him to his face. We'll find some way to part company with him, and then I'd like you to replace the divots wherever necessary."

"Sure, but aren't you a little oversuspicious?"

"I hope so."

They walked up the ramp to the spaceship, and Bill told Aaron to go on up, that he wanted to check the rejuvenation equipment first before going to the control room.

"All right." Then he took the elevator up to the control room.

Bill then went to the area that housed the rejuvenation equipment. He saw three rather large boxes marked Rejuvenation Equipment Spare Parts, with the letters *A*, *P*, and *D* marked on them and thought, 'Hello, Athos. Hello, Porthos. And hello, Dante. How are you doing?'

The robots answered that they were all doing fine and that it was good to hear, finally, from their commander.

Bill asked if they were all equipped with stunning rays.

The robots answered that they were.

Bill then asked how long a *Homo sapiens* like himself would be knocked out by these rays.

Porthos answered, 'It has been estimated that it would take approximately forty-five minutes for a person to regain consciousness, Commander.'

'That's good. Very good. Now, here is what I want you to do. It has been determined that this evening one or two — perhaps more — people will attempt to damage or sabotage the spacecraft. Porthos, I want you to guard the spacecraft. If any unauthorized personnel attempt to board from the ramp area, I want you to hit them with your stunning ray. Unauthorized persons are defined as anyone other than Chris or me. Athos and Dante, meet me in the alleyway of the apartment building I am staying in. I shall meet you at about 8:00 P.M. There is a critical job that I have for you. Now, Porthos, I want you to wait for Athos's and Dante's return before you dispose of the people you have caught. What I want you to do is to transport these individuals far beyond the confines of the NASA facility, strip them naked, and leave them to regain consciousness. Have you met Chris yet?'

Their response was that they had not met her.

Bill advised them that he would return shortly with Chris so that they would have the opportunity to meet her. Then he advised them that he had to go to the control room.

Athos, Porthos, and Dante said that it was a real pleasure to finally meet their commander.

Bill took his leave and took the elevator to the first tier, where he met Chris, Aaron, and Robinson.

Robinson chastised Bill for taking up so much time, which he considered to be very valuable.

Bill apologized in turn to Chris, Aaron, and Robinson for taking so long. Then he looked at Aaron, who had a perplexed look on his face. He looked at Chris and said silently, 'Don't worry about the small stuff. Everything is under control.'

'This guy Robinson is unbelievable.'

'Whatever you do, don't correct him.'

Robinson then very laboriously went over how to run the ship. After lecturing for two hours, Robinson concluded by saying, "Are there any questions?"

"Capt. Robinson, I would personally wish to congratulate you on your thoroughness and mastery on so complex a vehicle. I think that your explanations of everything in the control room and, for that matter, the entire ship were excellent. On behalf of Chris and myself, I thank you very much

35

for the job you have done here today and for the time you have spent to explain it all. Now, I know that you have more urgent matters to attend to, and I don't want to keep you any longer than we have. I think, though, that the lieutenant and I will stay here a while longer. After all, this is going to be our home for a long while."

Capt. Robinson looked at Bill rather disdainfully. "May I remind you, Mr. Anderson, that it is not *lieutenant* but, rather, Lt. *Col.* Chris Spalding whom you are making reference to. By your leave, ma'am, this civilian is right: there are more pressing matters that I have to attend to. If you wish me to hang around here any longer, I'm sorry, but it cannot be done."

"You may go, Captain."

All during this time, Bill was thinking, 'Capt. Robinson, you firmly believe that what you have told us is the only way to fly and operate this ship. You firmly believe that, and if you are ever to get a craft like this one, that is exactly how you would go about operating it.'

Robinson took his leave. After he was gone, Aaron looked at Bill. "Well, Bill, if you believed that guy, you're nuttier than I thought. Why didn't you stand up to him? Civilian, indeed! Why, you know more than this guy does with your eyes shut. To think that I am a part of this NASA crew."

"Aaron, that is exactly why I wanted you around when he gave us the wrong way to do things. What I would like you to do is to rectify what he told us. What I would like to do is to get to Alpha Centauri and back."

"I don't know what this stuff over here is, but I'm sure you are going to figure it out. You operate the direction and the speed of the craft by using these levers. First, you have to turn this thing on. You use this switch to do that. Then over here are your gravity controls, which will take you through space and our atmosphere. Over there is your speed regulator, and these controls affect your direction once you are in space. That's all I know about it."

"Aaron, what you've said makes one hell of a lot more sense than Robinson's explanation. Thank you very much. There's one more thing that I'd like to request from you. That force field runs on twelve-volt dry cells. Could you get us some spare batteries?"

"That's been done. There are five batteries in the spare parts and rejuvenation section with a gallon of distilled water. The batteries have not been activated yet."

"Once again, thank you."

"Good luck to you both. I have a hunch you are going to need it. I'd like to ask a favor from both of you: come home safely. I like seeing your ugly faces around here. It sort of makes my day. Now, if you two will excuse me, I'm going to leave." Aaron smiled and left.

Now Chris and Bill were alone. Chris looked at Bill and thought, 'You know, that guy Aaron Rugen is a nice person. Let's go down and meet your pets. I was listening to you talking with them. I gather that you are expecting more trouble?'

'Yes, there are twelve guards waiting for me in the park; and if the ship is to be sabotaged, it will be tonight.'

'All I can say to you is "good luck." '

'No, luck is what *you* are going to need. What I need from you is an aerial map of Peru. What we are looking for is the Bay of Pisco and the Polpa Valley, which will have the Plain of Nazca. Do you think that you can do that?'

'I can certainly try. Of course, that means the promise of another kiss. But why do you need them?'

'Of course there is the promise of another kiss. I need them because there is an ancient airfield in the Plain of Nazca which we are going to use after we capture that alien spacecraft, which is hovering directly overhead. Supposedly we are going to take this craft up for a test run!'

'Just how are we going to do that?'

'Very simply, my dear. The robots will fly the ship as we direct. Now, to get on with Peru, the Bay of Pisco, and the Polpa Valley. These are supposed to be archaeological finds. At the Bay of Pisco you are interested in the red-walled cliffs. There should be a gigantic trident inscribed on these cliff walls. This trident will lead us to the Polpa Valley and to the Plain of Nazca. Also, I want you to go to the library and get some information on the Pyramid of Cheops, or the Great

Pyramid, as it is called today. Check out the length of it. It should be ninety-eight feet high. You multiply this by one million, and it should equal the distance of the sun from Earth at our farthest point in our elliptical orbit around the sun. Now, the area of the base divided by two times the height should give you 3.14159, or pi. Please check this out and confirm it to me.'

Chris laughingly thought, 'Will do, professor.'

'Let's go down to the third tier and meet my "pets," as you call them. It must be remembered that these are highly intelligent beings and should no longer be regarded as mere pets.'

'Well, as you once said, that is a point well taken.'

They went down to the third tier, and Bill introduced the robots to Chris. In turn, each robot said that he was pleased to meet her.

'This is like something from Jules Verne.'

'I have some questions for you.'

Dante said, 'Yes, we can navigate this ship as per your orders. No, we don't have an instrument on board to measure either distance or the height of an object.'

'Can you get one on board and install it before tomorrow?'

Athos replied, 'That will require a direct computer tie-in. But, yes, it will be ready in time for takeoff tomorrow.'

Bill thanked them very much and hoped that this new project would not interfere with what he had asked them to do earlier. They replied that it was about time that they became busy.

Chris then said silently, 'Speaking about becoming busy, I'd better get you that information you require. You know, Athos, Porthos, and Dante, it certainly was nice meeting you. And please excuse me for calling you the commanders's pets. It won't happen again.'

Porthos replied that it was all right, and, after talking it over with Athos and Dante, he found that they agreed that they were proud to be considered the commander's pets.

All three said that it was a pleasure meeting her.

Chris and Bill took their leave. Chris then commandeered a jeep and took Bill to his apartment.

'Now I'm off to do some heavy reading and to get those maps you asked for.'

Bill thanked her for the ride, got out, and she drove off.

4

The Innocent Victim

BILL GLANCED AT HIS watch, which read 4:30 P.M. He walked up to the main desk and asked them to wake him at 6:00 P.M. This accomplished, he went to his room, didn't bother getting undressed, and hit the sack. He went right to sleep.

The next thing he knew the phone was ringing. Bill rolled over on his side in the bed and picked up the receiver. "Yes?"

"This is the front desk, Mr. Anderson. You asked us to awaken you at 6:00 P.M.."

"Thank you very much. Could you also awaken me at 5:00 A.M. tomorrow morning?

The voice said that it would.

After replacing the receiver, Bill showered and shaved. Then he went to the easy chair and sat down. 'I need some more things from you.'

'What is it, Commander?'

'I want my eyes to pick up infrared as well as to function normally. Also, I want the tip of my cane to have two rays; one for stunning a person for fifty minutes, and the other ray to revert a person back to the level of a six-year-old for as long as Chris and I are on this planet.'

'Those things that you have requested have been done. The way to operate the cane is quite simple. All you have to do is to point your cane at the person in question and tell them that they are either knocked out or that you have reverted them back to childhood. Now, the best way for you to test your eyes is to go into the closet, close the door, and look around.'

Immediately Bill got up, went to the closet, closed the door, and, to his amazement, could see everything as if it were day. He came out and thought, 'Thank you very much.'

40

Then Bill went down to the mess hall area. He looked around and immediately spied Krakowski, who was looking at him with a smile — no, a sneer — on his face. Bill ignored both Krakowski and the sneer and found an empty table to sit at. Presently a waiter came with a menu and Bill ordered straightaway. He then sat back in his chair and tuned into the wavelength of Krakowski.

'So, now I really have him. Yes, sir, just where I want this punk. My sixteen guards have been ordered to work him over real good before they take him in. What I would like to do beforehand is to have him tip his hand before I send him to that park next door.'

'Well, I thought there would be only twelve guards.'

Just at that moment Bill heard Andrea's voice. 'Oh, Bill, if you could only hear my voice. Stay away from the park. That informer that I was telling you about has turned out to be me! They came and got me from my apartment — all sixteen of them, including Krakowski. Then they told me to strip in front of them. I was so embarrassed. They had me lie on my stomach. While I was in that position, they gagged me and tied my hands behind my back. Then, after each of them had felt me up, they covered me up with a sheet. They transported me to the park bench and tied my legs spread out before them, with rope. They placed adhesive tape over my mouth and eyes, took the sheet off, felt me up again and went into hiding. They kept on saying as they were feeling me up, "You know what we are going to do to your boyfriend, doll? We are going to bash his head in. Then we are going to gang bang you. Doesn't that sound good?" Bill, please don't come here.'

'So, that is how Krakowski got his sixteen guards,' Bill mused. 'He needed Andrea's body as an incentive. Krakowski, you and I are going to have fun. We are going to have that little talk that you wanted. I think, though, that I'll wait a little longer. I can't eat before the hammer drops.'

Bill took one more mouthful and choked on it. He then got up from the table and threw his napkin down on it. He summoned the waiter over and told him to take that slop away. He wasn't through, though, and would be back for coffee as soon as he had a talk with Col. Krakowski. The waiter said that everything would be cleared from the table,

41

save the cup and saucer. Also, there would be a fresh pot of coffee awaiting his return. Bill thanked him and went off.

Meanwhile, Krakowski was viewing this whole scene. He was surprised to see Bill making his way toward him. Finally Bill got to where Krakowski was seated.

Bill murmured a polite greeting and, while he was still standing, said, "Col. Krakowski, it is imperative that I have a talk with you."

"Yes, go on."

"It can't be here. But it must be some quiet place. How about my room? No one can hear us in there."

"Let's go."

"No, we can't leave together. Why don't you use your passkey? I'll be up shortly. I'll see you in, let's say, fifteen minutes."

Krakowski agreed to this, saying that he would use his passkey and see Bill in his room in fifteen minutes. He then walked out of the mess hall.

Bill went back to his table, which had been cleared, and poured himself some new coffee.

Krakowski was elated. This guy Anderson was going right into Krakowski's trap and didn't even know it. He decided not to say anything until Anderson made the first move. He used his passkey and entered Anderson's room. Then he sat down in the easy chair and waited without saying a word.

Soon Anderson came in and, without saying a word, moved over to the nightstand, took the glass of water that he had previously poured, and, before Krakowski could stop him, took the bug out of the potted plant and placed it in the glass of water. Then Anderson turned around and faced Krakowski.

"Col. Krakowski, you are a dirty, rotten, no-good bastard. Human feces smell better than you do. In other words, I think that you stink. You had to use Andrea to trap me into a fallacious plot thought up by you and carried out by your nonthinking stooges."

Krakowski was dumbfounded. This is not the way he had worked it out in his little mind. "How did you know about Andrea? Who told you?"

42

"Let me say this. I am going through those sixteen guards like butter."

Krakowski was struck as if by lightning. "How did you know about the sixteen guards? No one knew that but me."

"I'm tired of talking to you." He then picked up his cane and pointed it at Krakowski. "You are nothing more than a power-hungry fool who thinks that he can advance by screwing other people. Therefore, I say that you are stunned and will not regain consciousness for a period of fifty minutes."

With those words, Krakowski slumped over in the easy chair.

"Just one minute. Krakowski, take off all your clothes. You can start with your shoes while you are still seated. Then I want you to stand up and take all your clothes off, including that sweaty T shirt and those jockey shorts."

Krakowski slowly responded by taking off his clothes, then he stood up and disrobed completely. All that he had left on were his socks.

Bill said, "All right, follow me to the exit stairway. That's right, sit down here. Everybody will be using the elevator so you can have a nice nap here."

He slumped down on the cold metal stairway.

Once again Bill pointed his cane at Krakowski's head. "Now you will revert back in time to six years of age. When you wake up, you will want to go down to the lobby and break everything that you see."

He then left Krakowski slumped on the staircase and went back into his room. He took the T shirt, the jockey shorts, and the shoes and put them all into the tub. As he was looking at them he thought, 'Disintegrate.' They immediately started to smolder. He then went back into the room and very carefully folded the blouse and trousers.

Bill went over to the potted plant and took the bug out of the water, made sure it wasn't dripping, and replaced it in the plastic fern. Everything was just the way it was before. While still carrying the clothes, he slipped out into the alleyway.

Bill met with Athos and Dante and described what he had learned to them. 'There are sixteen of them that we will have to find and take care of. What I want you to do is to find them, to stun them, and to take all their clothes off. Remember, we gather them all together, strip them, carry their bodies far beyond the NASA confines, and deposit them there. Do you understand?'

'Yes, Commander, we think that we do understand.'

Bill changed his vision to infrared and started to walk along the pathway that led to the oak tree and the bench. Suddenly he stopped short. 'There are two of them behind that hedgerow to the left. Give them time to warn their buddies by walkie-talkie that they have seen me and then stun them. This should draw the others out of their holes once they know which direction I am coming in.'

He started walking forward. Athos and Dante took care of those two. The others had been warned of Bill's approach. They did as was expected: they all gathered in a group. Athos approached from the left side and Dante came in from the right side. As soon as they had all been stunned, Athos went to get the first two. Dante had stripped almost all of them by the time that Bill got there. Athos came with the first two, and Dante started carrying the bodies away, four at a time. Athos picked up four bodies and was gone. Dante returned for another load.

'Thank you for your help. After you deposit this load, go back to the ship and help Porthos.'

'Thank you, Commander, we will see you tomorrow.'

Just at that moment Athos returned for his next load of bodies.

Bill also thanked him and told him to return to the ship to help Porthos out after he had dropped these remaining bodies off.

Athos said that he thought this was exciting, and he told Bill that if he had any more tasks like this, he shouldn't hesitate to contact him. Then Athos, too, was gone.

Bill walked up to the park bench and sat down beside Andrea. "You know something, lady? You have a very beautiful body." With that he started to untie her hands and then her legs. Very carefully she took the tape off her mouth and eyes. When she was through she flung herself into Bill's arms and burst into tears.

44

"I almost forgot," Bill told her, "Col. Krakowski was kind enough to give you his clothes. But before you put them on, would you please get up off this park bench? I would like to see the beauty that you really are."

With that, Andrea got up and slowly turned around.

"Thank you very much, Andrea. You know, I want to love you very much."

"Those guys also used their nightsticks on my breasts. They seemed to enjoy hitting them very much. I'm awfully sore, Bill."

"They were real bastards, weren't they? I'll tell you what; we can try it, and the first time you say "ouch," that's it. Okay?"

"Bill, I'm willing to try anything with you."

"Just remember, the first time you say 'ouch,' that's it."

Andrea looked around and wondered what happened to those sixteen guards. The place was devoid of them. Would they return? She wanted to get out of there. "Bill, we can't go back to your apartment. It's bugged."

"It *was* bugged; it isn't anymore."

Andrea slipped on the clothes Bill had given to her.

"Andrea, you will find a set of passkeys in the right front pocket of those trousers. That is how Krakowski and company gained entrance into your apartment. You can use those keys to get into your apartment and mine. My room is 208. What I would like you to do is to go home and to take a nice hot bath. There are a few matters here that I have to attend to. In the meantime, I want you to get those clothes that you have planned to wear tomorrow and whatever toilet articles you will need. You are going to stay with me at my place tonight. I want to make sure that nothing else happens to you. Also, discard Krakowski's clothes along the way to the apartment."

"Okay. Thank you for rescuing me. I'll see you in a little while." With that, Andrea was gone, and Bill found himself alone.

Bill started to retrace the scene of the action that had occurred just a few moments ago. He found all the clothes, nightsticks, and guns that the guards had used and carried. He strung up the guards' guns by their trigger housings, using the same rope that was used on Andrea, and placed them

45

behind the park bench, out of sight of any passerby. He went back to the pile of clothing and nightsticks. While looking at the pile, he thought, 'Disintegrate.' He stood back and watched the pile go up in smoke and then dissolve into nothingness. He never could get used to this. Then he walked up to his apartment building and went through to the main lobby. The place was in mass confusion. Bill walked up to the main desk and asked what had happened.

The clerk answered that one of the high-ranking officers had just gone berserk. He asked Bill how he had missed it.

Bill said that he had gone outside to try out his wobbly legs for a while. "By the way, who was it?"

"It was Col. Krakowski."

Bill looked as though he were thinking. "You know something? I think that I said hello to the colonel at dinnertime. He looked as though he had a lot on his mind."

"They took him away to the hospital for further testing."

Bill went to his room.

As he entered his room, Anderson made a fast check. Everything seemed to be in order. He walked over to the potted plant and saw that the bug was just where he had left it. He reached into the plant, removed the bug, and put it into the glass of water. He took a shower and shaved. He put on his jockey shorts only and sat down in the easy chair and waited for Andrea to appear.

Andrea came into the room, went to the closet, and hung up the clothes that she would be wearing that following day. Then she took her shoes off. After that she walked over to where Bill was. "You have me at a disadvantage. Here you have seen me naked, and I still don't know what you look like."

Bill stood up and took his jockey shorts off. Then he walked over to the bed and sat down on the side of it.

Andrea came over and sat next to him. She kissed him and explored his entire body. While she was doing this, Bill had taken off her blouse and skirt. He found out quite quickly that she was wearing no undergarments, and so he did some exploring of his own. Then he got two pillows that were on the bed and had her arch her back until he had placed them under her. Some two hours later they had both reached the ultimate in lovemaking.

"And you didn't say 'ouch' once."

"You know, I don't think that would have stopped us. Aside from that, you stopped any pain that might have been there."

Bill was still loving Andrea when the telephone rang.

"It's five o'clock, sir."

Bill thanked him and put the receiver back in its cradle. He turned over and looked at Andrea. "That was the front desk. It's five o'clock in the morning. Has anyone ever told you you are beautiful at 5:00 A.M.? Where in blue blazes has the time gone?"

"I don't know, but we had better get cracking. I forgot to mention that I have a date with a very handsome commander at 6:00 A.M. He is someone I would like you to meet. I think that I have fallen in love with him."

Bill cupped her face in his hands and, looking her square in the eyes, said, "Andrea, you know that can never be. All I can ask of you is to take this one day at a time. If you cannot do that, then walk out of my life now and forget you ever knew Bill Anderson. I have a mission to perform, and there is nothing on earth that will keep me from performing it. Please understand this. I think I am also in love with you. I, for one, would not like to see you walk out on me. I think I love you too much for that. All I can promise you is that I am yours while I am still here on earth."

"All right. I accept your offer, Commander. We will take it step by step, one day at a time. I could not hope to ask for more."

Bill smiled and kissed Andrea. "Thank you, Andrea." Bill rolled out of bed, took a fast shower, and shaved. He came back into the room, took the bug out of the water, dried it, and replaced it in the plastic fern in the potted plant. He went over to the chair and got dressed. Andrea had already gotten dressed and was brushing her hair when Bill came out of the bathroom. She was ready five minutes later.

As they were leaving to go downstairs, Andrea said, "Thank you, Bill. I have never been loved like that. I appreciate your taking your time to show me how beautiful it can be. How about a complete rerun sometime soon? Like tonight?"

Bill told her that he really didn't know what time they would be back. But she could use her passkey and wait for him if she wanted. He told her he had a very enjoyable time with her.

Andrea told him that she would wait for him.

They went to the mess hall area, and they both ordered big breakfasts.

"You know something? If we didn't do what we did last night, I would probably be down on men today."

"You have been through more in the last twelve hours than most people experience in a lifetime. You have withstood this very well."

"Not, sir, without your help."

They got their chow and ate it very slowly. Suddenly Bill looked at his watch. "Oh, my gosh, it is 6:45 A.M. Dodd is going to have our heads. Andrea, can you get hold of a jeep?"

"It's waiting for us outside. Let's get going."

Andrea and Bill got into Dodd's office at 6:50 A.M. Dodd hadn't arrived yet. Bill turned to Andrea and said, "Andrea, I don't know when I will be back. But when I do, I will need two hours' sleep."

Andrea said that she knew that and was planning a little surprise for him when he did come back.

"Okay. Say, will you get five cups of coffee, one of them for you? I want to surprise Dodd when he gets here."

Andrea left the room and soon came back with the coffee that Bill had asked for. Bill then proceeded to place one of the cups on Dodd's desk. Once again he sat down beside Andrea.

When Dodd finally came into the room, he was quite surprised to see Anderson.

5

A Test Flight and the Alien ————————

ANDERSON LOOKED A little peeved and said, "It's about time you got here. I was just about ready to call the guards out to look for you."

Just at that point Chris came into the office. She didn't even look at Bill.

Dodd went over to his desk and saw the coffee sitting there. He smiled and said, "Damned your watch, Anderson. By the way, thank you for the coffee, Andrea."

Chris finally turned and looked at Bill. 'I'm not the least bit jealous, Bill. It was a nice thing that you did for her. However, I had no idea that love could be so enjoyable. I want you to do the same thing to me that you did to her, and I want you to spend more time doing it.'

'All right, you have a deal. But first things first, as you have said to me. Let's get this show on the road.'

'All right. Once again, that is a point well taken.'

Dodd took three more sips of coffee and then said, "Well, it's my understanding that you were both checked out in the spacecraft. How about taking it up for a little try?"

"Well, General, I think that's what we're all here for."

"All right, then, let's go down and get you two fitted out in some space gear."

At that point Andrea said, "Good luck to both of you."

Dodd, Chris, and Bill finished their coffee and left the office. Before they left, Bill said, "Andrea, that fifth cup of coffee was meant for you."

The three of them went down to the provisions store, and

Chris and Bill suited up in astronautical gear. After that, they were driven to the spacecraft by Dodd.

"You're sure you both know what you're doing?"

The reply from Chris and Bill was that indeed they did know.

"Well, good luck to you. We will follow your every move on the ground. Take your time — this is only a trial run."

Chris and Bill entered the spacecraft through the ramp area. As they entered the ship, Bill called Athos, Porthos, and Dante. They met, all three of them, in the center area of the third tier. They stood in line and greeted Chris and Bill.

Bill asked if they had had any visitors last night.

Porthos confirmed that they had.

'How many of them were there?'

Porthos answered that there were sixteen.

'What did you do with their clothes?'

Porthos said that all the clothing was in the laboratory section.

'Very good. Are we all set to go?'

Athos thought, 'Yes, Commander, everything is in readiness.'

'All right, let's all go to the control room.' They all took the elevator to the first floor. Bill suggested to Chris that she sit down in one of the lounge chairs. Chris went over to one of the chairs and slumped down into it.

Bill looked at the robots. 'Okay, let's go. Athos, please close the ramp area and seal it. Porthos, switch on the television screen. Dante, turn this ship on and ascend to seventy-five thousand feet. Athos, after we reach the seventy-five-thousand-foot level, turn on the proton shield. Porthos, trade places with Dante as soon as the seventy-five-thousand-foot mark is reached. I want you to fly this craft directly south for one hundred miles. Athos, as soon as the one-hundred-mile mark is reached, put on the invisibility shield.'

After Bill gave these orders, he sat down beside Chris and asked her if she had the maps.

Chris said that she did but that there was no mention of the Plain of Nazca.

Bill told her that was both good and bad. He asked her if she had found out about the Great Pyramid.

She said that she had. The information about the height and the base were correct, just as he had said they would be.

Bill told her that was good, for it gave them a reference point.

At this juncture Porthos advised the commander that they had reached the one-hundred-mile mark.

'Porthos, hold the ship right here. Athos, after you turn on the invisibility screen, turn the television cameras up vertically and at the same time switch to six power.'

Bill advised Dante to pressurize the entire ship and to put on the gravitational field.

'Bill, I think I see it overhead.'

Bill then asked the computer how far away it was.

'Commander, it is hovering above us at six hundred miles.'

'Athos, make sure the invisibility screen is in operation.'

Athos then told the commander that the screen was in operation.

'Porthos, take it straight up to 625 miles. Make sure you do it nice and easy. I don't want us crashing into that craft.'

The ship slid past the alien's vessel. They were now hovering right over the alien.

'Porthos, lock your instruments and then come over here and switch the cameras down to cover the alien's spacecraft. This is like picking plums. It doesn't seem to me that he has seen us.'

'Athos, turn off the proton field. Porthos, bring our ship to within ten feet of the alien's craft.'

Porthos brought the spacecraft down to within the short distance that his commander had directed him. As they hovered over the craft, nothing happened.

Bill directed Dante to put the tractor beams onto the alien's vessel.

'It is confirmed, Commander, we have a capture.'

'Computer, what is the distance between the earth and the sun at this very moment?'

'It is 95,637,238 miles. The distance between the orbit as computed and the elliptical path taken corresponds to the height of the Great Pyramid.'

'Let's take this ship and the alien to the Plain of Nazca in Peru. Chris, show your maps to Porthos. Also, would you take

51

over now? I have some figuring to do. Remember, you are to land the alien craft, but hover over the spot where the alien's ship is. Don't land us.'

The spacecraft, with its tow, hovered over the coastline of Peru, then suddenly Bill identified the huge trident on the cliff wall.

'There it is. Now, if we go inland the way the trident is pointing, we should come across the Plain of Nazca.'

The ship moved slowly inland, and at that altitude they were able to pick out the ancient airstrip. They put the alien down on the ground. By using the television screen, they communicated with the alien's vessel.

"This is Cmdr. Bill Anderson of the star ship *Alpha Centauri*. We have captured your ship and now request that you leave it at once before we completely destroy your craft." 'All right, open up the ramp doors. Depressurize the ship and turn off the gravitational field. Athos and Porthos, I want you both down there. Athos, I want you to stun the being that gets out of there. Porthos, I want you to go into the ship and disarm the self-destruct mechanism. Dante, I want you to man the disintegration rays.'

The ramp of the alien craft was opened and a lone figure ran out of it. Athos was upon him almost immediately. He stunned the alien and removed the face mask. Porthos went into the ship and shortly after came out of it.

'Dante, I want you to land our craft near the alien's ship. Chris, let's go down there and see what we are fighting. Porthos, I want you to go back into the ship and make sure that all controls and communication gear is turned off.'

Then Bill turned off the invisibility screen, and their ship settled gently to the ground.

'Are you ready to meet our first alien face-to-face?'

'I'm not so sure.'

'I want you to bring that portable Geiger counter with you. Dante, bring all of that gear you got last night and put it in a pile on the ground.'

Chris and Bill were carried to the ground from the ramp area by Athos. They immediately went over to the alien. Chris took her readings and found that the creature was emitting no radiation.

Chris looked at Bill. 'Where is he? All I can see is his suit.'

'He's there, all right, but you need infrared to be able to see him. Here's his breathing apparatus. Have the computer check it out and find out what the gases are.'

Bill turned to the alien. He had already switched his vision to infrared, and he looked very closely at the alien's head.

He turned back to Chris. 'He's dead. This answers why they aren't waiting for us on the planet Ohg and why this creature didn't come down to planet earth. They're anaerobic, that is, they can't breathe oxygen; it kills them. Dante, Athos, and Porthos—load that craft into the ramp area of our ship.'

Bill went over to the pile of clothing that Dante had assembled and thought, 'Disintegrate.' The pile started to smolder, and a large amount of black smoke gathered. Bill went back over to the body of the dead alien and repeated the process. After the smoke had cleared, the body and the clothing it wore had disappeared without a trace. Nor was there a trace of the guards' clothing, their nightsticks, or their side arms. It was as though they had never existed.

All got on board again. Bill had Athos close the ramp area, retract the ramp, pressurize the entire ship, put on the gravitational field, and put the invisibility screen on. He directed Porthos to take the ship up 650 miles. At Bill's command, Dante put the proton field on as soon as they were aloft and started pumping in their own atmosphere. The ship climbed extremely rapidly.

Soon they were advised by Porthos that the 650-mile mark had been reached.

Bill instructed Porthos to hold and for Athos to turn off the invisibility screen. He had Dante aim the cameras at Houston and turn on the communicator.

Bill went to his seat beside Chris, picked up the communicator, and said, "This is Cmdr. William Anderson of the star ship *Alpha Centauri*. Is anyone picking up this communication?"

Suddenly they heard Gen. Dodd's voice. "Where the hell have you been? We completely lost track of your ship, but now we have you in our sights again."

"We took a fast trip around the moon and back. Everything here checks out fine."

"Anderson, that's just peachy. Here we are, wondering what pond you've landed in, and you tell me everything's fine. You're going to drive me to an early retirement. Get that thing back to base."

"Yes, sir."

Bill turned to the computer. 'Is there an evaluation yet on the gases in the alien's device?'

'Yes, Commander. The constituents are ammonia, 75%; nitrous oxide 10%; nitrogen 15%.'

'What about the skin graft I submitted?'

'It was 95 percent silica.'

'That's why you couldn't see him, Chris. You had to use infrared.'

'Well, there is one thing that I noticed. That form was well over six feet tall, and the gloves indicated five digits.'

'Very good, Chris. You and I are going to make one hell of a team.'

Then a voice called out, 'Commander, we all think that you have done a good job today. We also commend you on your knowledge of history. There is one thing that we would not like you to consider or, for that matter, think of again. That is the solar system of the star Sirius. The history of the planet that you are thinking of occurred some forty thousand earth years ago. Today, the star of Sirius does not have any planets revolving around it that are suitable for habitation. To our knowledge, the planets that encircle this star are not yet habitable. There was a nuclear war there that devastated all life on those planets.'

'Okay. I just thought that it would be a perfect place.'

'It was, Commander. But haven't you wondered that if things were as they had been, why we would even consider using Chris and you when we might have achieved the same thing?'

'Yes, I have wondered about that. For some reason you can't. I just have one question: Do you and yours believe in God?'

'Yes, we believe in God, for we know that he does exist. Chris, put your trust in this individual, and help him out when the time arises.'

Bill looked at Chris. 'Did you hear all that was said?'

'Yes, I did. And I have a question. Why were you even thinking about the star Sirius?'

'Back in the good old days there were two races of people: the Sumerians and the Egyptians. Now, for some reason, the Egyptians and the Sumerians based their calendar on the rising of Sirius. Question: Why not the sun? I can see right now that I'm boring you. I'm sorry, Chris, but these things are going to become important when we get to Alpha Centauri.'

'Computer, give us the coordinates for NASA, Houston.'

The computer gave the coordinates.

'Porthos, did you hear what the computer said?'

Porthos indicated that he did and already had a fix on Houston.

Bill then asked him to take them so that they would be five miles above the base.

Porthos indicated that he would.

'Chris, where did you get that necklace you are wearing?'

'It was given to me by a very old friend of the family about fifteen years ago.'

'It looks very beautiful on you. Whatever you do, don't take it off.'

'That's strange, but that's what she said to me.'

'Commander, we are now five miles directly over the base.'

Bill directed Athos to turn off the proton field. He picked up the communicator and said, "This is the star ship *Alpha Centauri* requesting permission to land and the coordinates with which to do so."

"This is the tower, *Alpha Centauri*. Permission to land is granted. Since you won't be needing a runway, set her down beside the hangar area. I trust your flight went very well and was a good one."

"Tower, this is *Alpha Centauri* again. We'll place the craft beside the hangar area. The flight went very smoothly, thank you."

"*Alpha Centauri*, this is the tower again, there isn't a bird within a radius of sixteen miles of you."

"Tower, that is a confirmation. Over and out."

Bill had Porthos settle the craft down easily beside one of the hangars.

'Athos, Porthos, and Dante, thank you for your help. But I think it is about time that the three of you went to the hospital section, out of sight of anyone who might come snooping around.'

'It was a pleasure, Commander.' Then all three robots left to go to the hospital section.

Bill turned around and thanked the computer for its help and information.

The computer told Bill he was welcome.

'Chris, I'd like to meet you at the ramp area after I open it.'

'Okay. I'll see you in a little while.' With that, she took the elevator down to the third tier.

Bill went over to the console and made sure that the power was turned off. Then he went over to the atmospheric and gravitational controls and made sure that they were turned off. After that was accomplished, he depressurized the ship, opened the ramp doors, and extended the ramp.

Then he went to the third tier to the edge of the ramp and found Chris waiting for him. Ladders and steps had already been placed against the extended ramp, and the maintenance crew were almost upon them. Bill told the sergeant in charge that they would find three empty boxes with the rejuvenation equipment. He asked him to remove them from the ship.

The sergeant said that that would be done immediately.

Chris looked at Bill. 'Thank you, Bill. You did a nice job up there.'

'Don't underestimate your importance to this little ride. It was you who first spied this bogey.'

'How're you going to explain this thing?' She was eyeing the alien spacecraft.

'If there is one thing about the military, it's that the left hand is never quite sure what the right one is doing. However, if a star was to be painted on our ship and stars painted on the tops and bottoms of the fins of the reconnaissance craft, both the left hand and the right one would be happy.'

Chris and Bill climbed down the ladders to the ground. There waiting for them were Brig. Gen. Alvin Dodd, Col.

Collins, Col. Abrams, Aaron Rugen, and Capt. Bill Robinson. All of them had smiles on their faces and looks of great achievement.

The general asked; "Well, how did it go?"

Robinson piped up, "I told you that with my expert guidance, these two had it made. They couldn't go wrong."

Aaron and Bill looked at each other and smiled.

Chris said, "General, everything went as smooth as silk. I let Bill handle the whole thing. All I can say is that I had an excellent ride."

Bill said, "Ride, my foot! I had her working her tail off up there."

The general said, "Who did what, where, or when is not important. The fact is that you work as a team. I'm glad you made it back safely. Chris, what I really want to know is whether you can put up with this lughead Anderson or not."

"In my estimation, you couldn't have found anyone who would be better."

"Chris, you're making me blush. General, I know this is probably not the time or place. But could you have a big star painted on the top of that ship, with letters going all around it saying *Alpha Centauri*, and also have stars painted on the tops and bottoms of those fins on the reconnaissance craft we have inside the ramp area?"

"Reconnaissance craft? I didn't even know there was one. Well, that's the military for you! Yes, I'll have someone get on it immediately. I have a surprise for you, Anderson. Tomorrow Chris, Collins, and I will accompany you to your hometown so that you can say good-by to your past wife and to your son. We also have your uniform ready as that of a commander."

"I'd better make some phone calls so they'll know we're coming."

"It's now 2:30 P.M. We'll leave at 0800 tomorrow. The next day we, or rather you, will depart for Alpha Centauri. Now, why don't you two rest up for this? Bill, you can try on your new duds. Also, here's a jeep for both you and Chris."

Aaron Rugen came up to Bill and said, "I'd like to talk to you, Bill. Maybe tonight at 8:00 P.M. at your place?"

"Aaron, you have a deal. I'll see you at 8:00 P.M."

After flipping a coin to see who would drive, Chris and Bill got into the jeep. Chris had won. As Bill settled back he said, "Home, James."

Chris turned to look at Bill and just smiled. 'I appreciate the opportunity of meeting your past wife and your son. I will make sure this is not going to be a catty session. I'm just curious to see where you came from and what the surroundings were like. I am quite interested in meeting your son.'

'It'll be hard on me, seeing them for the last time.'

'Bill, you're tired. I hope you might be able to get some sleep before morning.'

They pulled up in front of Bill's apartment building. He turned to look at Chris. 'Thank you for everything. You are a very beautiful and feeling person. Do me a favor—don't ever lose that necklace. Also, make sure that you wear it tomorrow and the day after. I think it looks great on you. From now on, I regard it as your lucky charm.'

'Don't worry. As far as I'm concerned, it will always be around my neck and never leave it. I would like to go to your apartment and see you in your new uniform, but I really have to get going. I'll see you tomorrow—you'll probably look better then. See you tomorrow!'

Bill got out of the jeep and walked up the front steps of the apartment building. He went to the main desk and asked them to call him at 6:00 P.M. and 5:00 A.M. The clerk said that he would and that he hoped that he would have a pleasant nap. Bill went upstairs to his apartment, didn't bother inspecting the place, and lay down in his bed.

He was awakened by Andrea's kisses.

"Oh, my gosh! What time is it?"

"It's 5:30 P.M."

"I have to make a phone call." He kissed Andrea full on the lips and said, "Hello."

Then he picked up the receiver and, after a long time, he finally got hold of his past wife. "Hi, Alice. I want you to do me a favor. I'm coming home tomorrow, but I'll be with some friends. Who are they? Well, let's see. There will be Brig. Gen. Alvin Dodd, Col. George Collins, Lt. Col. Chris Spalding, and Aaron Rugen. That should do it. Yes, I'm leaving the day

58

after tomorrow and probably won't be seeing you or our son again. That's kind of final, isn't it? Look, I want to make sure that both of you are home when I arrive. I won't be there too long. I'm taking a jet out of here about 8:00 A.M. and should arrive there about 10:30 A.M. Now, here is that small favor I wanted to ask of you. Could you make sure that my father, mother, and brother are there too? Okay, Alice, I'm counting on you. I'll see you all about ten-thirty tomorrow morning. Good-by." With that he hung up the receiver. He looked at Andrea and said, "You heard?"

Andrea was sitting on the bed crying. Bill went over to her and tried to soothe her. "Look, Andrea, you're just looking at a bum who has trouble walking. If I were you, I'd be happy that this bum is going out of my life."

Andrea turned to face Bill. "I wish that this world were filled with more bums like you. In my estimation, I've met a real man. Don't ever sell yourself short again."

"Okay," he told her gently. "By the way, they've given me a new uniform. Isn't it pretty? I thought we might have supper together." He held up the uniform for her to see.

"Kind of like the last supper? All right. But permit me to dress for this sumptuous feast. I'll be back in half an hour. Don't go away, bum!" Then she was gone.

Bill picked up the phone again and told the front desk that he was up. Then he showered, shaved, and tried on his new clothes. They fit him well — not at all like the fatigues he had been assigned. Then he went to the easy chair and sat down, waiting for Andrea to make her appearance. Just then there was a knock at his door. He got up to answer it, and there standing in the doorway was Capt. Andrea Webster. Bill took two steps backward and took a full look at her.

"Hello, bum. Are you ready?"

Bill only smiled and grabbed his hat. Then the two of them went downstairs. They walked into the mess hall, and everyone did a double take at the exquisite beauty that Andrea was.

They were immediately seated at one of the tables by the head waiter. They ordered two cocktails, and then, in a very subdued voice, Andrea said, "Don't look now, but seated behind you are four of the goons from last night."

The drinks came and Bill told the waiter that he and the

59

captain would be right back. The waiter nodded in agreement.

Bill got up from his chair and went over to where Andrea was seated. He pulled her chair back and said, "Let's go have a confrontation." Andrea and Bill walked over to the table where the four were seated. Upon their approach, the four immediately stood at attention.

"That seems quite odd. It seems to me that last night you were intending to bash my head in and rape Capt. Webster. Am I wrong in this assumption?"

"No, sir!"

"Well, I'm amazed that you got back so soon. I also think you owe Capt. Webster a sincere apology."

All four of them apologized in unison.

"Just remember, I want you four to watch out for the safety and welfare of Capt. Webster. If you don't, I'm coming back and do more to you than has already been done. Do I make myself clear?"

"Yes, sir!"

"I suppose you're wondering where you might find sixteen side arms. If one were to look behind the park bench, he might find them all tied up by their trigger housings with the same rope that was used on Capt. Webster."

The four thanked him very much and begged his permission to leave.

"Yes, go! Get out of my sight!"

They took a rather hurried departure.

Andrea and Bill went back to their table, sat down, and started working on those cocktails.

After a few sips Andrea said, "You know something? Those guys were scared as hell of you. It was like watching a field inspection of raw recruits. Okay, tell me what you did to them last night."

Bill smiled, had one more sip of his drink, and said, "Andrea, does Superman ever tell Lois Lane if he changes his underwear every time he gets dressed up in that ridiculous suit of his?"

"All right, so you won't tell me." She pouted a little. "It just so happens that as a bum, you showed more military presence than a lot of people I know. You commanded respect, and you got it. I am beginning to think that I really don't know Bill Anderson; I thought that I did. But now I'm not so sure."

Bill looked at his watch. It was 7:55. "Andrea, if I left you for a little while, would you still wait for me?"

"Promise not to be gone long?"

"I promise."

"Well, then, okay."

Bill left the table and met Aaron Rugen outside the door to his apartment. "Aaron, I'm sorry. I hope that you weren't waiting too long."

Aaron assured him that he had just gotten there.

They went inside and the first thing Bill did was to go over to the potted plant. He took out the bug from the plant and submerged it in the glass of water on his nightstand. "Now that we are alone, what's the scoop?" he asked.

Aaron said that he had brought along all of the prints on the rejuvenation equipment, the proton field, and the propulsion device. He had destroyed any and all copies that were made on these devices. Also, there was a complete set of ceramic replacement parts, which he had numbered accordingly for the proton device. He placed them all on the bed.

Bill thanked him very much but said he wondered why he was doing this.

Aaron's reply was a simple one. "During all of my days at NASA, I have never before met anyone who commands more respect than you do. All these things were drawn up by me, but they are certainly not my thoughts or ideas. They were given to me by someone, or some*thing* else. I don't know anymore. I only know that overhearing what some of the guards said about you made me perk up my ears. You were to be both feared and respected. It is my understanding that last night you took on a whole platoon of men and literally wiped them out of the picture. Single-handed! I'd say that was pretty good. What I have come here to say is that I am resigning — not because of you but because I feel it is about time I faced the outside world again. I'm going to start up my own company in the manufacturing of electronic controls and other

61

allied devices. For some reason, I wanted you to be the first one to know."

"Aaron, I'm elated. And I want to wish you the best of luck on this new venture. I do have a favor to ask of you. You know that I have a son. I would like you to come with me tomorrow and meet him. Would you give him a job when he reaches maturity?"

"Bill, if he has half the brain that his father has, yes — no question about it."

"Andrea is down in the mess hall waiting for me. I'd deem it an honor if you would join us for a couple of drinks. Thanks for the spare parts and the drawings. Better yet, why don't you go down to the mess hall, and I'll meet you both directly?"

Aaron told Bill that he had a deal and left the room.

Bill took the drawings and put them all into the bathtub and thought, 'Disintegrate.' All the papers went up in smoke. He put the spare parts in his pocket and went downstairs to the mess hall. He found Aaron and Andrea and pulled up a chair alongside them.

Bill found that he still had a glass of whatever it was and lifted his glass up high, saying, "To Aaron and his new venture." Andrea drank with Bill.

Aaron raised his glass. "To the best damned astronaut who has ever come along." Andrea started to cry again, but she raised her glass and drank with Aaron.

Bill looked quizzically at Andrea. "I hope you have had some food."

Andrea said that she had.

"Great, how about another round of drinks?"

"All right, Bill, one more. What time is the flight scheduled for tomorrow?"

"As I understand it, we leave at 8:00 A.M." They ordered another round of drinks.

Aaron gulped his drink down. "Andrea told me what went on last night. I hope you really socked it to them. It was swell. I'll see you two around."

Andrea and Bill were alone once again. Andrea pouted. "A fine last supper this was."

"Would you like to try for tomorrow night?"

"No interruptions?"

"It's a deal." Bill took another sip from his drink. "Now, how about coming with me, little young and pretty lady? I have some etchings upstairs that I would like to have you see."

"And here I thought you'd never ask. Let's go, bum."

Bill and Andrea spent a very pleasurable night. Too soon the phone rang. It was the front desk informing him it was 5:00 A.M. Bill turned in the bed to look at Andrea. One more time he made love to her. "Thank you very much, Andrea. I will always remember these last evenings." Andrea started to cry again. "What's this? Do you want to see a grown man cry too?"

Andrea laughed. "All right, it won't happen again."

"You know, I would like to see you in your uniform. Would you impress me again?"

Andrea said that she would wear it all the time that Bill was there.

Bill went into the bathroom, showered, and shaved. When he came out, Andrea was already dressed and had combed her hair. Bill hustled with his uniform and was through by the time Andrea was through brushing her teeth. Then they went down to the mess hall for breakfast. They had a slow and leisurely meal, but time for them went by too quickly. Without saying too much to each other, they got up from the table and went to the jeep. They got in and started driving to Gen. Dodd's office. Andrea commented that it looked like they were in for a beautiful day. Looking up into the clouds, Bill agreed with her. When they got to Dodd's office, Bill waited on the steps to the building as Andrea parked the jeep. Then they walked quietly together to Dodd's office. Inside they found Chris and Dodd waiting for them.

Without any quipping or wisecracks, Gen. Dodd asked Andrea to bring them all coffee, including herself. Dodd said, "You know, Andrea, you look very beautiful in that uniform."

Dodd commented that Bill had requested Aaron Rugen to go with them. Bill nodded his head in affirmation. Dodd said that they would be meeting him at the airstrip.

Bill glanced over at Chris and saw that she was wearing three of those necklaces. 'Power that knows everything, how many necklaces are there?'

'There should be five in all. The other two will arrive this evening.'

'That's good; you had me worried for a while there.'

Chris interrupted, 'What are you two talking about?'

'The necklaces. There are five of them. You certainly are going to look beautiful.'

'I wonder what this is all about.'

'You'll find out soon enough. I saw no reason why you should worry.'

6

Home, the Necklaces, a Different Type of Alien, and Andrea's Curiosity ————

JUST AT THAT MOMENT, Andrea came into the office with the coffee. This time it was Brig. Gen. Dodd who stood up first, closely followed by Anderson. Dodd said, "Andrea, why don't you bring in your coffee and join us?"

Andrea thanked him and said that she would be right back.

Dodd turned to look at Anderson. "Damned you, Anderson, this politeness is contagious."

"Good. It's about time."

Andrea came back into the room with her coffee cup in her hand. Once again Anderson and Dodd stood up until she was seated.

"Andrea, I hope that the same courtesy won't have to be extended after Anderson leaves."

"No, sir, I didn't even expect it while he was here. But it was nice to see."

"All right, let's finish up here. We have a plane to catch. Andrea, we'll be gone until about 4:30 P.M. I want you to handle things until I get back."

"Yes, sir."

They finished their coffee and went to the airstrip. They found Aaron Rugen and seven armed guards waiting for them beside a converted 727.

"Well, let's get on board. Where's Collins?"

"Here, sir," said Collins as he came running up to them.

They were no sooner in the plane when it started taxiing down the runway and then started to gain altitude.

Chris and Bill were seated together. Bill turned to look at her and said aloud, "Are we also going to see your folks?"

"I have no folks — or relatives, for that matter."

"Gee, I'm sorry, Chris. I didn't know."

"That's all right, Bill. The fact of the matter is that I have been on my own now for fifteen years." Then she changed to mental telepathy. 'If you're wondering about those seven armed guards, they are here for your benefit. It seems that a certain individual, who will go nameless, did a job of his own on some thirty-two well-trained guards. If anyone, on an occasion, were let loose on the countryside, you might imagine the havoc and destruction that person might cause if provoked. It has come to the attention of Gen. Dodd that your past wife has a boyfriend. It's the job of these seven guards to make sure that the two of you don't meet.'

'That's pretty ridiculous. Don't they know I wouldn't harm a flea?'

'I really don't know. I suppose that you would have to ask those thirty-two men for an opinion on that subject.'

At that moment, the captain of the 727 came up to Bill and said, "Commander, we have been talking it over and would consider it an honor and a great privilege if you would take over the controls for a while."

Bill said, "Captain, thank you very much for the offer. However, I haven't been checked out in flying 727s. You people are doing a splendid job. I'd hate to botch it up. Thank you, anyway, I certainly appreciated your offer." The captain smiled and left.

Soon the ship landed. There were three cars waiting for them when they disembarked from the plane. Within twenty minutes they had pulled up into Bill's old driveway. The seven guards stationed themselves beside the three cars, their guns drawn out and ready. Bill used his key and let Dodd, Rugen, Collins, and Chris into the house. He was met by his parents, brother, son, and past wife. He hugged his son and past wife. That was something that neither his parents nor his brother understood. His past wife was a very beautiful woman. Chris immediately spied the harpsichord and asked Alice if it was tuned.

Alice said that Bill was the expert in tuning the instrument. She didn't know how bad off it was, but Chris was welcome to play it if she wanted to. Chris immediately sat down before the instrument and tested the keys. Her first comment was that some of the keys or notes were definitely flat.

Bill said, "Chris, why don't you get up from there? I'll have the harpsichord in shape in no time."

Alice said, "I almost forgot. Chris, while he is tuning the harpsichord, there are two women whom I want you to meet. They said that they had traveled a long way to see you." At that moment two very elderly women appeared. Chris went to the back room with both of them.

When Chris reappeared, she was wearing five necklaces. Bill had just finished tuning the harpsichord. He seated Chris where he had been sitting. The two elderly women asked if they might sit down too. Bill got chairs for them.

Chris said, "Now, this is more like it." She played both Bach and Handel without any music in front of her. She played for a full hour uninterrupted. Everyone was amazed at her playing.

Finally Alice said, "You make me feel like quite a novice! Where did you learn to play like that?"

Chris replied shyly, "Before getting into this game, I was considered a child prodigy. I played for the Cleveland Philharmonic Orchestra." Then Chris looked pleadingly at Gen. Dodd.

Dodd looked back at Chris and then asked Alice if he might make a phone call. After Dodd reassured her that it would be a credit card call, Alice consented.

"A Sabatiel would do it, with an extra set of strings, a pitch pipe, and a tuning key."

Dodd looked at Anderson and said, "Damned you, Anderson, for reading my thoughts. Okay, that's what we'll get." He picked up the receiver and reached Andrea through the operator. He told Andrea what he wanted and also indicated that she was to find all the sheet music she could get her hands on and to put it and the harpsichord on board the *Alpha Centauri*, on the second tier, in one of the bedrooms.

The two elderly women thanked Chris and wished her luck and left the house. Bill looked at Chris. 'And five makes the set. Chris, I want you to stay close by me tonight. You will sleep in that room next to mine. Okay?'

'All right, but I don't see why you are making such a deal about this thing.'

Bill got up from where he was sitting talking to his son and said, "I want to thank you all for coming here today. What I wanted to say to you is that I am going on a mission. This mission will take a minimum of eight years. I realize that this is a long time. So the best thing I can say to you all is good-by. I hope that God will go with you all." Not a question was asked. And then Bill's son said, "Does that mean we will never see you again?"

"With God's help, I will return."

They all shook hands with him. Bill's mother kissed and hugged him, and then they all left.

There seemed to be a vacuum in the air, and then Bill turned to Alice and said, "Come on, get off that jazz. Why should you, of all people, have a tear in your eye? It was usually you who was laughing at me when I'd stub my toe. But then, that was before we got divorced, wasn't it? Col Collins here will discuss in detail the plans made for you and our son."

George Collins, said, "Boy, can you be tactless! I'm sure that you didn't mean all that you said. Ma'am, I will be making weekly trips out this way. If there is anything that you want or need, please don't hesitate to tell me. Now, young Bill is covered for expenses for four years at whatever college or university he chooses to attend. I'm going to be around to make sure you are all right."

"Alice, I think that George here is right. I've been tactless. That wasn't my intent. I'm going to miss both of you. The fact is that I've seen to it that both you and our son are to be provided for. One thing I realize quite well now is that this has been my prime thought ever since we started and I completely missed something more essential. I'm sorry. I guess I'll love both you and our son as long as I live. I hope you've found in your new friend this thing that I've been lacking."

Alice looked at Bill and said, "I'm sorry, too. I didn't understand what you were trying to do. Now that I do, you're telling me it's too late. As a matter of fact, I haven't found a new friend, as you put it."

"All I can say to you is good luck There are plenty of fish in the ocean. You're a very beautiful woman. There'll be someone who will come along and sweep you off your feet."

Then they left. Chris took Bill's hand. 'That was tough, Bill. I'm sorry that the two of you couldn't make it.'

They got to the airfield, boarded the 727, taxied down the runway, and were off back to NASA.

Gen. Dodd motioned to Bill that he wanted to talk to him. Bill went over to where the general was seated and sat down beside him. Before the general could say anything, Bill said, "General, could I see both that ring on your hand and the tape recorder concealed in the upper pocket of your jacket?"

The general was taken back. But he took off the ring, took the tape recorder from his pocket, and handed them to Bill. Bill made sure that the tape recorder was turned off and dunked the ring into a freshly poured cocktail. He looked the general square in the eyes and said, "How might I help you?"

"What you have done was totally unnecessary. None of these things which you were concerned about was really activated. What I want to do is to have a talk with you about your mission, Andrea, and that little test flight you took the other day. First, I want it understood that you are going to Alpha Centauri."

Bill nodded in affirmation.

"Secondly, there is Andrea. She has told me what transpired the other evening. I want to thank you very much for what you did for her — though I still can't see, understand, or even know how you took on and defeated an entire platoon of armed and trained guards. Thirdly, there is that little shakedown cruise that you took the other day. Our radar systems had been tracking an unidentified flying object that was hovering over NASA for three days. As soon as you took off and headed downstream, this unidentified object followed you. It stopped, and suddenly we lost you on our screens. The next thing we knew was that the unidentified object was coming down over Peru. Then our scanners picked you up again at an altitude of some 500 miles. When you landed, you had what you called a 'reconnaissance craft.' We've studied this craft very closely. We couldn't get inside her because we found no access doors. The metal is something that we are completely unfamiliar

with. Our torches don't even faze it. What are we dealing
with? What do you expect to happen?"

"Before we get involved, let's go back to your second point,
Andrea. She is a very beautiful woman, and I think that I love
her. But that is something that can't be helped. As you've said,
I am going on a mission. That will mean that both you and she
will have aged eight years and I will have aged only eight days.
It is my contention that you, too, are in love with her. Is this
assumption a correct one?"

"Yes, it's true. But I don't know how to handle it."

"You know, it would be nice if you told her how you feel. I
think that she likes you very much. Someone's going to have to
break the ice, and it might as well be you. All I ask is one more
night with her to say what has to be said."

"All right, you have it."

"Now that we have this understanding, let's get down to
some serious matters. Your assumption is correct; the craft
that we have is not one of ours. It is, in fact, an alien vessel.
While it hovered over NASA, people were acting quite dif-
ferently. All of their hatred and malice was directed at Chris
and me. Unfortunately, Andrea was mixed up in this whole
mess. It would be wise for you to arm any craft going up past
our own atmosphere from here on out. The best weapon that
you have is the laser. The fact is there are—and always have
been—aliens of one description or another. It is just that now
you are thinking beyond our solar system, these aliens are
becoming concerned. The craft that we captured is essential to
us because we have to find out what the weapons are on board
and somehow use it against them. It is our belief that the ship
was sent from the Alpha Centauri system. If this is true, then it
makes our mission extremely hazardous."

"I have no doubt in my mind that you will get there and
return. You are no ordinary person. I think that you have
some tricks up your sleeve which you are not telling me about.
When this is over, I would like to discuss the matter in more
detail. I am allowing you to keep the alien spacecraft."

"You have a deal, General."

At that moment Aaron Rugen came up to them and said,
"Bill, I had a nice discussion with your son. I think that he's
great. I'll keep close tabs on him for you."

70

"Thank you, Aaron, Now, if you gentlemen will excuse me, I think that I ought to get back to Chris." Bill left the two and went back to his seat. "Hi, beautiful. How's the ride?"

"It's fine." Then she thought, 'I think the general bought what you said to him.'

'Thank you, Chris, for your reassurance. Now I would appreciate it if you covered up those necklaces. We're going to have a hard night ahead of us. Porthos, do you hear me?'

'Yes, Commander. How can I be of assistance?'

'Porthos, I want you to wait for me on the second floor in the exit of the apartment building in which I'm staying. Dante and Athos, check the entire ship over for any stowaways — or, for that matter, bombs. Have the people come yet with the harpsichord?'

Dante thought, 'Yes, Commander, they have just gone.'

'Okay, Dante, be careful to check the instrument over. That is a perfect place for a bomb.'

'Athos, how are you doing?'

Athos replied, 'I'm fine, Commander.'

Bill looked at Chris, who was covering her neck with a scarf. He then thought as if he were thinking to himself, 'I don't know why, but I'm worried. I know that I shouldn't be, but I am.'

Chris looked at him. 'It's intuition working overtime. Now, tell me about the necklaces.'

'I hope that you're right about the overtime bit. Tomorrow morning I'll tell you about the necklaces. No, wait a minute. Are you up there and have you been listening to us?'

'Yes, Commander, that is an affirmative to both of your questions. We think that it is only fair to tell Chris about the necklaces. Does she have all five of them there?'

'Yes, you know darned well that she does. My question to you is, Are there any more of them?'

'There are only five of them, and Chris has them all. However, there are two women waiting for Chris's return who will try to give her other necklaces. But she shouldn't even try to put those necklaces on, for the moment she does, they will kill her and dissolve everything that she has on, including the genuine necklaces.'

The voice from above continued, 'Now, Chris, through a

71

process called an electromolecular synthesis, you are wearing three million, five hundred thousand people around your neck in the form of necklaces.'

'Wow! No wonder you guys didn't tell me.'

The voice thought, 'How did you know, Commander?'

'I really don't know. I just suspected it.'

'Your assumptions are right. We were smart enough in singling you out. Some two thousand years ago (earth years), there was a great upheaval in politics among the people. It was decided at that time that all work of colonization should be halted. Before they were caught and extinguished, they chose to be electromolecularly synthesized. There were over three and one-half million people who thought this way. A ship was assigned to take the necklaces to earth. As it had completed its mission and was going to its planet in the Sirius galaxy, it was shot down. They don't know to this day if we are dead or alive, but they are still trying to find out and make sure of it. Before he died, the physicist was forced to tell them what to look for. They didn't know it, but they lost a great man. That's the story in a nutshell, as Bill would say.'

'Thank you for telling me. It is because of the two women at NASA that you sent the two real women to Bill's house rather than to the base, isn't it?'

'Yes, that's the reason. You weren't supposed to meet those two real women until this evening. I'm sorry you're concerned. That wasn't really my intention.'

'Well, now that you've told me, I'm worried too.'

'We will have to take care of those two imposters, and then it will be my job and Porthos's to make sure that you will be safe until you get aboard the *Alpha Centauri*. You see, Chris, we're just out for a joy ride.'

Col. Collins came up to them. "Sir, would it be all right if I were to see Alice on a full-time basis?"

Bill looked at Col. Collins and said, "George, go with my blessings. I, too, like her very much, but I realize that it is now impossible for me to do anything about it."

Dodd came up to them. "About your 'reconnaissance craft.' What happened to the pilot?"

Bill turned to look at him and said, "He was anaerobic.

That is to say that he disintegrated as soon as he took his first whiff of oxygen."

"Oh, I see. Then both of you will need pressurized suits if you intend to use the craft."

"Yes, we will. Thank you, Alvin, for being so understanding."

"Anderson, you are going to have a lot to explain when you get back."

Their plane landed at the NASA base. They disembarked, and Chris commandeered a jeep. She pulled it up to where Bill was standing with Gen. Dodd, Col. Collins, and Aaron Rugen and said, "Gentlemen, your carriage awaits." Dodd, Collins, and Rugen declined her offer, saying that they had already made other arrangements. Bill thanked all three of them for the courtesy they had shown to him. It was nice seeing his folks for the last time. He got into the jeep with Chris and they were off to her apartment.

After they had cleared the airstrip area, Bill asked Chris if she would mind pulling over to the side of the road and stopping so that he could get his head in proper perspective. Chris pulled over and looked at Bill. She thought, 'You did a nice thing for both Alice and Andrea. You know, of course, that Alice is still in love with you.'

'I guess that makes me the biggest rat fink in the world. You know, I was right when I told Andrea that I was a bum.'

'Sure, you are. And that makes me Spider Woman.'

'No, I think of you as being Wonder Woman.'

Chris smiled and thought about what Bill had said.

'Okay, enough of this,' Bill interrupted. 'Let's get down to the matter at hand. When you pull up at your apartment, I'll go in with you. As soon as you are inside, immerse that bug in a glass of water. Then we'll knock the two girls out and have them put the necklaces on around their necks. After the clasps are fastened, stand away from them, okay?'

'Yes, sir.' Then she started the jeep and turned back onto the roadway. They arrived at her apartment some fifteen minutes later. Chris and Bill got out and started to walk to her apartment. On their way they met two good-looking girls who were waiting for Chris. Chris advised them that they were

73

expected. Bill, the two girls, and Chris went to her apartment. Before entering, Chris said, "Now, my room is bugged. What I have to do is take care of this first before any of us speaks." The two girls looked at one another and grinned. That is what they, too, had wanted. Both girls looked at Chris and nodded in agreement. Chris then unlocked her door, and they all went in. Chris had no sooner gotten into the apartment when she went to the bathroom. When she came out again, she was carrying a glass of water. She walked over to the potted plant, took out the bug, and submerged it.

Bill said, "You girls both speak with the same accent. Where do you come from?"

The two girls said that they were from Virginia.

Chris said, "You've brought me something. Could I see it?"

Both girls reached into their handbags and took out identical jewelry boxes. They invited Chris to try on the necklaces to see if they fit properly.

While the girls were taking the necklaces from their handbags, Bill had moved around behind them. He raised his cane, pointed it at one of the girls, and said, "You are now unconscious." The girl fell where she was standing. The other girl whipped around and immediately took a weapon from her handbag. Before she could complete this action, Bill had already pointed his cane at her and said, "You, too, are unconscious." She, too, fell where she was standing.

'Virginia, my foot. Don't touch those necklaces, Chris. Let each of these girls try one on for us.'

At his command, the first girl put on a necklace, and then the other girl did the same thing. Within seconds their necks were smoldering. Within minutes they had both vanished from sight. Everything, including their shoes, was gone.

Chris went over to where the girls' handbags were left. She upended them and took two ray guns she had found in the purses. 'You, sir, are very lucky. Those girls weren't horsing around.' Chris took the purses and put them into the sink. She then took careful aim with one of the ray guns and fired. The handbags had completely vanished along with a part of the sink they had been leaning against.

'Okay, put your playthings away, and let's get going. I want

74

to make sure that room is still vacant for you. And then there's Porthos.'

'You forgot to mention Andrea.'

'Why are you always throwing hurdles at me to jump over?'

'Because she's waiting for you right now.'

'Well, make sure that you take those two ray guns with you.'

'I'm all ready. Let's go, bum.' Chris and Bill sped to his apartment building. After some fast haggling with the desk clerk and the eventual passing of a ten-dollar bill, Bill got the room he wanted. Both went upstairs, and Bill asked Chris to wait at the door while he went and got Porthos. Bill told Porthos to keep a heavy guard on her.

'Bill, go to Andrea. If we need you for anything, we'll call you.'

'Okay. Good luck to both of you.' He then left to go to his room next door. Andrea immediately met him, and they embraced for a long time. Bill looked at her and felt an inner desire that said he wanted to be with her all the rest of his life.

"Andrea, you know something? I'm in love with you. But I know that we have only this evening left. Let's make the best of it. Did you know that Brig. Gen. Alvin Dodd is also in love with you? The fact of the matter is that, whereas you will be aging years on this planet, we will be aging only days on Alpha Centauri. But enough of that. I want to love you as no other person has or will ever love you again. This is our night, and no one can take that from us."

With that, he placed her on the bed and proceeded to undress her. They spent a delightful two hours, and then, as Bill was still fondling her, he said, "I'm sorry I was so late. Chris and I ran into a problem similar to yours. We had to eliminate it. I brought Chris back here with me. She's in the next room."

"That's fine, because I was given a present by one of two very fine girls to give to her before she took off tomorrow. Here, I'll show you." She got up off the bed and went to her purse. She took out a long slender jewelry box. Bill loved to see her walking around naked like that, but when she took out the box, he jumped to his feet.

"Andrea, give me that box. Then go over to the lamp on the

nightstand, unplug that bulbous lamp, and place it in the center of the room."

Andrea did what he asked.

"Go sit in the easy chair and watch." Reluctantly Andrea did what was requested and sat down in the chair.

During this time, Bill had removed the necklace from its box. He walked over to the lamp, fastened the clasp of the necklace around it, and hurriedly stood back. Within seconds the necklace started to smoke and the lamp started to disintegrate. Andrea watched in stark disbelief and terror. Within one minute the lamp, cord, plug, shade, and the necklace had vanished from sight.

"Two sweet little girls. They were sent to abort this mission."

"Who or what would do such a thing?"

"There are intelligent beings who are further advanced than we are. It was all right when we were just looking at the moon's surface or sending probes to our other planets. But now we have turned intergalactic. We are looking toward Alpha Centauri and are even contemplating greater distances. These beings don't appreciate that at all. They wish to throw obstacles in our path. That's the reason this mission is so important. If we stop now, we're doomed. It's for this reason that we must proceed with this."

"All right, I agree, but why you and not some other qualified astronaut? I love you, and don't you think that has anything to say for it? You're trying to tell me that you might not return, aren't you? I don't want to see you go."

Bill sat down beside her. "Andrea, there isn't anyone more qualified than Chris or me to go on this mission. Somehow I am coming back, but it will not be before you have turned old and gray. I signed on with NASA because there wasn't anything else left for me. Face it: I am a spastic guy on earth. As I see it, I have no future here. You do. You are young, beautiful, and intelligent. So, after tonight, forget me. Make the best of it. Let's make this night something that we can both remember; I'm never going to forget you."

"Okay, bum. I, too, will be a realist. You're right, and I'm wrong. It still amazes me, though, how one spastic bum can

76

take care of thirty-two trained guards or know about how necklaces can kill. You are one guy whom I'll never forget. We'll drop it there. All I can say to you is thank you."

They both walked back to bed and loved each other like there was no tomorrow, for in their case there wasn't.

Bill didn't get any sleep that night. The last time he had looked at his watch it was 4:30 A.M. Suddenly he was alerted by Porthos. 'Are you awake, Commander?'

'Yes.'

'Chris is also awake now. I am going to try to get back to the ship. I will see you on board.'

'Good luck to you, Porthos.'

Bill now turned toward Andrea. He was enthralled with her beauty. Her body was something to behold. Bill started to make love to her while she was asleep. As he started to fondle her sensuous curves, she started to cry. Bill looked at her quizzically. "Andrea, I love you very much."

"Oh, Bill, I love you very much too. I understand what you are going to do. It hurts me to know that we can't do it together. Remember me up there, for I certainly am never going to forget you. I am only crying because I am never going to see you again, and that makes me sad. I'll let you do whatever you want with me. After all, I'm yours." They made love for the last time.

They got dressed in silence. One could almost hear a pin drop. Together they went to the doorway. Andrea grabbed Bill and kissed him sensuously. "You know, I've been slowly putting things together. It all started with your taking care of those thirty-two men. We know that you had a wife and a child before you came here. The ship was built only by selected people. It has a drive on it that no one knows about. None of the engineers and maintenance men have been advised or required to make any changes. But changes are being made. On the third level there appear some sixty beds. The ship was not built by us, was it? In fact, I would wager that a duplicate craft could not be built by us for another one hundred years. Then there is you, a very extraordinary person. How many others are there on this earth like you? Where do you come from? What is this all about? Is Chris a part of this?"

Bill looked a little taken back. He immediately probed Andrea's mind and found that her questioning was for her benefit and no one else's. Bill grabbed her around the waist. "You look really famished. How about some breakfast?" 'Chris, are you ready to go get some chow?'

'Why, I thought that you'd never ask. Sure, I'm ready.'

"Andrea, let's pick up Chris, and then we can discuss your questions over some coffee."

Andrea looked a little puzzled. "Okay, Bill, if that is what you want, it's all right with me."

They got to Chris's door, knocked on it, and heard a pleasant voice answer, "I'll be right with you."

While they were waiting, Bill probed Andrea's mind. All that Andrea wanted was to keep Bill here and away from the mission. Chris stepped out into the hallway and said, "Why, Bill, I was expecting only you. Hi, Andrea." All three of them went down to the mess hall together.

They very quickly found a table and sat down. All this time, Andrea was looking at Chris, who had a very blank expression on her face.

"All right, I started this mess," Bill began. "I guess it is up to me to finish it. Andrea has come up with some very interesting questions. I think it is up to you, Chris, and I to answer them. Let me say this, Andrea: what we have to say to you does not go beyond this table. In the first place, no one would believe you. Let's start in a time period of some forty thousand years ago, when a group of space travelers came upon this planet and, through planned breeding and artificial insemination, developed what we call the Homo sapiens today. In the interim, wars were fought, people died, races were wiped out, and the balance of power shifted many times. Andrea, have you followed what I have said?"

"Yes, I think so. You are saying that these space travelers made man and woman as they are today, separate from the apes, rejected some of their experiments, and watched and observed our progress through the millenia."

"That is true, up to some two thousand years ago. For, at that time, they had a serious war themselves and were faced with extinction. It is then that the survivors came to this planet, earth, to escape their fate. They couldn't establish colonies or they would be discovered and slain by those people who were looking for them. So they entered into the very colonies of the Homo sapiens that they had made. They lost themselves in these cultures and became one with them. Now we come to present day. Every now and then a person comes along who genetically possesses the same kind of powers and mind as did the Elders of Egypt. At the present time, Chris and I are the only ones on earth that have these abilities. That does not mean that somewhere at this very moment others are not being born who might have greater powers. We have no idea as to the extent of these powers or of the race or color he or she might have or be."

"Above all the things I have said today, there is one underlying factor: it is the belief in God. I have found it to be a universal belief and certainly not confined to this planet alone. Now, to get on with Chris and me. In the Alpha Centauri system there is a planet called Ohg. There are some sixty people left on this planet that we have to get to, save, and relocate as soon as possible. This is why we are here. Now you know about us and our intentions. What are you going to do about it?"

Chris interrupted, "There is one more thing to consider. The ship as designed now is truly a star ship. All the plans for the gravitational field, the proton device, the power stages, and the ship itself were not thought up by anyone on this base. The fact of the matter is that it will be another one hundred years or so before any of your scientists come close to achieving this. There is no one outside of Bill and me who knows how to operate it."

"But Capt. Robinson checked you two out."

"If we followed what Capt. Robinson said, we both would be dead. Chris is right. Also, there is the question of our 'reconnaissance craft.' It is not one of ours. In fact, it is an alien spacecraft."

"What you have said, both of you, makes a great deal of sense. You know, Chris, I was also going to ask you about your necklaces. But I've decided, for reasons that have become apparent to me, to forget the whole thing. If I were to tell anyone of what was said here today, I am sure that I would be put away and the key thrown away. All I can say to you both is good luck and Godspeed. I am sorry that I even thought of botching this up."

"Andrea, it's all right. Just remember that both Bill and I love you very much. There is no way we would let anything happen to you."

Andrea thanked both Chris and Bill and said, "Hey, how about some chow?"

Andrea, Chris, and Bill ordered their breakfasts, and then Andrea said, "I certainly appreciate your telling me this. There were no fabrications, were there?"

"No."

After their meal was over, they went to Dodd's office. Bill went with Andrea, and Chris went alone. "Bill, I want to thank you for telling me what it was you were up against. The insight gave me a different perspective on this mission, which until now seemed rather pointless. I see now that it isn't pointless and that you will really have your work cut out for you."

"It's going to be a toughy. I just hope things work in our favor."

7

The First Aliens Are Encountered ———

THEY ALL REACHED DODD'S office, and Chris and Andrea parked right by the entrance. All three went up together and walked into Dodd's office. Dodd wasn't there yet. Andrea hurried out for some coffee. She came back just as Dodd came in.

"Andrea, thank you for the coffee. Hello, Chris and Bill. Are you two all ready?"

They said that they were.

Dodd invited them to have some coffee first before they went to the ship. When they finished their coffee, Dodd took them to the ship.

There waiting for them were Abrams, Rugen, Collins, and Robinson. There were also thirty-two guards in parade uniform whom Bill recognized immediately.

Before Chris and Bill climbed the stairway to the ramp, everyone wished them well. Then Chris and Bill climbed the stairs, turned, and waved to all of their well-wishers.

They went inside to the third tier, and at once Bill summoned the robots. There to meet them were Athos, Porthos, and Dante. Bill asked them if all was in readiness and if they, too, were ready.

The robots replied that everything was in order and that they were ready.

Bill suggested they all go to the control room.

Upon entering the control room, Bill requested that Dante retract the ramp and close and seal off the ramp area. He told Athos to bring the temperature to seventy-four degrees Farenheit, to turn on the automatic atmosphere, and to turn on the gravitational field. He told Porthos to turn on the viewing screen and then to take the ship up to seventy-five thousand feet and hold. The ship very quickly reached the seventy-five-thousand-foot level and held.

Bill contacted Houston. "This is the star ship *Alpha Centauri*. Do you copy?"

A voice came back over the speaker system, "*Alpha Centauri*, this is Houston. We are reading you loud and clear."

"I would like to speak to Brig. Gen. Alvin Dodd."

"Bill, this is Alvin. What's the problem?"

"Alvin, you were telling me the other day that radar had picked up a bogey at some five hundred miles. Do you see anything like that now?"

"This is Alvin again. Hold on. We are checking. Yes, radar picks up some very fast images headed in your direction at about three o'clock. There are three of them."

"Thank you, Alvin. Good luck with A. W. We hope to be talking with you again."

"Message received and understood. Good luck to you two."

'Athos, take Porthos's place. Porthos, turn on the proton device and make sure it's working right. Athos, take the ship up to the six hundred-mile mark and hold it there. Chris, man the computer. Take 360-degree sweeps above us and to the side of us. I don't know what we're looking for, but I'm sure it's there.'

Porthos, Athos, and Chris did what was requested of them. Very quickly the six-hundred-mile mark was reached. Chris thought, 'There are three bandits coming at us at a speed of two parsecs at three o'clock.'

'Athos, turn the ship around and head toward Alpha Centauri at a speed of two parsecs.'

'The ships are firing at us.' Suddenly Chris and Bill were thrown to the floor.

'We've been hit. Porthos, check the damage out. Dante, activate the invisibility screen. Athos, turn the craft at a ninety-degree angle, go twenty-five miles, and hold the ship in place.'

Chris turned to the big viewing screen. Both Chris and Bill

watched as the three ships kept their course and went right by them.

'Are they leaving a trail behind them? Something we might track and follow?'

'Yes, it's radioactive material. Their trail would be a cinch to follow.'

'Porthos, how is the proton field holding up? Was there any damage done to our force field or to the ship?'

'No, Commander. Both the force field and the ship suffered no damage.'

'I wonder what they threw at us. Dante, turn the proton device off. Get ready to fire the disintegration rays. Wipe out their propulsion devices and sectors only. Athos, bring our ship to within firing range of those three ships.'

Athos increased the speed of the craft to three parsecs per hour and decreased the range considerably. As they came up to the alien ships, Dante aimed and fired one short blast at each of the vessels. After he had finished and immobilized the ships, Athos circled back and hovered over them, finally coming to a stop.

'Chris, what speed could we travel if we had those alien ships under tow? Also, would our force field cover them as well as ourselves from meteor showers?'

'Hold on a minute. With the relative weights of those vessels, the maximum speed that our craft can go is five parsecs per hour. The force field will cover them if they are close enough to our ship.'

'Chris, also have the computer make a reference point between our sun and Alpha Centauri.'

Bill had Athos get as close to the alien craft as possible. Then he directed Dante to put tractor beams on each craft. He had Porthos put the force field on again.

'All right, let's go see where those ships came from. Athos, with the help of the computer, follow the trail of pollution that these craft made at a rate of four parsecs per hour.'

Bill turned and put the main viewing screen on to three power, adjusted it to straight ahead, and sat down on one of the lounging chairs. He invited Chris to sit down too. Chris got up from the computer console and came over to where Bill was and sat down beside him on the other chair. Bill turned the communicator on and said, "This is the star ship *Alpha Centauri*. Why did you fire upon us?"

"You are considered enemies. Therefore you had to be stopped."

"We are taking you back to where you came from. After we return you, you will have exactly sixty minutes to evacuate your base. We will then have to completely destroy this base of yours. Where are the life-support systems to be found on this base of yours?"

"At the far end of the base." All the time the alien was thinking, 'It is really in the center, but I would never tell him that.'

"Thank you for your help. Remember, you have just sixty minutes to leave. End of communication."

'I didn't realize that all of them speak English,' Chris thought.

'They don't. It is the communicator which translates for both us and them.'

Bill became pensive. 'Oh, Chris, you're going to love it at Alpha Centauri, You see, there are three stars orbiting each other. The makeup of these stars is 95 percent hydrogen helium. There are 106 other elements. But it is exactly like our own sun. Having three suns means that there is always sunlight.'

'That's fine, Bill. Here you are, speaking of a beautiful place where we have aliens waiting for us, and, to boot, you are heading away from Alpha Centauri.'

'It's just a little detour. Porthos, make sure the invisibility screen is on. Dante, increase the power to six on the viewing screen.'

When the viewing screen was increased to six power, Chris saw a large formation of meteors.

Bill told Athos to pull up and go over the meteor field. After this was accomplished and the meteors were passed, Bill had Athos resume the path left by the spacecraft. Athos complied with this request.

'Computer, in what direction are we headed?'

'Yes, Commander, we are headed toward Sirius.'

Athos started to reduce speed. He indicated that the space platform was dead ahead.

Bill couldn't believe his eyes. 'Chris, get back on that computer again. Find out all there is to be known about that thing out there. Athos, put the ship at a dead stop until we know more about this space platform.' Both Chris and Athos complied with Bill's request. The ship came to a halt. Never before had Bill seen anything like it. The platform was huge.

Chris came back with the computer's findings. 'The measurements are as follows: three hundred yards long, one hundred yards wide, fifty yards thick. It has life support in the center, along with power and light systems. Food is produced in the uppermost section. It has twenty-five launching pads, all elevator operated. Its holding capacity is 125 spacecraft; at the present time they have only 75 spacecraft. The crew is four hundred strong. The main control room is located at the far end of the base.'

'Dante, do you think that you can blow a hole in the center of this thing from top to bottom, measuring twenty-five yards in diameter?' Dante's reply was that he could easily do it, providing they were close enough.

'Okay, let's do it. Athos, bring in the crippled spacecraft so they are lying on one of the pads. Porthos, when this is accomplished, turn off the tractor beams. Make sure that the craft are resting on the pad first before you release them from the holding beams. Dante, turn off the proton ray. Athos, as soon as the three craft are deposited and released on the pad, take the ship up one mile from the base, invert it, and then fly around to the underside of the platform. Go to the center of it and then lower the ship to within twenty-five feet of the platform. Dante, as soon as you are within twenty-five feet, turn your disintegration rays on the platform.'

The robots answered by saying that they all understood.

'Athos, after Dante is finished, go around again to the front side, reinvert the ship, and take it away from the platform to twenty-five miles above it and hold. Porthos, after the twenty-five-mile height is reached, turn on the proton shield again.'

85

'Bill, what do you want me to do?'

'Man the radio tie-in with the computer. Relay any message you hear to me at once.'

The alien spacecraft were placed on the pad. Porthos turned off the tractor beams on the ships. Athos took the ship up one mile and inverted it. He flew around to the underside, got to the center, and lowered the craft to twenty-five feet above the platform. Dante directed the disintegration ray at the center of the platform. Within less than one minute he had cut a path through the platform and continued in an ever-increasing circle, finally equaling twenty-five yards in diameter. Dante turned off the ray and Athos flew the ship to the front side, reinverted it, and climbed above the platform to a height of twenty-five miles. Porthos put the proton shield on. Reducing the focus to one power, they all watched on the screen at the hole that had just been made.

Issuing from the hole was an enormous amount of gaseous material and destroyed equipment. It was obvious that the thing that they were after — the life-support system — had been impaired and also, very possibly their power generation equipment.

Bill then went over to the lounging chair and picked up the communicator. "This is Comdr. Bill Anderson. Is there someone on the space platform who is reading my communication?"

"Yes, we hear you. What do you want?"

"Both this platform and the three spacecraft that we have returned to you are in violation of the parameters that have been clearly established. You are off limits and therefore must return to wherever it is you came from. I gave your men and am now giving you approximately sixty minutes to vacate this base, at which time it will be permanently destroyed. This is my order and directive, and I cannot go back on it. I now give you and yours sixty minutes, and that is all."

The commander of the space platform replied, "You speak of defined parameters and limits that have been clearly defined and established. Why is it that I have not heard of them?"

"You are considered as aliens with no rights or privileges.

Your sixty minutes are fast elapsing. This is my last warning to you. Go, my friend. End of communication."

'Commander, a communication with their main base was just sent. In it the commander of this base says that he is under attack by an alien who claims that they are aliens. Their life support and power have been obliterated. There is no way that it can be repaired. Their mechanics are trying to raise the elevators to the pads so that escape might be possible. They have been given one hour to get away from this base. They have estimated a minimum of two hours required to raise the platforms or pads. Can the commander of the main base help? The answer that he has gotten back is that some 250 ships are being made ready to come to the aid of the people who are trapped on the space platform and to capture this alien spacecraft.'

'Chris, have you gotten a fix on the radio transmissions?'

Chris said that she did and had already given the information to Athos.

'Oh, great and wondrous voice from heaven, I would like to hear from you now. Are these people the same ones who made your people go into hiding? Am I doing the right thing?'

'Yes, Commander, to both of your questions. You are now engaged in a great battle that could have been avoided and could mean disaster to you both. I'm only sorry that you have brought this upon yourselves.'

'If we can wipe out two space stations and wipe out 325 spacecraft in the process, what will they be left with?'

'You will have reduced their power by seven-eighths.'

'What have these people done for humanity?'

'They really haven't. They have used their power and might to impair others from growing and reaching their own levels of success.'

Bill was amazed. 'What you are saying here is that they have been able to hold on and hold back progress for over two thousand years.'

'Yes, hold it back and, in some instances, retard it.'

'All right, our course of action is quite clear. We're going to attack. Athos, head the ship toward those radio communications. Computer, take a fix on the space platform below. Athos, proceed one thousand miles in the direction of those radio communications and then stop. We are going to wait for our adversary. Porthos, check to see if the invisibility screen is working all right, and make sure that our force field is on. Dante, stand by those disintegration beams. Chris, man the computer and monitor any and all radio transmissions. Athos, use seven parsecs per hour speed.'

The trip of one thousand miles put the ship in a direct line with the second space platform. Bill had switched to six power and was watching the amassing of 250 spacecraft. The pattern was one of a group of threes. After a while there were eighty-three sets of three. Then slowly the elevator pushed up one lone and larger spacecraft. Slowly this ship moved fifty feet into formation with the rest of them. Each group of three moved fifty feet from each other. They formed a wedge with the line covering over one mile. The main and larger craft was enveloped by sets of three craft on the top, bottom, and sides. This larger spacecraft lay well behind the wedge at fifty feet.

'Well, that is very impressive. Dante, break up this wedge by destroying the first six sets of three spacecraft, in the apex of the wedge. Athos, after Dante has broken the wedge, fly our craft to within Dante's range for firing on the larger ship and its escorts. Dante, totally wipe these ships out. Then Athos, go to the far end of this broken wedge. And Dante, wipe these ships out as Athos goes down the line of this wedge.'

'It's the commander to all spacecraft. "This is a time of emergency. Someone or something has dared to attack us. We cannot, we will not, let this go unheeded. We must destroy this craft before it has a chance to go any further. We have had a good thing for a long time and we will keep it or die in the attempt. That is all. Go get that interloper." '

'Porthos, make sure that the proton device is turned off.'

Porthos responded and Athos brought the ship into the range of the apex of the wedge at approximately 1,000 yards above them. Dante turned on the disintegration rays, eliminating first the center and then alternating from one side to the other. As soon as he had finished, Athos brought the *Alpha Centauri* up in a wide arc, settling at last about 750 yards behind the escort ships. Dante turned on the disintegration rays, knocking out the first three sets of three escorts, then the larger ship and the set of three escorts on the bottom. Athos flew the *Alpha Centauri* to the end of the broken wedge, and Dante directed his rays at one set at a time as Athos finally arrived at the end of the wedge.

'Good work, Now let's invert the ship and go to the center of that big space platform. Athos, get to a height of fifty feet above the underside of the platform. Dante, blast a hole that has a diameter of forty yards right through to the other side of the platform. Chris, please find out what the dimensions of this thing are.'

Athos swung the ship around, inverted it, and proceeded to the center of the underside.

Chris thought, 'It measures six hundred yards by five hundred yards by seventy-five yards. This space platform has elevator launching pads for two hundred spacecraft.'

After Athos got on the underside and had proceeded to the center, he lowered the ship to an elevation of fifty feet. Dante turned on the disintegration rays and worked through to the other side and proceeded to widen the hole by ever-increasing circles.

Chris thought, 'This platform has one life-support system, which you have just taken out. The control room is on the other end and controls the auxiliary power. I think that you have also knocked out their main power source. This base manufactured space vehicles.'

'Athos, take this ship to the end of the base. Maintain the same elevation. Dante, I want you to halve and then quarter this thing. Athos, when Dante turns on his rays, proceed down the length of it very slowly. Then come back to the center, and Dante can cut through from one end to the other of the width. Make sure that the cuts you make go clear through to the other side of the platform. I want four distinct sections. Chris, thank you for your report about this platform. Here I thought the first platform was big. This one was a monster!'

Athos did as he was commanded, and Dante turned on his rays. The platform was halved and then quartered in less than two minutes.

Bill had Porthos put tractor beams on each of the four

sections. Then he had Athos tow these sections so that they were fifty miles apart from one another.

Bill had Athos go to the first platform at seven parsecs per hour. They were there in a very short while.

Bill turned on the communicator. "This is Comdr. Bill Anderson of the star ship *Alpha Centauri*. Is anyone receiving this communication?"

"Yes, Commander, we do hear you."

"How are you coming with your departure?"

"As you can see, there is a vehicle on one of the pads now."

"Commander, I said total and complete evacuation. Is there a self-destruct device on board the platform?"

"Yes, there is such a device on board. But it has been quite a while since we have thought of using it."

"Well, take as many people as feasibly possible. Arm your self-destruct device to go off in five minutes, and then leave the platform."

"You seem so sure of yourself. How do you know that I didn't send for help?"

Bill took some time in answering. "It is true that you did send a distress call and asked for help. We picked up your call and followed it to another and larger space platform. We watched some 250 spacecraft assemble and form a perfect wedge. It was a perfect striking wedge. I must commend you on your display of tactics. The wedge with ships in groups of three, extending for about one mile, made the whole group very formidable. We drove a big hole in the center of that wedge and attacked a larger ship that was in the background. We then went back and took that wedge apart. There isn't a single spacecraft left. We then took care of the platform, dividing it into four equal parts. This is not pleasant for me to talk about. But you are a warlike people who have never lived in harmony with anything or anyone. This is something that I know you won't understand. We regard life, anyone's or any-ing's, as sacred. We take life only when we are threatened. I say this once again for the last time. Go back home from whence you came, and choose your passengers wisely."

There was a long pause and then the voice came back over the communicator. "We have been trying to raise someone at

90

the main base and also the attack force. We have been able to do neither of these things. Perhaps what you say is true. If it is true, then you have destroyed what has taken us many years to build. I will choose my people, get the required fuel on board, and set the self-destruct mechanism. You have won. I hope that this makes you feel very happy."

"Remember, the only place you are going is Sirius. We will make sure of this. Also, take off any armament you might have on this craft of yours."

"Yes, we understand."

Bill carefully looked over the platform. Suddenly he spied the three ships that they had first encountered, resting on the same pad they had deposited them on.

'Oh, mighty ones, are you still there? Are you listening to this conversation?'

'Yes, we are. What is it you require, Commander?'

'I would like to deposit these people on your old planet rather than kill them. What do you think of this idea?'

'That would be all right. We can guide the ship or ships there.'

'Do you trust them?'

'Not as long as they have power.'

'Your meaning is well understood.'

Bill got on the communicator again. "This is Comdr. Bill Anderson again. Do you read me?"

The voice of the commander of the space platform responded by saying that he did copy.

"Instead of one vehicle, there are now four that you can use. My craft would shuttle them back to where they belonged. This would increase the number of personnel that could be saved. Also, there is no problem with fuel since you won't be needing any."

"That would mean that you plan to ferry the three disabled craft to their destination." Then he thought, 'This will give me an opportunity to shoot him out of space before he knows what hit him.'

Bill turned and looked a little dismayed. 'Dante, use the beams once again to cripple the ship on the pad by wiping out his engines.'

Dante took careful aim, fired, and completely wiped out the engine section.

Bill picked up the communicator. "Commander, you have exactly three minutes to get on board the spacecraft. I am really late on my schedule."

"All right, we are coming now."

Bill watched as the commander boarded and then all the rest of the people got into the spacecraft and the others boarded the three disabled spacecraft. There were forty aliens who got into their craft. When everyone was on board, Bill had Athos take the craft to an elevation of fifty miles, after Porthos had put the tractor beams on them. Bill had Porthos release the tractor beams and directed Athos to return and land on the space platform. Dante was to turn off the proton field. Bill picked up the communicator. "This is Comdr. Bill Anderson. Does anyone copy on the space platform?"

The voice that returned Bill's communication was feminine. "Yes, Commander, what is it that you want?"

"Has the commander of this platform taken any women with him?"

"No."

"I want sixty women on top of this platform right now. We will pick you up. Don't get any firing devices, and keep clean of all weapons."

"That is all of the women there are on this base."

Bill had the women get ready and go on top of the platform. He got Porthos to pick them up and to stay with them until they disembarked.

'Under no circumstances are you to leave these people alone. If they try anything, knock them out. They are not to go near the ship that we have or to go up to the second or first tier.'

'Thank you, Commander, for giving me this opportunity. I was beginning to wonder what my function here really was.'

'Porthos, Athos, Dante, Computer, and Chris, all of us on board have functions to perform. Don't ever think that you are being wasted in any way. Now, Porthos, tell us when you are ready in the ramp area. When this ramp area is fully depressurized, we will extend the ramp, open the outer doors, and turn off the invisibility field. You will then bring the women up by groups of four, advising each group in its turn to stay against the far wall away from the spacecraft. Tell them not to go near the craft for any reason. As soon as you have brought the sixtieth woman on board with you safely inside, we will retract the ramp, close and reseal the outer doors, and repressurize the entire third tier. The women will stay in the middle section of the third tier and will not go beyond this area. We will then raise the ship and turn on the invisibility screen.'

'Bill, the commander has sent a message to a third platform. In it he advises that he is under heavy attack and is a prisoner to the alien. He advises that he deliberately did not set off the self-destruct sequence because, in his way of thinking, they would be needing this base again.'

Suddenly they heard from Porthos. He was now in the ramp area. Bill closed off the ramp area from the center section of the third tier, depressurized the ramp area, opened the outer doors, and extended the ramp. At the same time he made sure the proton device and the invisibility screen were turned off.

Chris kept listening to the radio to get a fix on the position of the third base.

'This is the first time they will have seen us.'

Porthos had brought in all sixty women and himself on board the *Alpha Centauri*, and Bill closed the outer doors and resealed them. He retracted the ramp and repressurized the ramp area. He opened the doors to the center area, and Porthos ushered them into the center area. As soon as everyone was in the center area, Bill closed the doors to the ramp area. Bill then instructed Athos to bring the ship up by one thousand feet, invert it, and head for the end of the platform. He requested that Athos proceed slowly, and that Dante quarter this platform as he had done with the other one. He turned on the invisibility screen again.

'Bill, the commander has been relaying urgent messages to their third base ever since you turned off that invisibility screen. He has said the following: "The ship is almost as wide and one-half the size of the platform; it is disklike in appearance; it must have many levels to it, judging from its thickness; a ramp has been extended from the ship; one of the inhabitants of the vehicle is getting off; this is an extremely fat and round creature, small but very strong." The commander of the third base asked what this person was doing. We now have the coordinates of the third base. The commander replies that this person is putting people on board the vessel, carrying four at a time. The commander of the third base said that he was to keep in touch at all times.'

'Thank you, Chris. Now, how would you like to give Athos his instructions and drive us to that planet that the Elders are going to tell us about on Sirius? But first I want Dante to quarter that thing out there and then pick up each quarter section and locate it fifty miles from the other sections. Dante, use the tractor beams when you are ready.'

'I would love to be in command of driving this ship.'

'The proton shield has been turned off, and we are awaiting Dante's handiwork.'

Athos pulled the craft to a level of fifty feet above the space platform on its underside. Dante started his division of the platform with Athos going forward in a straight line until he got to the middle. Dante then directed his beams at a ninety-degree angle and divided the platform in half. Athos then continued on a straight course. Dante kept on with the rays. After quartering the platform, Dante put his tractor beams on one section at a time, and Athos towed each away so that each section was fifty miles from each other. Athos then went back to the disabled ships, and Dante put the tractor beams on these.

'Are you still with us?'

'I will always be with you. I am listening also. We have already programmed Athos as to the location of the planet to which you wish to go.'

'Thank you very much. Please forgive me. I don't wish to sound disrespectful.'

'We understand. This planet has been uninhabitable for some time now.'

'We plan to check out the atmosphere before we set foot on it.'

'Good luck to you!'

'Okay, Chris, the proton shield is on now. Take it away.'

'Yes, sir, Commander. Athos, take the ship to orbit around the planet we are going to.'

Athos swung the ship toward the star Sirius and increased the speed to four parsecs per hour. Dante moved away from the disintegration rays.

Bill sat down in one of the lounging chairs. He picked up the communicator and advised the computer that this would be for intership communication. "This is Comdr. Bill Anderson again. I want to thank you and welcome you on board the star ship *Alpha Centauri*. We will be letting you all off shortly. At the present time I want you all to remain calm. It is not our intent to hurt you or harm you in any way. At the present time we are towing four of your disabled craft. It is my hope that you will all be reunited again." 'Porthos, how's it going?'

'All is going well, Commander. How did you know that these people breathe the same atmosphere as you and Chris do?'

'It was just a hunch. Chris, how would you like some coffee?'

'I'd love some, thank you.'

Bill went over to the dispensing machine and got two cups of coffee. Then he went over to one of the lounging chairs and handed a cup to Chris, keeping one of the cups for himself. He sat down and asked Chris how she was doing.

'Everything is doing fine. Thank you for the coffee.'

'Make sure that you keep your eyes on the screen. What you will be looking for are black holes or truly inverted suns.'

'Yes, I will keep my eyes open for them because I know the enormous gravitational pull that those black holes have.'

For the next twenty minutes things went by very slowly. Bill had a chance to take a nap. He didn't know why, but it felt very good to close his eyes.

Athos suddenly started decreasing speed. He thought, 'We are entering orbit around the planet.'

'I had better get a readout on the atmospheric conditions.' Bill then went over to the computer. 'Wow! These people must have involved themselves in a nuclear holocaust. Chris, would you turn the viewing screen down on the planet's surface and magnify by six?'

Chris turned the viewer on to six and directed it straight

95

down upon the surface of the planet. All they saw were the grotesque and warped forms of buildings. On most of the buildings some sort of foliage had taken over so that now most of them were buried in rich green. Some fifty species of animals were counted. The planet had large lakes and seas. Nowhere on the planet could they detect higher animal life. Vegetation was flourishing. There were many types of trees, grasses, and shrubbery. Both Chris and Bill studied the landscape for about an hour.

'That report on the atmosphere should be complete by now.' He got up and went over to the computer and started to read off the gases. 'Nitrogen, 78%; oxygen, 21%; argon, 1%; water vapor, .01–4%; carbon dioxide, .03%; cobalt, .001%. The atmosphere measures four hundred miles. The gravity here is almost the same as that on planet earth.'

'The atmosphere is now safe for human life forms.'

'Yes, but that cobalt count worries me.'

The Elders said, 'It's all right. The count is now low enough that these people can live with it without its affecting them.'

'Chris, how would you like to see what these women really look like? Porthos will be with you the whole time.'

'I thought you'd never ask. Yes, I would like to see them.'

'Dante, go to the ramp area. I am opening the doors to the center area and the ramp. I am also turning off the proton field. On your order I will close the doors to the center area and depressurize the ramp area. When we are just about ready to set the four craft down on the ground, we will open the doors to the outside and extend the ramp. I want you to be on the ground when these craft are deposited. I want you to knock out all that disembark from their ships. Then line them up one hundred yards from the ships. When you have done this, double check the craft and make sure there is no one inside. If you do find more beings, knock them out and put them one hundred yards from their craft. When that's done, make sure that these people do not have weapons of any kind. Those weapons that you do find are to be put in one of the damaged spacecraft. After that's accomplished, get back to our own ship, get into the ramp area, and advise us of your return.'

96

Dante acknowledged what his commander had said and left for the third tier and the ramp area. Chris went down to the third tier with him.

'Athos, put the ship down over that mountain chain that we just passed.'

Athos responded by changing course and then descending into the atmosphere. Just at that moment Dante reported that he was inside the ramp area.

Bill then closed the doors to the center area, depressurized the ramp area, opened the outer doors, and extended the ramp. At the same time he made sure that both the invisibility screen and the proton field were off.

Athos put the four craft down and stopped his forward motion. Bill turned off the tractor beams that were on the four ships. Dante was already on the ground and had gone to the ships before anyone had appeared. Very proficiently Dante went about his work. Soon all forty men were knocked out and Dante was carrying them beyond the scope of the force field. Then he checked each person out and confiscated what weapons he found on them. He took all the weapons and put them into the first ship that he came to. He then checked the spacecraft over to make sure that he hadn't missed anyone. It was when he had gotten to the fourth spacecraft that he found a radio operator still there. He immediately knocked this alien out, confiscated his weapon, and put him with the others. Dante went up to the *Alpha Centauri*, got into the ramp area, and advised the commander he was back.

As soon as Bill got confirmation from Dante that he was back, he closed the outer ramp doors and retracted the ramp. He repressurized the ramp area and then put tractor beams back on the four craft. He had Athos go to an elevation of one thousand feet and then take the ship out to sea. He asked the computer to remember the coordinates on the place they had just left.

'We are going to have to let these women off at the same place as soon as we dispose of these four ships.'

Athos got the ship up to an elevation of one thousand feet and then went out to sea. Bill found a likely spot and turned off the tractor beams. He watched as the four ships hit the water and then sank. Bill had Athos go back to his original position with the computer's help. Athos then landed the ship, and Bill depressurized the center area and the ramp area. Then he opened the doors to the ramp area, opened the outer doors, and extended the ramp. Dante helped Porthos put the women beside the bodies of the unconscious men.

After they were all out and down, Chris reassured the women that the men were only unconscious and would soon wake up. Chris said this not in English but in the women's own tongue. Chris, Porthos, and Dante went into the center section, and Bill closed the outer doors and the doors to the center area. He retracted the ramp, repressurized the third tier, and sealed the doors. He had Athos go up to one thousand feet. After this was reached, Bill turned on the invisibility screen and activated the proton device. Bill had Athos go beyond the planet's atmosphere, orbit the planet, and fly by the third space platform at a speed of two parsecs per hour.

Just then Chris appeared with Porthos and Dante. Bill looked at Chris rather quizzically. 'How is it that you spoke in the tongue of these people?'

Chris said that she didn't know how she did it, but she was quite sure she was able to converse with these people as if she had been doing it all her life.

Bill's only comment was that they both seemed to have powers that were still unexplored. He wondered about that.

'Where are we off to now, Commander?'

'I thought we might drop by the third platform and say hello. What I am hoping for is that they might go after us, thereby forming our invasion fleet to Alpha Centauri.'

Chris looked very skeptically at Bill, 'You really are a dreamer, aren't you?'

'Now, Chris, where would we be today without the typical "dreamers," as you call them? I'm glad you got those sixty women off the ship. Porthos and Dante, congratulations on a job well done!'

Porthos and Dante were murmuring to themselves. Finally Dante thought, 'Commander, you did say sixty women, didn't you?'

'Yes, there were sixty of them. It amounts to fifteen trips by both of you.'

Dante thought, 'It is true that fifteen trips were made by Porthos and myself. However, the number of women deposited was only fifty-eight.'

'There were sixty women. That is what Porthos took on board with him. Porthos and Dante, we have two stowaways on board. Find them and bring them here. This means searching the ship tier by tier, until you find them. Now go. They must be found. Athos, stop this ship until we find these aliens.'

Chris thought, 'I even checked the third tier. There was nothing left there. I thought we got them all.'

'Don't worry, we'll find them. Now, what was it you talked about when you visited with them?'

'Nothing special. I just told them how life was on our planet. That no special merits were required on the basis of sex, but that ability was the prime concern.'

'That's nothing to concern yourself with.'

Just then Porthos and Dante appeared with the two women. They were brought to Bill, who seemed to be studying their features. In reality he was probing their minds. What he found out was the hope they shared: that they might become one with them. The life they had left behind was very dismal, to say the least. All the men required of them was sex. They had been excluded from any decision that had to be made. Their whole training and existence was to be subservient to men. Chris had instilled in them something new. The idea of equality was something new, and they couldn't get their minds off it.

'Chris, if there is any one thing that might be said of you, it is that you inspire people. These are the same individuals you talked to, aren't they?'

'Yes, they are.'

'Chris, you know something? You are quite a girl. Now, since you speak their language, ask them if there is anything we can get them to eat. They must really be hungry.'

8

The Alpha Centauri *Gets an Escort* ——

CHRIS TURNED TO THE girls and, in their own language, asked if there was something the commander and she could get them to eat.

Both girls turned and looked at Bill. He read their thoughts. Both of them were asking him if it would be all right. Bill calmed their fears by answering telepathically, 'Yes, it is true you have nothing to fear. Order your food through Chris. There is one thing, though, I will need your help. Will you do what I ask?'

They both thought, 'Yes, we will! We will do whatever you want.'

'Thank you. Your time is fast approaching. Now, order your food through Chris verbally.'

The girls then ordered their food through Chris. Both Chris and Bill got the food that was ordered and gave it to the girls.

While the girls were intent on eating their food, Chris looked at Bill. 'Do you think it was wise to talk to the girls with telepathy?'

'Only when I am directing my thoughts at them can they hear or understand what I am saying. From now on, it will be your job to direct these girls in their own tongue. They are very poor at receiving and are not good transmitters. I want them to talk to the space platform we are going to. Through the communicator, they are to advise those on the platform that they are being held captive aboard the *Alpha Centauri* to be transported to a zoo. We are collectors and have many specimens. They are to ask for help. They have no idea where the others have been placed. They need their assistance immediately. I want you to tell them this in their own tongue and to supervise their conversation. I will communicate to the girls only through you. I want nothing more to do with them.

'Athos, fly this ship to within five miles of the space platform and hold it there. You can use seven parsecs per hour if you want. Porthos, make sure that the invisibility screen is turned off and that the proton field is turned on. What I want is for the whole contingency to follow us to Alpha Centauri. Do what you can in this direction. Okay, gal?'

'Yes, Commander.'

Chris went over to where the girls were seated and said in their own tongue what she wanted to have them say. Their reactions to this were utter amazement. Chris assured them it would be all right, that the commander wanted the ships to follow them. The girls agreed to do this. They had thought that the commander had something else on his mind. Chris assured them that this was not the case. It just wasn't so. The commander was very busy and had much to do.

At that point Athos advised them that they were nearing the space platform. The ship came to an abrupt stop.

Bill picked up the communicator and said, "This is Comdr. Bill Anderson of the star ship *Alpha Centauri*. Does anyone on the space platform read my communication?"

"This is the commander of the space platform. What is it you want?"

The girls heard Bill and their commander speaking a language that was completely unfamiliar to them. They were wondering about this and asked Chris to explain. Chris then told them that this was their original language and that a voice scrambler converted their language into ours and vice versa. The girls said they had never before heard of this process. Both wondered how it was that Chris spoke in their tongue. Chris advised them that she wasn't sure. She didn't know why, but she found no problem in this feat.

Bill held the communicator up to his mouth again. "This is Comdr. Anderson again. We have plotted your position and find that you are within the confederation's established parameters, and therefore I have no bone to pick with you.

We are now going back to our home base. Live in peace and God's good graces."

Bill looked on the screen and saw a long tubelike object being raised from the platform. 'Everyone brace himself. I think we are about ready to be attacked. Dante, get to that beam bank. Porthos, man the lever for the invisibility screen. Chris, get on the radio tie-in with the computer and report anything that you might hear.'

The two girls looked with amazement and fear as Chris, Porthos, and Dante changed their positions as if it were one motion. They were afraid, and Bill sensed this fear. Without saying anything, he went over to where the girls were on the lounging chairs and motioned to them to stay where they were.

Then the space platform fired on the ship. The shock was heard and felt through the ship.

'Porthos, turn on the invisibility screen. Athos, take the ship up in a big arc and put the ship within one thousand feet of that laser beam. Dante, get ready to fire.'

Bill adjusted the viewing screen and turned it on to one power. Athos made a big arc and came to within one thousand feet of the space platform.

'Dante, line up that laser gun. Obliterate it and leave a big hole where the gun once was.'

Dante fired the disintegration beam at the laser gun. The two girls were amazed as they lay back and watched the gun disappear and a big hole appear where the gun had been.

'Athos, take the ship up to a range of one hundred miles above the platform. Porthos, turn on the proton device and turn off the invisibility screen.'

Bill picked up the communicator. "This is Comdr. Bill Anderson. You have fired upon us, and we have gotten rid of your laser device. Since I have no quarrel with you, we will be leaving. But before we go, I would like you to hear from two people whom we have collected."

Chris immediately got up from where she was sitting and went over to the girls. "Now, you both know what to say?" Chris asked them in their own tongue. The girls said that they did. Bill handed the communicator over to Chris.

Chris advised them how to use the communicator and asked

them if they were ready. The girls said they were and started to talk over the communicator, telling how they were abused, that the spaceship they were on had six levels, that the men were all about 4'5" and very fat, that these people plan to put them on display when they returned to their base, that they needed help to escape from these beings, and that they needed their help immediately.

Bill took the communicator away from them. "There, Commander, you have heard how wonderfully we are treating these two specimens — I mean people."

Chris was back at the radio again. 'You really struck a vein. The commander is calling all his ships to battle status. He has asked these ships to assemble under the space station. They are to attack as soon as they can.'

'Athos, it is about time that we got out of here. Continue on to Alpha Centauri at a rate of one and one-half parsecs per hour.'

Athos started moving the ship forward. Bill asked the computer how far it was to their destination.

'Yes, Commander, the distance to Alpha Centauri from here is 4.8 light-years.'

'I wish that our escort would hurry it up a little.'

'Bill, the escort is formed, and their commander has given them their final instructions. They are catching up to us at four parsecs per hour.'

Bill went to the viewing screen, changed to six power, and couldn't see any obstacles. Then he turned the viewing screen by 180 degrees and watched as the fleet of some seventy-five ships bore down on them.

'Athos, increase your speed to four and one-half parsecs per hour.'

The escort maintained four parsecs per hour. Bill watched for a while and then swung the viewer around by 180 degrees and still was on six power when he saw a black hole coming up fast.

'Athos, take this ship up vertically by one million miles from the present course. Level off at one million miles and proceed to Alpha Centauri.'

Athos veered the ship until it was exactly one million miles off course. Then he leveled off on a straight line to Alpha Centauri, still maintaining the four and one-half parsecs per hour.

Bill turned the viewing screen back by 180 degrees and saw that the escort followed his idea and the ship at four parsecs per hour. As he swung the viewing screen back to the front by 180 degrees and saw that they were passing the black hole, he told Athos to bring the ship back to their original line of travel by dropping down one million miles. Still on six power, he saw that his escort had not altered its course and that the way ahead was clear of any hazards. He then put the viewing screen up by 90 degrees and watched the escorts. He told Athos to cut the power back to four parsecs per hour.

Athos reduced the speed of the craft.

Bill turned the viewer forward and watched awhile. The universe looked calm and serene. There were no obstacles all the way to Alpha Centauri.

'Chris, will you take over for a while? Porthos, will you show me where the washroom is?'

The two girls watched Bill use his cane to navigate as he and Porthos left the control room. Chris came up to them and asked how they liked the ride so far. The two girls said that they never before had seen so much go on without a word spoken. Then they asked what was wrong with the commander in that he had to use a cane to get around. What was it that he did during this whole trip that made him the commander? As far as they were concerned, this commander of hers had done nothing through this whole thing.

Using their own tongue, Chris straightened them out. "In the first place, our commander doesn't use his voice. He projects his mind images to everyone and everything on board. Nothing moves unless it is his wish that it moves. In this way he gets a response from me and the robots. I am endowed with the same abilities. But he is first and foremost the commander of this vessel."

The girls looked a little amazed and said, "You mean the disintegration of the laser gun and that detour around the black hole were done under his guidance?"

"Yes, they were. He may be physically impaired, but his mind is as sharp as a tack."

The girls apologized for what they were thinking. Chris reassured them it was all right. Nothing could change her, the robots', or the computer's opinions of their commander.

The girls said they just didn't understand and couldn't because of their ineptness.

"Just remember, both the commander and I think that you are two of the most beautiful creatures we have ever seen. Never before have we seen beauty like yours. If it were up to me, I would have directed this ship and left you on that planet we were on. But the commander kept you on board. I don't mind telling you that this made me very jealous. But the commander allayed my fears in a conversation we had that you didn't even know was going on. That is all I am going to say about it."

The girls thanked her for her honesty. If she had so much faith in such a person, so did they.

Chris sat back and scanned the universe through the viewer. She made a mental note that the escort was still with them, though they hadn't altered their speed or direction. They were still one million miles above them.

Then Bill and Porthos appeared. 'There is one thing I would like to say to you all, and that is congratulations and thank you all for a wonderful job well done.' Bill thanked them all for putting up with his tyranny. 'Now, Athos, you must be tired. Let Porthos take over for a while.'

Athos advised that he appreciated the change. He got up and let Porthos take over.

'Porthos and I have been over the alien ship. It is our opinion this alien and the ones above us will be evenly matched. I think that it would be a good idea if you were to show this alien ship to our two guests. I want them to watch the viewing screen for alien craft. We will be coming into their zone in about twenty minutes.'

'Yes, Commander.' Chris got the two girls, and all three of them went down to the third tier. Chris took them into the ramp area and showed them the alien craft. "Get a picture of this ship in your minds. Picture this ship without any stars painted on it. Within twenty minutes we will be approaching the realm where these ships come from. I want you to see these things before they see us. As soon as you see one of these craft, sing out loud and clear. These people are waiting for us, but they don't know what they are waiting for."

Some moments later, Chris came back with the two girls. The girls went to the viewing screen and started their vigil.

Bill asked Chris to monitor the radio.

Chris said that she would and went over to the computer.

'Are you there and can you hear me?'

'Yes, Commander, we are here and we do hear you. What is it you require?'

'It is the girls. Why do you want them?'

'Have you seen how lovely they are?'

'Right now I am not interested in beauty. What is your reason for having them here?'

'All right, we will stop beating around the bush. They are here because we find we are two women short. We need these women to complete a set, so to speak. Is that answer short enough?'

'Yes, it is clear and concise. Let me add something to this. The girls will go with you only if they want to go. We have agreed to transport you to your new home, wherever that might be. After that, Chris and I are free to go. This has been our understanding and therefore the law, so to speak. We have gone to a lot of trouble for you, and in return we want some consideration from you. I want this ship, the robots, the computer, Chris, and everything else we have now, including the other computers and their banks of stored information.'

'Commander, you are right, and we have to admit we are wrong. It isn't every day that we admit to this. The girls will have their choice, and so will you. You will also have your ship and everything on board her. Everything is to function as it is now. Commander, you are a great warrior and, I might add, a leader of men.'

'Thank you for the appraisal that has been made. It is greatly appreciated. I also appreciate your taking your time to reestablish our agreement. I will not bother you any further except to ask you if there is anything you will require of me.'

'Yes, there is. Since there now exists the possibility that you will not be with us, we will need three spacecraft equipped with lasers.'

'All right, you have them. Athos, turn on the invisibility screen. Porthos, take us up one million and two miles, just above the spacecraft that is escorting us. Dante, put the tractor beams on the last set of three ships. Porthos, as soon as the three ships are captured, take us down by one million miles before anyone becomes cognizant of the missing three ships.'

'Bill, I have been listening to your conversation. I had no idea that we might have trouble this way. It seems odd that things have worked out this way.'

'Don't worry that pretty little head over the small stuff. We have a job to do. Let's do it to the best of our abilities.'

Porthos brought the ship up in such a way that they were directly over the far edge of the wedge. They were still traveling forward at a speed of four parsecs per hour.

'Computer, what would be our maximum speed if we were to bring three of those ships under tow? I would also like you to compute the drag effect if we were to use our tractor beams.'

'I am computing, Commander. The maximum speed the ship will go is five parsecs per hour. The drag effect of the tractor beams is of negligible importance. Don't allow your conversations to have any bearing on your performance. We are all with you 100 percent.'

'Thank you, Computer, for both your help and advice.'

One of the girls called out that she had one of those ships in the viewing screen. Bill looked, and there was one of the ships hidden behind a rather large asteroid. That gave Bill an idea.

'Okay, Porthos, get into position at the edge of the wedge and hover over the last three spacecraft about fifteen feet above them. Athos, turn off the proton field. Dante, put your tractor beams on.'

'Commander, we have a capture!'

Bill inverted the screen and confirmed that they had three ships. 'Porthos, take the ship down by one million miles and proceed on course at five parsecs per hour.'

The ships didn't even notice the three ships diving straight down from them. 'We have one hope, and that is that the scout ship didn't notice them yet before they peeled off. When the ships pass the scout ship, the war is on. Athos, how are those three ships doing? Put on the proton field and turn off the invisibility screen.'

Athos replied that the three ships under tow were doing fine.

Chris went over to look at Alpha Centauri when the viewing screen had been inverted to straight ahead. 'There are ten planets revolving around the larger sun. Four of them are too close to the orbit of the other suns. The fifth and sixth planets look as though they might be inhabited.'

'What are the distances of the planets from the major sun? I'm not sure, but I think we will find the right planet at a distance of from ninety to one hundred million miles.'

Chris said that she would check with the computer and would be right back.

Chris came back directly. 'It is the third planet of this solar system that is exactly 93.284 million miles from Alpha Centauri.'

'What about the fourth planet? How far away is it?'

'The fourth planet is 110 million miles away.'

'Porthos, take this ship to the fourth planet.'

In a few moments Porthos advised that they were entering orbit around the planet.

'Chris, will you find out what gases exist and the relative height of the atmosphere?'

Chris said she would be right back. In the interim, Bill turned the viewer down on the planet's surface. As he studied it, he saw that life was abundant but that none of the higher forms of intelligent life existed. There was an abundance of foliage, trees, and grasses.

Chris came back, 'With the exception of cobalt, the gases are the same as that on the other planet we visited. The atmosphere measures some six hundred miles.'

'That's beautiful. Porthos, take the ship down into the atmosphere. Athos, as soon as Porthos has done that, open up the ramp area, extend the ramp, depressurize the entire ship, and turn off the force field. Dante, get down there first and knock out all the people on the three ships. We are going to release the ships as soon as they are on the ground. Dante, collect the bodies and deposit them one hundred yards from their craft. Disarm them and put all of them in the first ship. Then go through all the ships and disarm the self-destruct mechanisms and make sure that everything is turned off. Athos, help Dante out. After everything is completed, load the ships on board with the other alien spacecraft. Good luck to you both.'

Porthos went straight down. There was a large field there. Bill went over to the viewing screen and inverted it straight down. Athos and Dante were there even before the ship had gotten there. Porthos settled the three ships down on the ground. Bill went over and turned off the tractor beams. Then he picked up the communicator.

"This is Comdr. Bill Anderson. I would suggest that you get out of your ships as fast as you can, before I exterminate them. We have checked out the atmosphere and find it is compatible with yours." The ramps of the spacecraft were extended, and one person from each ship ran out.

As soon as they were outside, Athos knocked them out. In the meantime, Dante was going through the ships, disconnecting the self-destruct devices and making sure that everything was turned off. Athos came back with the weapons he had gathered. All weapons were placed in the first ship.

Bill had Porthos land the ship close to the other three and asked Athos and Dante to load the ships on board with the alien craft.

By stacking the ships, Dante and Athos got all of the ships into the ramp area.

Bill then walked up to the two girls and mentally asked if they also would like to get off. Both of the girls answered that they didn't.

'Okay, this is your choice, not mine. I want you to tell me anytime you want to get off, okay?'

The girls said they understood, and then one of them thought, 'How could we leave so handsome a man?'

Bill smiled and shook his head. 'Athos and Dante, are you both inside the ramp area?' Both Athos and Dante said that they were.

Bill retracted the ramp and closed and sealed the ramp doors leading to the outside. He pressurized the ship and set the temperature at seventy-two degrees Fahrenheit. He had Porthos bring the ship up beyond the atmosphere and hold. He put on the proton field and made sure the tractor beams and the invisibility screen were off. Athos and Dante came back to the control room.

'Is everything put away all right?' Both Dante and Athos thought, 'Everything is fine.'

'Porthos, take the ship to the third planet, which should be 16.716 million miles from here.'

'Do you want us to orbit this planet first?'

'Yes, I do. Chris, how are you doing? How about some coffee?'

Chris turned and looked at him. 'That was a nice try on your part to get rid of the girls. Yes, Commander, coffee sounds fine. It would be my honor to have coffee with one who dared talk on an even plane with the Elders.'

'Let's not make a big deal of this.'

9

The Relocation of the People of Ohg —

CHRIS AND BILL GOT their coffee, found two chairs, and sat down.

'You know, Chris, I haven't heard you play that harpsichord yet. Some Handel or Bach would certainly go good right now. I think a little Brandenburg or water music would be just fine.'

'You haven't heard any music because I have a real task-master for a commander. So you can blame it all on him.'

'Oh, Chris, I hope we can get out of this thing in one piece. I never expected this—any of it. This universe is just crawling with creatures so far advanced in science and technology that it makes me wonder what we are doing here.'

'Your points are indisputable. We are here, though. You are making changes that will affect many peoples and worlds. I am glad to have come along with you as far as we have gone. Through your direction we have disposed of a tyrannical power. A dreamer's notion. You are a dreamer, did you know that? I'm in love with a dreamer. That's really a kick in the pants.'

'Thank you, Chris, I'm in love with you, too. I don't think it's the situation we've found ourselves in. It goes back to NASA and my first meeting with you.' He held her hand and felt an energy he had never felt before. 'I must talk to the Elders.'

'Yes, Commander. What is it you require?'

'Yes, tell us about God.'

'God is very important and never should be overlooked in any way. It is he who created the firmament. The firmament is all of the galaxies as you know them and all forms of life

111

thereon. It is naive to say that either you alone have a god or that he doesn't exist because you alone travel through space. In effect, it is he that created all living things. He is universal in concept. He does exist. Those whom you have conquered have lost sight of this fact and tend to think they are the only ones in the universe. You have very rudely awakened them. They don't know how to handle this — to think they have been supreme in their sector of the universe for such a long time, and here you are beating them back! It doesn't matter how far advanced they are in science and technology. They have forgotten one thing: God.'

'That is very powerful and thought-provoking. Does this mean that you will keep God in your hearts when you are free?'

'Yes, it does.'

'Thank you for your help and the time you have spent with us now.' He looked at Chris. 'Now, let's go over to those two girls and make them feel more at home.'

Chris nodded in affirmation, and they went over to where the girls were. Speaking in their own tongue, Chris asked them how they were doing.

The response was that they were doing fine. They had been keeping watch on the screen and saw three ships leaving the orbit of the planet they were headed for.

'Athos, put the invisibility screen on.'

Bill turned to the girls and telepathically said, 'Is there anything we can get for you?'

The girls looked at him and telepathically said, 'No, thank you, Commander, we are both fine.'

'Keep your eyes wide open on the screen for alien craft.'

'Chris, I think you better get back to that radio.'

'Yes, sir, Commander.' She turned and went to the computer.

Porthos thought, 'We are now entering orbit around the third planet.'

'Computer, what is the readout of the atmosphere? Please give your findings to Chris.'

Bill scanned the horizon and saw no obstacles. He inverted the viewing screen downward by ninety degrees and turned the focusing to six power. After a while he thought, 'Wow! It looks as if we had another atomic war here. Wait one minute. Porthos, stop our forward motion and hold the ship right here.'

Porthos complied with his commander's request and stopped his forward motion, holding the craft in place.

'Chris, come here and look at this!'

The computer had just finished its atmospheric evaluation and printed it out for Chris. As soon as the computer was through, Chris went over to where Bill was standing with a piece of paper in her hand. She gave the paper to Bill and looked at the viewing screen. 'Why, Bill, those are pyramids down there.'

'Computer, what is the height of the largest pyramid down there?'

'Commander, the height is ninety-six feet.'

'If one were to multiply by one million, you might find that the farthest distance in elliptical orbit that this planet travels around Alpha Centauri happens to be ninety-six million miles. Computer, is that right?'

'Commander, the farthest distance that this planet travels around its sun is ninety-six million miles.'

'Computer, if you were to take the area of the base and divide it by two times the height, would it give you 3.14159, or pi?'

'I am computing. Yes, Commander, it is 3.14159265.'

'Chris, we have found our planet. Porthos, take the ship down to sixty-thousand feet. Computer, take a reading of the atmosphere at the sixty-thousand-foot level. Porthos, take the ship in an easterly direction and do it slowly, at about 750 miles per hour. Computer, take a reading of the atmosphere at twenty-minute intervals.'

Bill then went to the computer and took the readout card. This was compared with the original card that Chris had given to him.

'Chris, the upper atmosphere and the northern hemisphere are shot. But the cobalt count in the southern hemisphere is not that bad. It's still a killer, though.'

They had passed by a continent and were now passing over a sea. Suddenly they came upon another continent. There it was, inscribed upon the cliff walls, a trident. Bill asked Porthos to hold the ship down in speed to about twenty-five miles per hour and to lower the craft to a level of five thousand feet. They seemed to be crawling until they saw the old runway. He told Porthos to stop and still maintain the five-thousand-foot level elevation. Bill asked the computer for a readout on the atmosphere. After a few minutes the computer came up with the atmospheric conditions.

'Well,' thought Bill, 'here it is: Nitrogen, 78%; oxygen, 21%; argon, 1%; water vapor, .01–4%; carbon dioxide, .03%; cobalt, .003%. They really did it, didn't they? This is the only area left on this globe where the atmosphere is still breathable. Boy, the same thing could happen on our planet.'

'It kind of frightens you, doesn't it? The people are right ahead of us.'

'Athos, turn off the invisibility screen and the force field. Porthos, land the ship. I will depressurize the ramp area and the central area to the third tier. I will then extend the ramp and open the ramp doors to the outside. Athos and Dante, retrieve the people. Put them all in the center area. Keep them clear of the alien ships we have in the ramp area.'

Athos and Dante left the control room and took the elevator down to the third tier. By the time Bill had depressurized the center area, the ramp area, and extended the ramp and opened the ramp doors to the outside, Athos and Dante had reached the third tier. They immediately went out the ramp and started to collect people. They brought them aboard four at a time until all sixty people had been collected. There were twenty-nine men and thirty-one women. Both Athos and Dante got into the center area with the sixty people. Bill then closed the ramp doors to the center area as well as to the outside and retracted the ramp. He repressurized the third tier and advised Porthos to take the ship straight up through the atmosphere and to hold it there. Porthos started a very rapid ascent. Bill told Athos to stay there and Dante to come to the control room. When Dante got there, Bill asked him how the gases were holding out. Dante assured him that their atmospheric condition was fine. Even with their sixty passengers they had enough gas to last them for a full month. Bill asked

Dante to go down to the third tier and check out the rejuvenation equipment.

'Chris, I don't know why, but you are the communicator in our little group. Go down with Dante and speak to their chief person. Find out if they would have any objection if we were to deposit them on the fourth planet and advise them that it would be perfectly safe to go there.'

'You make reference to a chief person. It would be either male or female. I am going right now. Watch out with these two girls. I don't like throwing temptation at you.'

'Okay, your point is well taken.'

He went over to the console and put on the invisibility screen and the proton field. He put the viewing screen up by ninety degrees and changed the power to three.

'Porthos, take us back to the fourth planet and land at approximately the same spot that we were before.'

Porthos started forward at a speed that would put them there in thirty minutes.

Bill walked over to the computer. 'Computer, are you alive? I know this is a funny question to ask you, but a while back you offered me comfort when I needed it.'

'Am I alive, Commander? That is a difficult thing for me to say. I feel as though I were.'

'I want to thank you. Now can you tell me what happened on the third planet?'

'Computing. It is difficult to say without additional information what actually happened. It is obvious that three cobalt bombs exploded in three of the northern sectors of the planet.'

'It is apparent there were three powers that had the cobalt bomb. Someone got itchy. One of the bombs was exploded. As soon as the other powers found out about it, they decided to get their bombs over to the enemy and explode theirs so that they would all die at the same time. Stupid, stupid, stupid.'

Chris came back and told Bill she had spoken with the leader. 'By the way, it's a he. Anything we can do would be appreciated.'

'Did you have any trouble in speaking to him?'

'I had absolutely no problem in conversing with him. The

115

fact of the matter is I can converse in any language I come into contact with. It's weird. I always had trouble with languages of any kind.'

'Chris, I want to meet this individual. Would you please introduce us?'

'Let's go. I'd be happy to have him meet you.'

Chris and Bill went down to the third tier. As soon as they got there, all sixty people stood up. Bill telepathically addressed the whole group.

'Please sit down as you were. I have come to talk to your leader and to find out what happened on the planet Ohg. We are here not to interrogate you but to find out what happened. What we do know is three cobalt bombs were dropped and exploded in the northern hemisphere. What I would like to know is why.'

A spokesman for the group addressed Bill telepathically. 'Commander, we all want to thank you for getting us out when you did. We certainly appreciate your kindness and consideration. We will all sit down now as you have requested. Our leader is over there. To have been able to find us tells us that you are one of us.' He pointed to an elderly gentleman in the corner of the room.

'Chris, please introduce me.' Chris went over to the elderly gentleman and, in his own language, introduced Bill and made mention of the fact that he seemed to be very deep in thought. The man looked up. Then he stood up, saying that he had expected a visit from Bill. Very studiously Bill looked at the man standing before him. The man was taller than Bill. He had a massive forehead, a long pointed nose, and six digits on each hand. In one of these hands he was holding a fairly large book. The man offered the book to Bill. After leafing through the book, Bill ascertained it was a Bible. It was the story of creation and the ten rules to live by. Bill handed the book back to the man.

'My name is Comdr. Bill Anderson, as my cocommander has already said. We have studied the fourth planet in your solar system and have found it suitable for life forms. What we don't know is whether the three suns that revolve around each other will continue to do so. Do you have an astronomer who can answer this question?'

116

'Yes, we do.' He went over to a woman who looked very much like him and brought her over to Chris and Bill. He explained to her what Bill wanted to know and asked her if she had any opinions on the subject. She looked at Bill very carefully and thought, 'We have been studying this situation now for many millennia. It is our opinion these stars will not collide or fuse together for many millions of years to come.'

Bill thanked her and said that he honored her opinion. He then turned to the man. 'All right, sir, it is the fourth planet we will be taking you to. There is one small detail. What happened on Ohg?'

'On the planet Ohg there were three great political powers. It was decided that one of these powers had to go. In their infinitely small minds, they decided to drop and explode a cobalt bomb on this power. They forgot, even though they were warned, that a cobalt bomb would be carried by the winds once it was detonated, destroying everything that it came in contact with. In retaliation, the other power exploded two of their cobalt bombs. That was the beginning of the end.'

'There is one thing that confuses me. Where are the children? There is not one child with you. Can these people reproduce?'

'Yes, we can reproduce. There are no children here because they were conscripted into the service by one of the powers. They thought by going that we might escape and would not be further harassed. We are very proud of them, for they knew they were going to die.'

'I'm truly sorry. All right, then, it's settled.'

The astronomer thought, 'Your choice is a good one. For quite some time now we have known about the fourth planet. We could not check this out because of the aliens. I am surprised you were able to get through to us.'

'I must take care of this as soon as I drop you off.'

Both Chris and Bill said that it was nice talking with them.

'We have to go upstairs and see how things are going. Under no circumstances are you to leave this area. The robot is programmed to make sure of this.'

'We will stay here. You will not have to worry about that.'

'Bill, it is strange that these people don't resemble us physically.'

117

'That's not so, Chris. If you were to look at the wall drawings of ancient times, you would see exact duplicates depicted of these people, from their foreheads to their six-digit hands. These people are the same race that visited us over forty thousand years ago. The reason we're not the same is that we are offshoots and they are the real McCoy.'

When they got to the control room, the two girls told Chris that they had seen no aliens and that the way was clear ahead. Chris thanked the two girls and asked them to keep their eyes on the screen and to report anything suspicious immediately. They said that they would do this.

Bill asked Porthos how it was going and how long it would be before they came to the fourth planet.

Porthos advised him that everything was fine and that the estimated time of arrival would be ten minutes.

'That gives us time for another cup of coffee.'

'You're on.'

Bill went to the dispenser and got two cups of coffee. He went to Chris and gave her a cup and sat down in a chair beside her.

'It's strange, though, that our two stowaways are physically like us and not at all like those people down on the third tier.'

'Is it so strange that there can be throwaways like us? These two girls are a result of crossbreeding, like us.'

'I wonder how these girls got to where they were. I didn't have the opportunity to take a look at the others. Where the heck is the difference?'

'There was a difference. There was a big difference. Some of the women had six fingers on each hand, high foreheads, and a big stature, quite unlike the two girls that stayed on board. I will ask them and try to find out.' Chris asked the two girls over to where she and Bill were sitting. Chris then asked them in their own language how it was that they didn't have the high foreheads and the extra digit on each hand. The girls replied that they were taken captive from their own planet. Their primary purpose was to serve their captor in whatever way they could. Their captors were a mixed breed of men. Some had six fingers on each hand and high foreheads, while others were very similar to them. There did not seem to be any difference in responsibility between the two types of individuals. There seemed to be a definite caste system between the women. The women had no say in the decisions made. There was a definite discrimination made between the men and the women.

Porthos thought, 'Excuse my interruption, Commander. But while you and Chris were down on the third tier, these two lovely women were discussing how they might take over this ship. They seemed to have a great knowledge about the ship and how it works.'

'Thank you, Porthos. How were they to take over the ship?'

'They were to dispose of you through a guise of sexual pleasure. You were to have your hands and feet tied. They were to get Chris by overpowering her. They have no idea of our capabilities and think we can be turned off or neutralized and therefore become ineffective. The ship will become theirs. I have already advised Athos and Dante about this.'

Bill thanked Porthos once again and turned to the two girls.

'What exactly were your jobs on the space platform?'

'Our job, Commander, was to design and renovate spacecraft.'

'Oh? What speeds were you able to design these craft for?'

'Four parsecs per hour.'

'Then you might say your jobs were rather important ones, despite your lack of being able to make decisions?'

'Yes, you might say that. There were times when we took these spacecraft up for a little test flight.'

'What, if anything, do you ascertain to be different between the spacecraft you have worked on and ours?'

'The only difference that we see is in the size of the craft. We have estimated the speed to be about the same.'

'If this craft were yours, where would you take it?'

'We would take it back to our own planet.'

'Thank you very much. We have evaluated your opinions and appreciate them very much. Your job right now is keeping an eye on the televiewer. I would appreciate it if you would return to this task. As you are doing this, try to picture your-

119

selves back home right now. You have learned and seen too much to ever be able to fit into the society that you have known and loved. Please think about this.

'Porthos, please orbit the fourth planet until further advised.'

Chris looked at Bill. 'So, these girls are not the small likable people we thought they were. This makes our job a little more hazardous than we thought. From now on we should take one of the robots with us wherever we go.'

'That is a good idea. We'll do it.'

Porthos thought, 'We are now in orbit around planet four.'

'Computer, have you now translated the language of the people on the third tier, and can you now speak their language?'

'Yes, Commander, I can.'

'Computer, this is an intership communication to the third tier.'

He picked up the communicator. "This is Comdr. Bill Anderson. We are now in orbit around the fourth planet. Before we touch down, I want you to be apprised of a situation that might make a difference in your thinking. We were requested to confiscate three alien spacecraft. This was done and the pilots were deposited on this planet. They are without weapons and should pose no threat to you. Do you still want to live there?"

A voice spoke up. "Yes, Commander, we will accept these people. Put the ship down in approximately the same location these three pilots were placed."

'Okay, Porthos, put the ship down where we were before.' The ship left its orbit and descended into the atmosphere. The girls were watching Bill with apprehension. They were thinking how they might duplicate the apparent calmness that this individual had. Bill had them tuned in and was listening to everything they were thinking.

Porthos thought, 'This is approximately where we left the three.'

Bill went over to the console and turned off the force field and the invisibility screen. 'All right, set her down.' Then he depressurized the ship, opened the doors to the ramp area and

120

the outside doors, and extended the ramp. He then turned to Chris. 'Take Dante with you. Break out the rejuvenation equipment and start replacing the gases that we have expended.'

'Okay, but what about the two stowaways?'

'I'm glad you brought that up. They are going to help with the disembarkment of the people we have downstairs. They shouldn't have a moment to themselves.'

'This climate is warmer than I thought. Just two minutes after you depressurized I started to feel it.'

'Computer, I wish to talk with the third tier again.'

'All right, I'm ready for you.'

'We have landed.'

'Thank you both.' Bill picked up the communicator. "This is Comdr. Bill Anderson. We have landed on planet four in the area where we have left the three pilots. We will be down shortly to assist you in your disembarkment. If there is anything you will need, it is a good draftsman and an architect. Please advise if you have these individuals available."

'Porthos, turn everything off and then follow me out with the two girls.'

Porthos went around and made sure that everything was turned off.

Bill went up to the two girls. 'If you two lovely damsels are ready, we will go now to the third tier. We have some people to let off.'

The girls immediately got up and followed Bill who, in turn, was followed by Porthos. When they got down to the third tier, they immediately spotted Chris and Dante moving the rejuvenation equipment to the ramp area. Attached to this equipment was a lot of hose.

Bill looked at the two girls. 'I want you two to be the first ones off the ramp area, with the help of the robots. Once on the ground, I want you to guide these people approximately one thousand yards away from the ship. When you are through, you will come up the same way you got down. Is that understood?'

The girls nodded in agreement.

Bill summoned Athos and Porthos and told them to deposit

the girls on the soil and then come up again for their next load of people.

He went over to the astronomer and the elderly man. 'Do you have a draftsman and an architect?'

The man turned and told Bill everything was fine and that they had everything that was needed.

Bill advised them that both Chris and he had some unfinished business to transact and would be right back as soon as the matter was taken care of. Right now what they needed and were taking were some gases which were vital to their existence.

The astronomer took Bill's hand and smiled. 'Thank you, Commander. We would like to wish you the best of luck with that unfinished business. I couldn't help noticing the necklaces on your cocommander's neck. They are very old, aren't they?'

Bill looked at her very quizzically. 'Yes, they are old.'

The man interrupted them. 'You see, Commander, we are only curious and don't mean to pry. You will notice that we haven't even brought up your having to get around with a cane.'

Bill straightened up. 'That is a point well taken. If I were to bring other people here, would you also accept these individuals? Let it be clearly understood that there are to be no slaves here. Everyone is to be democratically the equal to everyone else.'

'That there be no slaves is understood. Everyone is free to decide which course of action he will be taking. Everyone is democratically the equal to everyone else. On this point you have our pledge.'

'As I have said, I will be back. I will bring with me a detailed map of all the riches of this planet. With this map you will know where every resource can be found.'

'I know you are one of us. You certainly don't look like one of us. But I know it. Your mind is fantastic. Once again, thank you for saving us.'

'Commander, in answer to your initial question. We will accept with open arms anyone you bring here. They will be accepted as one with us.'

Porthos and Athos came up to them as the man was talking. 'Commander, everyone is off the ship, save these two.'

'Thank you, Athos. All right, take me down along with the others and stand by my side.'

The robots conducted all three down to the planet's surface. Bill walked up to the two girls.

'There has been a change in plans. Since you both speak in the tongue of those downed pilots, it will be your responsibility to find them and bring them into the fold. We will be back to pick you up shortly. Understood?'

The two girls nodded in assent.

In the meantime, Chris and Dante were trying to manage the rejuvenation equipment. Both of them were puzzled as to how to make it work correctly. Chris finally hit upon the right procedure. She and Dante were busy getting the required gas into the appropriate cylinders. After approximately ten minutes, all of the cylinders had been filled. Chris suggested to Dante that they go upstairs to try out the gas. They went upstairs to the first tier, and Chris closed off the entire ship, save the ramp area, and pressurized it. After several minutes they concluded their efforts had been fruitful and that they had done it correctly. Chris then depressurized the entire ship and opened up the center area to the ramp section.

10

The Encounters

BILL SOON MADE HIS appearance with Athos and Porthos and immediately went up to the first tier with them. He came in, went to the dispenser, and got two coffees. He sat down in one of the lounging chairs, and Chris came over to get her coffee. She, too, sat down in one of the lounging chairs. Bill looked a little dismayed and troubled. He looked up and asked Chris if she had any trouble with the rejuvenation equipment.

Chris reported that she had had a little trouble but that she thought everything was taken care of and that now they were breathing fresh gas.

Bill nodded his approval and then went into deep thought.

Chris sensed that something was wrong and asked Bill what it was.

Bill looked at Chris. "Chris, what in God's name are we doing here?"

Chris looked a little astonished that he spoke and didn't use his telepathy. For the first time during the entire trip he spoke aloud. Certainly he had done so when using the communicator, but not while addressing her, the robots, or the computer. She saw that something was really bugging him, but she had no idea what it could be. "All right, let's speak in our own tongue. What's bothering you? Up to this point you have done an excellent job. You have done things which I wouldn't have had the faintest idea of being able to do. Now I sense something is wrong. What is it?"

'I'm really not sure, but there seem to be many questions

forming in my mind. I'd rather not say right now. Mainly because my thoughts are not really formed yet. Let me get them together, and then we can have a long talk. I don't know why I feel this way, but you can bet it isn't out of line.'

Chris tried to probe Bill's mind but found nothing tangible there. All his thoughts seemed to be in mass confusion. "At what point did you learn to close your mind off from mine?"

"When I realized that it could be done. Chris, I'm not closing my mind off to you but, rather, to them. This is what they have done to us."

Chris couldn't fathom this whole thing. "I look forward to our discussion." She went over to the computer console and sat down.

Bill turned to the robots. 'All right. Athos, take over Porthos's place and give him a well-deserved rest. Porthos, go over to the atmospheric controls and pressurize the ship. Make sure that all doors are closed to the outside, including the ramp area. Also, retract the ramp. Athos, take us up beyond the atmosphere, turn on our proton field and the invisibility screen. Dante, stand by the disintegration buttons.' The robots shifted their positions and awaited further orders.

'We are now orbiting planet four.' Porthos put the shields up.

'Athos, take us within approximately two million miles of the sun, Alpha Centauri. Then level off and hold it right there. Dante, place the viewing screen level and change the focus to six power. Chris, are you picking up any radio communications?'

'No, nothing as of yet.'

'Commander, we have reached the two-million-mile mark. Our ship is melting because of the intense radiation.'

'Break through the gravitational field produced by Alpha Centauri and take the ship to a level of twenty million miles and then hold.'

Athos soon had the ship at a level of twenty million miles. 'This is better, but we are still too close.'

'I am now picking up some radio communications,' Chris apprised them. 'It is coming from 125 degrees to the left.'

'Athos, turn the ship 125 degrees to port and hold. Porthos, has there been any deterioration to the craft because of our close proximity to the sun?'

Porthos reported that nothing had been damaged because they did not stay there that long.

Bill asked Chris to look into the viewing screen and tell him what she saw.

'This increasing to six power makes one feel as though they were closer than they really are. Yes, I see two types of alien craft. It looks as though that wedge is a very effective way of fighting. I approximate that the ones with the wedge have some fifty craft left. Whereas the other group has only twenty-five ships left. Wait one minute, there is yet another space-craft off at a distance to the right of these other craft. The size and shape of it is like ours, or at least it looks like ours.'

'Computer, how far away are these spacecraft?'

'Computing, Commander. The approximate distance is 15.3 million miles.'

'Athos, take this ship straight ahead 15.3 million miles and hold. Dante, switch the focus on the viewing screen to one power. Porthos, check out the invisibility screen and make sure that it's functional.'

Soon Athos reported that the 15.3 million miles had been reached and that he was now holding.

Bill looked at the viewing screen and confirmed they were in the right area. Porthos advised that the invisibility screen was in operation and that everything seemed to be functioning all right.

'Dante, destroy all of the craft on each side but one on each end of the lines. Athos, take care of that wedge first. Put Dante within range and then proceed in a straight line to allow him a good shot. After you do this, put Dante within range of the other line of spacecraft and then proceed down along the length of it.'

Athos positioned the ship along the far end of the wedge, and Dante commenced with his destruction, leaving only one ship on the end free from harm. Athos swung the ship around and placed it along the far end of the other alien's line and proceeded forward. Dante made short work of these ships, leaving only one of them untouched.

Bill asked the computer for lines to both of the remaining ships.

After a pause the computer said it was ready.

Bill picked up the communicator. "This is Comdr. Bill Anderson of the star ship *Alpha Centauri*. There was no conflict here because I wanted it halted. May I suggest you return to your respective bases of operation so that no harm will further befall you? Henceforth this entire area is off limits to your people as well as yourselves. You have handicapped the growth of planets too long. This will not occur again. We will make sure of this. Now, may I suggest that you both take your leave now?"

The two remaining spacecraft turned around and left. They immediately gained speed and disappeared. 'Athos, turn in the direction of that other ship. Come to rest about one hundred feet above it. This spacecraft did nothing to stop this fight but just hung in the background and watched. I wonder if this is the third set of aliens. Porthos, as soon as we are above the craft, turn off the invisibility screen. Make sure the proton device is working correctly. Dante, stand by the disintegration rays. Computer, I want to hail that ship on all frequencies. Chris, what do you make of this craft? I want to know how it is powered, its atmosphere, how many decks it has, and how many people are on board her.'

Athos reported that he was hovering at one hundred feet above the spacecraft. Porthos turned off the invisibility screen. Dante turned up the focus on the viewing screen to two and directed it on the ship below. Then he went to the destruct buttons and awaited his commander's orders. Chris got all of the obtainable information that she could get on the alien space vessel and went to Bill with the information. The computer advised Bill that all channels of communication were now opened to him. Porthos made sure that the force field was on and in operation.

Bill asked Chris to stand beside him, which she did without hesitation. Bill picked up the communicator. "This is Comdr. Bill Anderson. Is anyone receiving this communication?"

Moments passed by and then the picture of a being appeared on the screen. "Greetings, Commander. We have been awaiting your arrival now for some time. We have felt your

127

probes and know you have all the information as to our weapons, the number of people we have on board, the construction of our ship, and the type of drive we are using. Unfortunately, we have also tried to probe your vessel. Our probe beams keep on returning to us. We do not have the data you do. What is it you want?"

"You are making me blush. What I would like to know is where you come from and if you might have room for 3.5 million people? Please excuse my probing of your vessel. It seems difficult for me to accept we record some 450 people on board your ship."

"It is harder for me to believe that you have 3.5 million people on board your vessel; although your craft is larger than ours. You are a technologically advanced race of people. We have been studying you for many hundreds of years. Every planet you have started to develop has, for some reason, backfired. We have to admit your craft is more sophisticated and more highly advanced than ours. This takes a lot of admitting on our part, in that we are supposed to be protecting this galaxy. But we have seen you do things with this vessel that would be impossible to do with ours. We will do you a favor and go after and eliminate the alien race you have found breathes no oxygen. In our estimation, by holding back progress, they have done more harm than any other despotic race. We have to ask you — no, implore you — not to go any farther than you have in the universe. this is the council's decision, until you develop a race on one of the planets which will not turn on us in the end. We give you the choice to repair the damage you have already started or go on. The choice is yours to make. If you do repair the damage on one of the planets, then you will go with our blessing. We of the council think this is imperative."

"We will need time to think about this."

"We have to go now to chase an adversary. Take all the time you need."

"All right, but promise us one thing. At all times we will keep our radio on and the channels open. If you need help for any reason, give us a call and we will come running to help you out."

"It is agreed. If we run into any trouble, you will be the first ones advised."

"Thank you and good luck. We have to go to establish life on one of the planets in this solar system of Alpha Centauri."

"You mean reestablish, don't you? At any rate, good luck. We will meet here again when we both get through."

The alien spacecraft started to move out. Chris and Bill watched as the ship gained momentum and soon was gone.

Bill asked Chris to take over the helm while he sacked out. He advised her to set course for planet four and then go into orbit around the planet. He had promised the people there a resource map.

She said that she would do this and that she hoped he would have a nice nap.

Bill left the control room. He was beat, physically exhausted. Chris knew this and watched as Bill hobbled off and took the elevator down to the second tier.

'Porthos, Athos, Dante, and computer, this is the first time I have actually been alone and given the command. I will need the help of all of you to make sure everything goes along smoothly. Porthos, turn on the invisibility screen. Make sure the proton field is on. Athos, take this ship to planet four and then orbit around it. Dante, readjust the viewing screen to straight ahead at one power. Computer, after we get into orbit, make a map of the landmasses and then depict all of the raw materials and natural resources that are available. Now, I am going to rest too. Call me if anything extraordinary occurs. I will be right here if you need me.' Chris went to one of the lounging chairs and lay down. Soon she, too, was fast asleep.

Time slipped by. Soon Athos was reporting that they were now in orbit around planet four.

Chris snapped out of a heavy sleep. 'Computer, get ready to get a printout and a depiction of all of the available resources.'

'Yes, Commander, I am starting a resource readout right now.'

At that moment Bill reappeared. He went to the dispenser and got himself a cup of coffee. He went to where Chris was seated and sat beside her in one of the lounging chairs. 'You know, that was a pleasurable three-hour nap. How are things going with you? I see that we are in orbit around planet four.'

'I hereby pass the command over to you.'

'That was very unfair of me, leaving the helm and taking a nap like that. I'm terribly sorry. Why don't you go down to the second tier and take a long-deserved rest? After you return, we can have that long-awaited discussion.'

Chris admitted she was tired and perhaps a rest was in order. She got up from where she was sitting and went to the elevator.

When she was gone, Bill asked the computer how it was coming and how much longer it would be.

The computer replied it would be finished in about one hour.

Bill advised the computer to take its time, perhaps enabling it to make two maps, one of which he wanted to keep.

The computer reported that this would be done.

Bill then asked the computer how long they had been away from planet earth in earth's time.

'You have been away from earth for seven and one-half years.'

Just then Chris came into the control room. Bill turned to look at her.

'Chris, you are just as beautiful as the first time we met. I don't think you have aged any at all.'

Chris rubbed the sleep from her eyes and looked at Bill as if he had a screw loose. 'What are you talking about?'

'According to the computer, we've been living together for seven and one-half years, and we have yet to have our first domestic quarrel. That seven and one-half years I refer to is in earth years. Of course, we haven't had any sex. This could make a difference.'

Chris blushed. She kept on thinking what Bill had said. This seven and one-half years had only been a very short time to her and Bill. She kept on thinking how relative this idea of time actually was. 'Oh, you don't want to admit that I now have wrinkles, my hair has turned completely gray, and my teeth have all fallen out.'

Bill laughed at this summarization. For he was quite aware

he and Chris had only experienced days while earth had gone through years.

'Chris, I've been thinking. I believe it would be a good time for us to have that little discussion I referred to. This has become very important to me, and I would like to have you and the Elders know my thinking on this matter.'

'Of course, Bill. I will summon the Elders and you speak your mind. You have taken us through a lot, and I'm sure they will listen to you. Are you listening to us talking now? Our commander has something he would wish to discuss with you.'

'We hear you, Commander. What is it that seems so pressing?'

Bill started his long dissertation. 'I have given a great deal of thought on what we have experienced and learned about several cultures. We have destroyed your tormentors and are about to eliminate another race of people. We are doing so because these cultures were impeding the progress of others on other planets. I agree that this situation was not a good one. Planets and peoples on them should be unhampered in their natural progress and should be allowed to communicate with other people living on other planets without being impeded in any way except by God. We went to a planet called Ohg, which had just experienced a total conflagration, to rescue only sixty people on a planet that must have had forty million people. This made me think of earth, where Chris and I come from. It makes me shudder to think of the idiots we have put in power because of the lack of a better way. At any time these people can destroy millions of individuals just by pressing a little red button. This is what happened on Ohg. If it happened to the planet Ohg, it can certainly happen on the planet earth.

'Then in the course of our travels we meet another group of people in a spaceship very similar to ours. What we find here are supposedly the guardians of the galaxy. This is very hard to believe. I smell a big brown rat here. But they admit, both freely and openly, that we do possess some superiority over them. I know that they are just dying to find out. However, they ask us to stop and think about what we have accomplished so far in our efforts to develop civilizations on other planets. Something that you have to admit to has become obvious even to the common layman. You have failed miserably. Why is this so? I think the answer is quite clear. Even though you have given these people a technological edge, we have forgotten these people cannot handle the emotional aspect of what they have achieved. They therefore have made these advancements into weapons and think in terms of superiority. Rather than looking at the good they have, they think only in terms of how they might deploy these weapons against what they call the bad guys. We must put an end to this. I think we should start with planet earth. We can still do this, and I think we should make every effort to. Certainly we can go on, but why? We have an obligation here to clean up the mess we started. I, therefore, implore you to go back. I will go anywhere you wish, but I do think we must go back to make sure things are set right.'

There was a long pause. 'We have listened to you, Commander. We have learned what you think should be respected. What is your plan of action? For, surely, you have a plan.'

'Yes, I do. It is a very simple one. But I think it can also be effective. It is to take all of the ICBM's and stockpile them on the Plain of Nazca in Peru. We then do the same thing to all of the nuclear submarines. Then we introduce ourselves at the United Nations and tell them what we have done and why. They will not be prepared to receive what they term aliens, and suddenly they will be thinking about a new type of worry. The next thing for us to do is to establish a self-contained base in Peru. All of our foodstuffs could be produced under the ground, and our air could be gotten from underground ducts that will surface at the South Pole and at the Equator. The city, which will be built above the ground, will be protected by a transparent dome, which will be impenetrable to people, gases, bugs, and hydrogen bombs. Our demands made to the United Nations will be that they find a peaceful way to use the technology they have at their disposal and not use it as weapons to kill each other. I figure that I will need six hundred people from the necklaces to pull this off. That, in essence, is my plan — subject to revision, of course.'

132

'All right, Commander, we are with you. That is what we will do.'

'Thank you very much.'

11

The Elimination of the Second Set of Aliens; Gurkha and Aryana; The Discovery of the Third Set of Aliens ——

THE COMPUTER BROKE into the conversation. 'Commander, it is the space ship *Alpha*. They are sending out a distress signal.'

'Send a message to them. Tell them to keep their key and transmitter on. We are leaving immediately. Also, keep a fix on Alpha Centauri. Athos, bring the ship up to seven parsecs per hour and get the directions from the computer. Computer, guide Athos in his directions.'

'We are in agreement, Commander, with one contingency, or stipulation, as you might call it.'

'All right, what is it?'

'That you never close your mind off to us, as you have done.'

'All right, I promise.'

'Thank you, Commander.'

'Porthos, put on the proton device and the invisibility shields. Set the viewing screen to straight ahead and adjust the focus to six power. Dante, stand by the disintegration buttons. Chris, get to the computer and listen for the open transmitter.'

Bill was intent on keeping an eye on the viewing screen. After twenty minutes had passed, he spotted the craft with a mass of alien ships hovering around it. He thought he could see that the engines were impaired and the ship couldn't move. It would be a matter of time before its shields broke down.

'We are half a minute away.'

'Thank you, Athos. Dante, get ready to fire. Just remember, don't touch the larger ship. You are interested only in the elimination of those hornets which are circling for the kill.'

'Don't worry, Commander, I'll be careful.'

'Now I can make out their base. Athos and Dante, after you free the larger spacecraft, we are going to cut up that base into little pieces.'

In a short while, the *Alpha Centauri* was upon the scene. Dante very precisely took care of the hornets, as Bill called them. Athos paused only briefly to allow Dante to hit the ships, and then he went on to the space platform. He inverted the ship and came to a dead halt in the center of the platform at a height of five hundred feet. Dante made short work of cutting a hole right through the platform, and then he cut it in half. Athos went to the end of the space platform and, very slowly, proceeded to the other end. Dante sliced a hole clean through all the way down the entirety of the platform.

Athos inverted the ship and went around to the front side. He hovered one thousand feet above the platform. Porthos inverted the screen downward, and they all watched as a voluminous amount of steam and gas escaped. The now four parts of the platform were beginning to drift apart. Two craft emerged from the sections and started to move away. Dante fired again, this time at the two craft, and disintegrated them. Athos turned the ship and proceeded toward the larger ship. He got within five hundred feet of it and held his position.

Bill picked up the communicator. "This is Comdr. Anderson. How are things with you?"

"Things are just fine, if you don't mind having no power and the life-support systems going."

"Do you have people on board that can make the repairs?"

'Computer, how fast can we get back to planet four of the Alpha Centauri system?'

'I am assuming you will be taking that ship with you in tow? You can make five parsecs per hour. The time required will be fifteen minutes.'

'Are you sure about the time?'

The computer replied it was quite sure.

'Then how is it that it took over twenty minutes to get here?

135

We were traveling at seven parsecs per hour.'

'That point makes me wonder also. The radio beams were constantly changing in direction.'

'Then what you are saying is that the vessel was traveling around. That it was not here all the time.'

'That's right, Commander.'

The Commander of the other spacecraft replied to Bill, "Yes, we do have a maintenance crew that can repair the damage done. But the type of work required will have to be external."

"How many minutes of life support do you have?"

"No more than one hour, converted to your earth time."

"What type of gas do you breathe? Can your ship withstand the atmospheric pressure exerted by a planet of the Alpha Centauri system?"

"We breathe the same type of gas you do. We can land the vessel on the planet, but we will need an assist to get into space again."

"That's understood. I want it understood by you that no one is to come on board this vessel. If they do, they will die."

"You have such a lovely way of putting things, Commander. No one will attempt a transfer to your ship."

"Brace yourselves for tractor beams." 'Porthos, put your towing beams on that ship below us. Athos, as soon as the tractor beams are set, make your way to planet four of the Alpha Centauri system, at a speed of five parsecs per hour. Get the directions of navigation from the computer. Porthos, turn off the invisibility screen.'

The two craft continued on course to planet four. Everything was going along quite smoothly. 'Porthos, please adjust the viewing screen straight ahead. Set the focus power to two. Dante, make sure the proton shield is up and on. Chris, how about a cup of coffee?'

'Has anyone ever told you that you drink too much coffee? I'll pass on the coffee, but give me some hot chocolate.'

'That's a deal.' He went over to the dispenser and got his coffee and a hot chocolate for Chris. Chris said she would be right over. She got up from where she was sitting at the computer and sat down beside Bill.

'That spaceship we are towing has just sent a message to its home base and has advised that an alien craft has saved them from impending disaster and is now towing them to planet four of the Alpha Centauri group for repairs. The answer they have gotten back is "well done." A fleet of three vessels is being dispatched immediately and will arrive in approximately seventy-two hours.'

'Let's hope that it won't take that long to effectuate repair.'

Bill handed Chris her hot chocolate and proceeded to take a sip of his coffee.

'Bill, I think your plan to intervene with the political structure of planet earth is a good one. It might work. If it does, then we don't have to worry about this.'

'Thank you, Chris, for your vote of confidence; it's important to me. Just remember, we are playing this thing by ear. At any point we might change our whole approach. Every suggestion you can make will not go unheeded. I was surprised the Elders accepted what I had to say. I do think, though, it is important to them that they do something right. So far this idea of colonization has been nothing but a big mess.'

'We are now entering the atmosphere of planet four.'

'Thank you, Athos. Take it slowly and easily. I think the shell on the craft we are towing is a fragile one.'

'Understood, Commander. Where would you like them deposited?'

'By the colonists of planet three.'

They traveled the same route they had before. They could see that changes had been made. There were small towns and farmed tracts of land.

'Computer, how long has it been since we have left these people?'

The computer replied it was almost three years to the day.

'Chris, I don't think I will ever get used to this new concept of time. It really baffles me.'

'It's not only baffling, but we have yet to sit down and have a meal together. And already seven and one-half years have gone by.'

'We are now over the original spot where we first let the sixty people off. There's a flare.'

137

'Athos, let the ship down easily. Porthos, get ready to turn off the proton field. All right, cut it off. Now get ready to turn off the tractor beams. All right, cut them off. Athos, after the tractor beams are turned off, land the ship close to the one we are towing. Chris, get over to the computer and listen for any and all radio communications. Computer, give Chris both maps showing the resources of this planet. Dante, depressurize the ship and then open the doors to the ramp area. Extend the ramp to its fullest.'

'Your assumption was right. The ship is now in touch with its home base. The base advises that the people on the ship are to do their darnedest to get the plans of our drive, invisibility screen, and our weapons. They are to stall, as long as possible, until the reinforcements arrive.'

'That does it! Porthos, drop both Chris and me off on the planet. As soon as you have done that, get back on board. Dante, close the ramp area and retract the ramp as soon as Porthos is on board. Then activate the invisibility screen. Athos, take the ship beyond the atmosphere and orbit the planet. Dante and Porthos, make periodic checks of all tiers of this ship. If you catch anyone, knock him unconscious and dispose of any weapons or communicators he might have. Chris and I will contact you when we are ready to come on board. Let's go.'

Chris, Porthos, and Bill went immediately to the ramp area. Porthos deposited Chris and Bill on the ground.

'Thank you, Porthos. There are two things I forgot to mention up there. Make sure you activate the proton shield when you are in orbit, and give yourself some atmosphere.'

Porthos advised he would do this, wished them the best of luck, and went back to the ramp area. He disappeared from their sight.

The first one to greet them was the astronomer and then the elderly man. Their greetings were very warm and friendly.

Bill asked Chris to take out the maps and to give them one.

Chris gave them one and folded and tucked the other away in her jeans.

'You know, I was so busy the last time that I completely forgot to ask both of you what you are called.'

The elderly man said that he was called Gurkha, and the astronomer said she was called Aryana.

'You know that we are called Chris and Bill. I had no idea we were conversing with the gods of ancient earth times. Chris, let me introduce Gurkha, the most feared war god in all history, and Aryana, the goddess who had twenty-seven children.'

Chris bowed ceremoniously. 'It is a pleasure to meet you both.'

'I thought both of us would be forgotten by now.'

'Our history has forgotten you. But I do remember your names and your deeds.'

'You do us a great honor.'

The hatch of the craft they had towed opened, and two beings appeared. They were dressed in space garb and were helmeted, so when they emerged their entire appearance was not known.

The astronomer, Chris, the elderly gentleman, and Bill watched this whole scene with a great deal of interest.

The people dressed in space garb finally realized they were being watched. One of them struck the hull with two hard blows. Bill realized this was a signal that the air was breathable. The hatch was again opened and two more suitably dressed people emerged.

'It's odd that these people have no way of testing the outside atmosphere except by trial and error.' He pointed to the people on the craft. 'These are supposed to be our big protectors. I am beginning to wonder about this.'

Chris asked Aryana about the two girls they left on the planet. 'All is fine. They will be along shortly.'

Chris asked if they had found the three pilots that were also left there. Gurkha replied that the three had been found and fit into the group very well. Those three were out on one of the farms, tilling the soil.

At that point the two voyagers who were suitably garbed reached the ground by means of a ladder and had come up to the four spectators. Their first question was, Where was the spacecraft that had brought them here?

Bill answered them telepathically. 'As soon as your ship was down safely, our craft took off again. They have left us here to make sure everything was all right.'

The two looked a little dumbfounded. They mentally heard what Bill was saying and understood it. But they didn't see his lips moving at all. Finally one of them said, "We were hoping to have a closer look at your vessel."

Chris spoke up this time. She heard their language being spoken and could now speak it herself. "I am sorry, but this will not be possible. When your ship is ready, it will return to take you through the atmosphere."

The two looked at Chris. "How is it you speak our language and know so much about our ship?"

Bill looked at them. 'If you will remember, we probed your vessel. From this we have all the pertinent data collected about your ship and its relative weaknesses. One weakness we perceived is the vessel was assembled and constructed in outer space. You therefore rely upon molecular transference to arrive either upon a planet or in another ship.'

The two looked a little shocked. They asked Chris if she would like to come on board to have a closer look at things.

"Thank you for your kind offer, but until the ship is repaired and ready, I have no desire to see it."

The two thanked Chris and Bill for saving their lives. They said that they had to return to the ship to look after the repairs but that they would return.

After they left, both Chris and Bill probed their minds. One of them said, "This is going to be tougher than we expected. Somehow we are going to get one of them on board the ship to use the mind scanner. We better contact the base to get further instructions. I am beginning to believe they are aware nothing is wrong with our ship."

Bill looked up toward the sky. 'Computer, do you read?'

'Yes, Commander, I am reading you loud and clear.'

'Computer, lock onto and record any and all radio communications sent from this planet or the three craft that are coming here. Relay any and all messages to me at once. Understood?'

'Will do, Commander.'

'Thank you very much.'

Chris looked at Bill. 'I honestly thought their ship was damaged.'

'Yes, I did too. Now we find we have been thrown a sucker play. One thing I do know, though, all of a sudden you and I are inseparable.'

Chris looked at Bill and giggled. 'You know, that might be fun.'

'You see, that proves my point. There is a light side to everything.'

After a while the two people came back from the ship. Bill asked them how long they thought it would take to repair the ship. They answered that they thought it would take approximately sixty-eight hours.

Bill looked at Aryana and Gurkha. 'Can you feed us?'

Gurka looked at Bill. 'If you will please excuse me, I have been listening to everything that has transpired. In answer to your question, yes, we can feed you and your newfound friends. I am wondering how you are going to get out of this.'

Bill looked at Gurkha and thanked him both for his concern and for his hospitality. 'In answer to your question, right now I'm not sure. But you will be the first one I will advise on this matter.'

Chris smiled and informed the two aliens that they were welcome to eat with them.

The two looked at one another. One of them said, "This isn't in our plans, but let's play along. It gives us the time we need." The two turned and thanked Chris for her kind offer and advised her they would be more than happy to accept her kind invitation.

Chris and Bill faced Aryana and Gurkha, still keeping the aliens tuned in. Aryana nodded her head as if she were being spoken to. The two aliens observed this and then one of them said, "This whole thing is a little weird. All right, we're safe, but I still don't like it."

The first one said, "Somehow we are going to have to interrogate these people, get out of here, and get back into space again."

The other one replied, "Sir, that is not going to be as easy as you might imagine. I have a funny feeling about this whole thing. I think these people are far more intelligent than you have given them credit for."

Bill turned to the two and pointed his cane at them, knocking them out. 'Sit down and don't move. How many craft do you have in this federation of yours?'

'We have twelve of them, including ours.'

'How many planets do you oversee?'

'One hundred thirty-two of them.'

'If I were to destroy the three craft that are being sent here plus yours, that would mean your forces were only 75 percent effective to service 132 planets. Plus the loss of some twelve hundred personnel. That doesn't make much sense, does it?'

'No, it doesn't.'

'May I suggest you immediately get back on your spacecraft and take off? My ship will be waiting for you to take you through the gravitational field and into space safely. From now on, the group of planets we call Alpha Centauri will be considered off limits to you and the ships of the so-called federation. Do I make myself clear on this matter?'

'Yes, perfectly clear.'

'You have five minutes to raise this craft of yours and to get out of here. Now move it.'

The two got up and immediately boarded their vessel. Soon the ship was in the air. Bill had his ship come down and escort and tow the ship past the gravitational field surrounding the planet. He also had his ship follow the craft as it moved into position to intercept the three ships that were coming to help them out.

Through radio communication the vessel advised the other three ships to change course and to head back to their home base. The other three craft reported that they were changing course and asked why they were requested to do so.

The craft the *Alpha Centauri* was following said, "We have met individuals with greater intelligence than ours and also greater weapons. We have been advised to steer clear of this star grouping or else they will destroy us and our ships. This is no idle threat. We have documented their capabilities and know this to be true."

"Were you able to interrogate them?"

142

The vessel *Alpha* answered, "That is a big negative. We think we were interrogated. They can also read minds."

The other ship replied, "All right, we have changed course. We expect to meet you back at the base."

With that, the *Alpha Centauri* changed its course and went back to planet four.

In the meantime, Chris and Bill had found their stowaways. It was a very happy reunion. The two girls told Chris, in detail, everything that had happened since they had last seen each other.

Finally Bill broke into the conversation. 'Were you able to find the three downed pilots?'

Their smiles were overwhelming. 'Yes, Commander, we found them.'

Chris thought, 'It is our intention to take you back to your planet and people. How does that sound to you two?'

The girls thanked Chris and Bill but said they would rather remain where they were.

'Well, that's just fine. Here the two of you were instigating to take over the control of the ship, and now you say you don't want to come back with us even when we invite you to go back home.'

The girls looked at Bill, very embarrassed. 'You knew what we were talking about all the time. We're sorry we even thought it. We've met others here we are able to get along with quite nicely.'

Chris said, "Don't feel embarrassed. We understand. In fact, it saves us a trip."

Bill looked at Aryana, Chris, and the two girls. 'Women, women, you are the bane of my existence.'

Aryana then looked at Bill. 'How is it, Commander, you are so smart in some things and so dumb in others? Come with me, there is something we must talk about.' Aryana then looked at Gurkha, Chris, and the two girls. 'He reminds us of someone, doesn't he?'

Aryana was quite a woman. Although her earth age was two thousand plus years of age, she looked as though she was in her thirties. A woman who was as vibrant and pulsating as a young girl. She took Bill to a clearing and sat down beside him. 'I said what I did because I wanted to get Gurkha aroused and to make Chris a little jealous. This is not like fighting an enemy, but coercive force.'

'Aryana, you are a very beautiful woman. All of the lines about you suggest you are still young and, in fact, can bear children. Is this not so?'

'Yes, it is true. I can bear children. But the child I bear cannot be just any child. It must be Gurkha's child.'

'If that is true, I can see your problem. Gurkha's only sign of age is that his hair has turned gray.'

'And yours, my friend, is that you must navigate with that stupid cane.'

'How is it you became the astronomer for this little group? I hope your little strategy works. You know I'm crazy about Chris.'

'I became the astronomer when I knew about all of the constellations. Yes, I know how you feel about Chris. There is something else about you and Chris that Gurkha and I haven't put our finger on yet. Time will tell us what we need to know.'

'You must be very careful and observe precisely. It isn't necessarily the movement of stars as much as it is the movement of large bodies such as planets and being able to plot their course.'

'I have been most meticulous in watching the movements of heavenly bodies. I can also see you are not going to tell me what I want to know about you and Chris.'

'If there were something to tell, you would be the first to know. Perhaps it would be better if we were to go back to the group now. Thank you, Aryana, for your help and understanding.'

'Certainly. I will be the first to know, just as Gurkha was the first to know when you took care of those aliens. Thank you for a purely enjoyable time. Let's go.'

As they were leaving the clearing, they met Gurkha, who looked as though he were on a dragon hunt. Bill very casually thought, 'You know, you amaze me. Here you have been with this very beautiful woman for so long. She is yours, you know. Here it has been so many years and you have yet to make an advance toward her.'

144

Gurkha's countenance changed. 'Thank you both for being so wise.' He smiled and took Aryana's hand, and together they went back to where Chris and the two girls were waiting for them.

When they had all gotten back, Chris thought, 'That really must have been some talk you had. Did you solve the world crises? Is it safe to unlock our doors at night?'

Bill immediately sensed Chris was ticked off. 'Chris, I think the world crises you make mention of are definitely over. Aryana and Gurkha are now together after two thousand years have passed.'

Chris was very apologetic. 'For a moment there I thought she had gotten to you and you were her next catch. I didn't know what you two were planning.'

'Chris, thank you for caring. Let's all go and try this wonderful chow we have heard about but have not seen yet.'

Aryana came up to Chris and thought, 'Don't worry, Chris. You see, I have what I want. Come, let's all sit down to a feast prepared by none other than the two girls you left behind.'

"Why is it, Bill, you have not advanced a pass at me since we left?"

"Because I don't want to do anything while 3,500,000 people are looking on."

"I wasn't sure what your reasons were. That's perfectly understandable."

"Chris, I think the world of you. I wish that it could be different. But the main thing is that we do have time. All I can do is wait until then."

'Commander, we have been listening to your conversation with Chris. From this time to when you board the *Alpha Centauri* again, we will terminate any and all communications. This will mean you will not have any sort of an audience. We hope this will make you feel better. Good luck to you both.'

'Thank you very much. I appreciate what you say. Chris, how about testing that chow? After the meal, let's get lost. Okay?'

"All I can do is follow your orders, Commander." Chris smiled.

The meal the two girls had prepared was excellent. It was served with a very tasty wine. Chris and Bill hadn't tasted anything better before.

Bill stood up and raised his wine goblet. 'I would like to make a toast, if I might. First, I would like to thank Aryana and Gurkha for their hospitality.'

They imitated Bill since this was the first time that they had ever heard the word *toast*. They all raised their wine glasses and drank.

'Secondly, I would like to thank the two people who prepared this meal and who did such an excellent job in doing it.' Bill looked at the two girls, who blushed. He raised his goblet in their direction and emptied it. Then he sat down.

Then it was Gurkha's turn. 'Commander, you have taught us a new word and very definitely a new custom. I, too, would like to make a toast to Chris and you. First, for bringing us here, and secondly, for ridding us of the parasites from above.' They all drank to that. By this time Bill had his wine goblet refilled and he drank too.

Bill got up. 'You know that Chris and I have not seen all of the changes that have been made. If you will excuse us, we will take a tour.'

Gurkha looked at Aryana, and they both smiled. Gurkha thought, 'By all means, take the tour. I hope everything will meet with your satisfaction, for both of you.'

Bill thanked him and, taking Chris by the hand, left the table.

They found a meadow close by, and he and Chris sat down. Bill worked over Chris very slowly and deliberately, feeling every curve and hollow that she had. Chris reciprocated with Bill, and very slowly they reached the climax they were both seeking to achieve.

A little while later, Chris thought, 'I never believed it could be so beautiful. Let's do it again.'

'Madam, your every wish is my command. We do have time. Did I ever tell you I love you?'

'No, Commander, never. Have I ever told you that I love you?'

Bill looked at her in disbelief. 'Why, no, Chris. That is hard to believe. How is it you have chosen such a bum? I don't know if I approve or not.'

'I had forgotten what you were or are. However, it still doesn't change the way I feel. Bummy Commander, Commander the Bum. I don't know. It just doesn't sound right.'

They both laughed. Bill loved to hear her laugh.

'You know something? I still haven't heard you play that harpsichord. How is your Handel these days?'

'Even after eight years, it is mean, man.' That made Bill laugh even harder.

Time had gone by very quickly for them. They hadn't realized the time they had used up was five hours. They were now experiencing the twilight of another sun. Bill turned to look at this new sunrise and advised Chris that they had to get going.

Chris was indignant at first, and then she realized that Bill was right. They both got dressed and quickly made their way back to the encampment.

At the encampment Aryana and Gurkha were silently awaiting their arrival. Aryana was the first to see Chris and Bill approach and she immediately got up. Gurkha followed her lead. Chris and Bill were amazed to see them still there. Aryana was the first one to speak. 'We have stayed up to see you off and to wish you good luck. Please feel free to return here anytime you wish.'

Gurkha thought, 'Yes, please remember us, no matter where you go. As far as we are concerned, this is your home. If there is anything we can do to help you out, don't hesitate to let us know about it.'

Chris and Bill thanked them for their offer and sincerity.

'We'll be back.' Bill then hailed the ship and told Porthos to turn off the invisibility screen.

Chris turned to Aryana and Gurkha, thinking, 'There is still much we are going to do for you. I'm sorry we didn't have the time to do that which we wanted to do.'

Gurkha thought, 'Perhaps it is good you didn't do them. It will mean we will see you again all the sooner. What we want to do is to build our own spacecraft, using our own specifications and design. There might come a time when we

147

will need them to escape from here. We will watch the heavens very closely. We have the engineers and the astronomers to accomplish this feat.'

Just then the spaceship *Alpha Centauri* landed, and Porthos and Athos came down from the extended ramp. The invisibility screen was off and the big ship loomed in the sky. They immediately went up to Bill. Porthos thought, 'Is everything all right, Commander? Are you ready to go?'

Bill looked at Chris and then at Porthos. 'Yes, we are ready.'

Then he turned to Aryana and Gurkha. 'Thank you both for a very nice time. It makes our leaving here a very sad thing for me. But I realize we have no alternative but to go.'

Chris thought, 'The happiness we have found here will never be forgotten.'

Bill said good-by to Aryana and to Gurkha. Then he looked at Porthos. 'All right, take us both back to the ship.'

12

The Return to Planet Earth————————

PORTHOS TOOK BILL UP to the ramp area and was closely followed by Chris and Athos. Together Chris and Bill watched the world that they had become accustomed to. Below them they could see Aryana, Gurkha, and now the two girls. Chris and Bill waved good-by and then went inside the spacecraft. They then went through the main section of the third tier and with Athos and Porthos went to the first tier by means of the elevator.

'Athos, take us beyond the atmosphere of this planet. Porthos, close off the ramp area and pressurize the entire ship. After we get beyond the gravitational field, put on the proton field and also the invisibility screen. Computer, how far away is planet earth?'

'The distance is now 4.3 light-years away.'

'Athos, get your distance and navigation from the computer. We are returning to planet earth. Use a speed of seven parsecs per hour.'

Athos replied, 'Yes, Commander. It is good to have you on the bridge again. It is good to hear that barking voice again.'

'Thank you for that off-handed compliment. I missed all of you, too. Now, when we get back to planet earth, orbit the planet. Don't go in there until we know what has happened and what the atmosphere looks like.'

'Commander, how about some coffee?' Chris went over to the dispenser and got two very hot cups of coffee. Then she brought them over to where Bill was. She gave him his coffee and sat down beside him.

149

After Chris had made herself comfortable, the voice came back again. 'I hope you were both having an enjoyable time. Commander, are you sure you are doing the right thing?'

'Right now I'm not sure. But I will be as soon as we find out what condition earth is in.'

The voice went on, 'You have been made aware of our definite superiority over the so-called federation. What is your point for not going on?'

'Gentlemen, it has also become obvious to me your planned stocking of various planets has ended in failure. We must find some way to maintain and keep this plan in force. It is my thought that it is not enough to start something and then walk away, saying things will evolve. That is illogical and must be corrected.'

'Once again, Commander, we bow to your way of thinking. Your plan, though, is not quite clear to us.'

'Then let's see what needs to be done in this regard. We can only know this when we arrive there.'

Chris thought, 'I'd like to go on record as saying I agree with Bill. Say, Bill, did you know this coffee is better than the hot chocolate? I, too, would like to see a social order which will continue to grow without the people killing themselves off.'

The voice thought, 'All right, we will see.'

Bill and Chris had just finished their coffee when Athos advised them he was just starting to orbit around planet earth. 'Wait one minute. There seems to be a structure up ahead. It is not a spaceship but, rather, a space platform. We should come up to it in one minute.'

'Computer, make a scan of this thing. Porthos, make sure our invisibility screen is up.'

Athos thought, 'This platform is in rotation and is following a definite path of orbit around the earth.'

'The scan is complete; the information is being recorded.' The computer had the printout moving very rapidly. Finally it was finished. Chris came up to look at it.

'Chris, what does it say?'

'Population is 1,250 people; atmosphere is the same we have. There is no weaponry on board at all; their rotation is to maintain temperature; there are three craft inside: one for shuttle to the earth, one for exploration, the other for fairly long range work. All drives are sublight; the medical laboratory is extensive, but very inferior to ours; the sun is the prime source of their heat and power.'

'Athos, stop our ship right over the platform. Computer, I want you to try all hailing frequencies to contact the platform.'

Bill picked up the communicator. "This is Comdr. William Anderson, commander of the star ship *Alpha Centauri*. Who are you? What are you doing here?"

There was a pause, and then a voice answered, "Comdr. Anderson, we show no record of your ship, the *Alpha Centauri*, or, for that matter, you. We not only find no record or listing, but our scanners cannot even pick you up. Is this some kind of a joke? Please advise."

"Sorry about that. We are right alongside of you." 'Porthos, turn off the invisibility screen.'

The voice on the radio said, "Wow! We see you but we don't believe what we are seeing. You are larger than our whole platform. Are you from planet earth?"

"That is an affirmative, Platform. Brig. Gen. Dodd can confirm our existence."

"We are checking this confirmation. Please hold. Did you just scan our platform?"

"That is an affirmative. With 1,250 people on board, you must be crammed for space."

"That Brig. Gen. Dodd you allude to is not registered. Do you have any more references?"

"His name is Alvin Dodd. For all I know, he might have been promoted to a full general or cashiered out of the service, which I doubt."

"We are checking again. We have located Gen. Alvin Dodd. Please hold on a minute."

"We have reached Gen. Dodd. The spaceship *Alpha Centauri* is confirmed. The general would like to talk to you."
There was another long pause, and then the general was wired into the frequency. "Bill, is that really you? Can you put Chris on?"

"Hi, General. Congratulations on your promotion. Yes, Chris is here. I'll put her on."

"Hi, General. Congratulations on your promotion. There is

151

one thing we are both wondering about. Did you and Andrea get married?"

"My God! It really is you. The last time we saw you was through the screen being chased by three bogies. We honestly thought you had bought lunch. In answer to your question about Andrea, yes, we finally did get married."

Bill said, "That makes us very happy. Please say hello to her for us."

"Will do. Hey, when am I going to see you two again?"

"We don't know whether we will see you again. We ran into a cobalt atmosphere. We believe our ship is highly radioactive. If we do meet again, it will be in one of the smaller ships we have on board. Where are you living these days?"

"The same place in Houston."

"We still have some unfinished business. We will be in touch with you as soon as we know what we're going to do."

Chris said, "There is one more thing, General. Did you have any children?"

"Yes, two boys."

"Oh, that's wonderful. We'll be in touch with you again through the space station. End of communication."

But Bill continued to the platform, "All right, the ship is not called a spaceship with the name of *Alpha Centauri*. It is in fact a star ship. Now that we have all of the red tape cleared away, I have some questions for you noncombatants. In the first place, you haven't answered any of my questions. Who are you, and what are you doing here? Aside from your construction of an interplanetary hedge hopper?"

"Your scanners have been very busy. You also know we do not have such a device. We do not even know the principle under which it operates. What more can we tell you?"

"Let's start with my original questions. Who are you, and what are you doing here?"

"We, in essence, are an independent planet. We exercise our own individual rights, independent of any power on earth. We are also in charge of space exploration, although we have not had the means to do so right now. We are of mixed nationalities. All countries represented are a part of the United Nations."

"Then not all of the countries are represented. Do the

countries not represented have atomic power?"

"That is an affirmative to both of your questions."

Chris said, "Does this mean that all sides have nuclear submarines and all sides have missiles with nuclear warheads?"

"Yes, that is also true."

"Then your primary duty is one of a police force. If any power does something that even seems like a warring move, you immediately tell the others."

"Affirmative," was the reply.

Bill said, "Thank you very much for your help. We will be in touch with you again." 'Porthos, put on the invisibility screen. Athos, after the screen is on, make a lower orbit. Computer, get me detailed maps depicting all of the missile silos and launching pads on all of the continents. Also, pick up any and all nuclear submarine activity in the oceans of planet earth. Chris, monitor all conversations between the space station and earth.'

'They are back on the pipe with Dodd. They are asking him about our space drive, the type of weaponry we have on board, our probing device, our invisibility screen, and how the ship was constructed. Dodd is saying he doesn't know. All he knows about is that the ship was constructed with two hulls. The drive and the other things were put on after the arrival of its commander, Bill Anderson. An exact duplicate of the ship was made but a Capt. Robinson tried to fly it with four others aboard. He and his crew were reported lost at sea. They instigated searches for it, but they always came up empty-handed. The only ship of its kind is the *Alpha Centauri*. A man called Aaron Rugen was an engineer who supposedly designed the force field and the drive. Rugen now claims Anderson added parts to his prints. Rugen has no idea what these changes were and that his memory of this whole thing was a complete blank. In short, they built the inner and outer hull. That is as far as it goes. There can be found no prints or schematics of the craft. These have disappeared. Nothing that was done can be duplicated except by commanders Spalding and Anderson. As far as Dodd knew, the ship had no probing device or invisibility screen. This was the first that he heard about it.

'Dodd reported that some strange things went on at the base

which he could never explain. For instance, his top security man went bananas, his secretary was attacked by thirty-two well-trained guards and defeated by Anderson. When the ship came back from its maiden voyage, it had acquired what Anderson called a "reconnaissance craft." But this craft was built of a metal which was impervious to their torches.

'The space platform believes the only way to get answers is to get on board the *Alpha Centauri* and question the commanders. Dodd says his country can't demand custody of this craft because the statute of limitation applies.'

Bill thought, 'That is very interesting. Computer, how are you doing?'

'One more pass at the planet and I will have all of the required information.'

'Gen. Dodd has a good memory. He has called the platform back and is telling them to watch out for Anderson. This person has MS, but he took on and defeated an entire platoon of armed and trained guards. They are to handle him with kid gloves.

'The space platform wonders how a person so stricken could be so harmful.

'Dodd's reply to this is that he was. "Don't ask me how, but he was." In his opinion, they are not dealing with a normal individual. His brain processes are greater than the normal individual.' Chris thought, 'He has really hit upon you and your personality.'

'Thanks for the compliment, Chris. Computer, also take a scan of the Plain of Nazca, Peru. I want to make sure there are no people around.

'I think it is about time we consulted with the Elders. Chris, please call them.'

The voice called out, 'Yes, Commander, we await your plans.'

'My plan is a simple one. Take all of the toys away from the supposed powers and make them look elsewhere for a feeling of power. It is not enough to get hold of their weapons. We must advise them who has done it and why. This will be done by Chris and me or, very possibly, one of you people. We are thinking about constructing a city in the Plain of Nazca, in

154

Peru, which will be encased in an impenetrable dome. This dome will not allow bugs, people, or bombs in. The only thing that can enter this dome is this ship. Air for the city will be gotten by pipes going to the Equator and to the South Pole. Five miles beneath the city will be our farm with infrared and ultraviolet lighting to permit anything to grow we might have need for. All power required will come from the center of the earth for heating and electricity. We want these people to believe we have no need for anything they have to offer. The plan I have conceived of will require only six hundred people at the present time. It will be these people's jobs to prepare for the rest of you. Are you in favor of my plan? We can always go somewhere else. Please advise me on this.'

All was quiet for a long while, and then the voice thought, 'We have heard what you have said. You realize, of course, that without weapons, which you are planning to take away, there might be a change in power between those who hold the big stick now and those who might in the future.'

'The type of warfare might also change. We could easily be looking at germ warfare. They might even get together and plan for outer space. Face it; anything would be better than the use of the cobalt bomb.'

'All right, Commander, we will build your city, establish a power source for it, protect it with a dome, make your farming fields a reality, build your air ducts to the South Pole and to the Equator—in short, make everything a reality as you have envisioned it. The taking away of the toys will be left up to the robots, Chris, and you. We are not going to contact the United Nations; that, too, will be your job. If this works, it will be amazing. In return, you will give us form again. It will be the first time in two thousand years that we will be given this opportunity. There is one thing that we have never discussed. It is that you are to be our king and queen. Do you accept?'

Chris and Bill looked at one another. Chris thought, 'I'm willing if you are.'

Bill told them it was all right. But he wondered what this entailed.

'We've been watching Chris and you now for some time. We believe that as our king and queen you will protect us satisfactorily. In turn, we will make sure that no harm befalls you. You are two of the best inferior specimens of the lot.'

Chris thought, 'Thank you very much.'

'That means a lot to us. You see, Chris, you are pregnant.'

Chris blushed. 'How is it you know that and I don't as of yet?'

Bill forgot himself and kissed Chris.

'That is what we mean. You are both honest and compassionate. In addition to this, you don't let power go to your heads.'

'Computer, what do you have for us?'

Porthos, Athos, Dante, and the computer all congratulated Chris and Bill on their new addition.

'Yes, Commander, here is the information you requested. You will find that no one is living on the Plain of Nazca. Also, most of the atomic submarines are in the northern hemisphere, as are the missiles.'

Bill took the maps from the computer and studied them very closely.

'If everything is in order, let's go and see our new home.'

'Athos, take us down to the Plain of Nazca in Peru. Porthos, turn off the proton field, and, after we are down, turn off the invisibility screen. All right, Athos, put us down on the runway. Chris, let's go with Dante to the second tier. We have some people to revive. Let's go, Dante.'

They all went down to the hospital section. Chris very ceremoniously took off the first necklace. Then they fed the necklace through the machine and very patiently waited. As for the machine, all knobs were set in accordance with the instructions and were properly turned on.

The first person popped out of the machine. He looked fairly young. Bill guessed this person looked as though he was in his mid-thirties. The person that had just entered into their time had six-digit fingers, a large forehead, and a fairly long straight nose. He was well over 6' and, with no clothes on, looked very wiry. Bill took this person over to a large pile of clothing that was on a table next to the machine. The next person to make an appearance was a woman. Her characteristics were the same as the man's, except she had long

156

flowing hair. Bill very politely took her by the hand to the table of clothing. Chris was astonished at the woman's appearance or, rather, at her proportions, and was a little put out at all the fuss Bill seemed to show her. Soon they had six hundred people — three hundred men and three hundred women. All of these people looked very young. All of them had similar features.

'We've landed at the required area. The ramp is now being extended, the entire ship is being depressurized, the ramp doors to the central area are being opened, the invisibility screen is now being dropped, and the doors to the outside are open. Both Porthos and Athos are on their way to the medical section.'

Bill picked up the communicator and thanked the computer for its information.

Just then both Porthos and Athos made their appearance. Bill looked at Porthos, Athos, and Dante. 'This place is getting a little crowded. I think it is about time you showed these people the planet and transported them down to it.'

The first man who had come out of the machine thought, 'Your Highness, you have one more person in process. After he makes his appearance, please turn off the machine, retract the necklace, and allow us to set up our base of operations. We have much to do before any more of us come into being.'

The last person made his appearance, and Bill turned off the machine, took out the necklace, and asked the people how he might be of assistance.

The first man advised Bill they would need the last three ships he had confiscated. They needed these craft to bore holes into the ground. They intended to use the lasers to lay the pipes, to make the agricultural fields, to cut and to transport stone for the city. The last man was clothed and all 601 people went down to the ramp area. Chris and Bill followed them down. The people were transported down to the ground by the robots. As soon as this was done, the robots came back and transported the three spacecraft down.

Chris and Bill wished them good luck. There was a big round of applause and shouting from the 601 people for Chris and Bill.

Chris, Bill, and the robots went immediately to the hospital section and made sure the machinery was turned off. Chris had already replaced the necklace with the others around her neck. Then they went to the first tier, and Bill had Porthos retract the ramp, close the outside doors to the ramp area, close the doors from the ramp section to the center area of the third tier, and repressurize the entire ship. Then he sat down with Chris and took out the maps again.

'Chris, I think we should stage multiple raids on those powers who possess nuclear weapons. We take the missiles, including the warheads, and deposit them far away from earth. What do you think?'

'I think the best thing you can do is to send all of these missiles into the sun and give the sun a minor charge. How do you intend to get these missiles? They should be under heavy guard.'

'The main thing is to cut the umbilical cords to the missiles, warheads, guidance systems, and the power. Then it will be our responsibility to raise these missiles from the subterranean depths by using our tractor beams and tow them into outer space. I like your idea of sending these things into the sun. It certainly wouldn't hurt the sun in any way, and we would be rid of them.'

'Which of these powers will feel our wrath first?'

'It appears to me that what we know as the United States has the most missiles. Or it looks as though they do. We can work our way northward and completely take over their complexes. From the United States we will wend our way over and on to Siberia and then on to China. After each raid, we will take our prizes to the dark side of the moon. Our pattern will not be a straight one. During each raid I will be taking Athos, Porthos, and Dante with me. During this time you will be in full charge of the ship. You will maintain the invisibility screen at all times. Does this meet with your approval?'

'I think it would be best if you were to leave Dante with me. He would be able to guide you back to the ship and also operate the destructor beams in case of trouble.'

'You have a very good point there. Having Dante would also insure your staying at the helm. I like it. This is our method of madness. One more thing, we must make sure the people on the space platform are completely unaware of what we are doing. We will need the help of the computer for this.'

'Computer, keep tabs on the space platform. We will need to know where it is at all times. Can this be done?'

'That is an affirmative, Commander—or should we now call you "your Highness?" '

Bill blushed a little. 'No. To all of you I am nothing more than the commander. These fast titles are a bit confusing. We came here to do a job, and that is what we are going to do. Athos, raise the ship to ten thousand feet. Then proceed to our first target as outlined by the computer's maps. Hold above the target at a level of ten thousand feet until we check it out. Porthos, make sure that the ship is pressurized and that the invisibility screen is on. Computer, where is that space platform now?'

'Commander, the space platform is just making its way over the United States. It will be back in another thirty minutes.'

'Good, that gives us time.'

Athos thought, 'We are now over our target.'

'That was fast, Athos. Porthos, direct the viewing screen down on the target. Use six power infrared. Move the screen at five degrees every two minutes.'

Porthos moved the screen into position and moved it at five degrees every two minutes.

'The missiles are housed in those silos. Chris, land the ship in that clearing over there. When Athos, Porthos, and I are free of the craft, go to one thousand feet and hold. Dante, take your orders from Chris. Porthos, depressurize the ship, open the ramp doors, and extend the ramp. Then you and Athos follow me down to the ramp area. Let's go, guys.'

Bill was on the elevator going down to the third tier. Athos and Porthos followed him down. Suddenly Chris found herself at the helm of a very large ship. She moved the ship very slowly down until she had landed it. She received a telepathic communication from Bill, praising the way she was handling the ship.

Bill, Athos, and Porthos went out on the ramp. Athos carried Bill to the ground, and Porthos followed. As soon as

Chris saw that they were free, she raised the ship to an elevation of one thousand feet. She then watched their progress through the screen. It seemed the main body of soldiers were intent on the outer limits and not the three who were all ready inside.

Bill, Athos, and Porthos made their way to the main building. They easily got inside. As soon as they got into the building, they were immediately confronted by guards. There were five guards. By using his cane, Bill rendered them unconscious. Bill then asked them how many silos there were. One of the guards told him there were fifteen of them. Bill asked how they could get to them. He was given a plastic card that was perforated. This card, when placed in a slot, would open up the elevator doors, which would take them down to the firing room. Bill took the plastic card from one of the guards. He also took two of their automatic weapons. He put the card in the slot and two panelled doors opened, baring the elevator behind them. Bill, Athos, and Porthos got on, and Bill pushed the only available button. The doors closed and the elevator moved downward with amazing speed. It came abruptly to a halt. The doors slid open, and Bill found himself in an elaborate computer room. Bill stepped off and was immediately attacked by four technicians. Before Bill could get on his feet again and turn around, Athos and Porthos knocked them out. Bill walked up to one of the technicians and told him to open the silo doors. All fifteen of them. The technician got up and went to the console and pushed fifteen buttons.

'Porthos, go out there and sever all of the umbilical cords to the rockets.' Porthos was gone. He returned again after a short while.

Bill emptied both of the automatic weapons on the console, destroying any possible recovery or ignition attempt. Bill, Athos, and Porthos left the same way they had come. Athos signaled Dante to come and pick them up. The ship descended and the three got back on board.

'So far, so good. Now, let's all get to the first tier on the double. Porthos, repressurize the entire ship and close all doors. Put the proton shield on when we get to five hundred feet. Make sure the ramp is retracted. Dante, raise those missiles by using the tractor beams. Stack them all up in that field. When you are finished getting them out of their holes, put the towing beams on all of them. Athos, relieve Chris at the helm.'

They got to the first level. Chris came up to them and saw that Bill was hurt. He had a gash on his head that wouldn't stop bleeding. Athos immediately took the helm. Chris said that she was going down to the laboratory and would be right back.

Athos had increased the altitude to five hundred feet. Porthos had put on the proton field. Dante was busy extracting all of the missiles from their silo bases and piled them up in the field. Porthos had closed all the doors, retracted the ramp, and was now repressurizing the ship.

Bill saw what had been done and told Dante to put the towing beams on all of the missiles. He told Athos to go to the dark side of the moon. Athos took the ship straight up. Soon it was orbiting the moon.

'The time that has elapsed is exactly thirty minutes. The space platform is now over the target area. By radio communication they have filed a formal complaint with the American government. They call the opening of silo doors an aggressive act and wonder why this was done. The U.S. Government says they are totally unaware of this action and are checking into it.'

'Thank you, Computer. Keep your sensors open for anything that is going on at earth.'

Just then Chris came back with a pan of water and some swabs. She went up to Bill, placed the pan with the swabs beside him, and looked at his wound. 'It looks as if you were hit in the head with an ax.' She began to clean Bill up a little and stopped the bleeding.

Bill thanked her for her help and concern. 'Computer, is there any more communication between the space platform and earth?'

'Yes, the space platform has noted unusual activity of construction in Peru.'

'Athos, find a crater and have Dante deposit his catch in it.

161

Computer, make a notation as to where these missiles are. Athos, when Dante is through, put the craft down over the target area in Russia. Advise me when you are ready.'

He then turned to Chris. 'Hey, beautiful, how about some coffee?'

Chris got up from where she was leaning over Bill. She went to the dispenser and got two cups of black coffee. She went over to where Bill was and handed him a cup. She kept one for herself and sat down beside him. 'You took an awful chance a few moments ago.'

Bill looked at Chris and just smiled. 'Look, gal, we have to take a few chances if we are going to keep this planet alive.'

'Commander, the situation has gotten out of hand. SAC has launched its retaliatory aircraft and has directed them to strike against Russia. The planes — there are six of them — are entering the Pacific Ocean area.'

'Athos, intercept those craft. Dante, get ready to put your tractor beams on them.'

'We are right above those aircraft now.'

'Thank you, Athos. Dante, put your tractor beams on all these ships. Porthos, make sure these ships are protected by our proton shield. Computer, make a clean sweep with your antenna. Pick up any communications at all. We must nip this in the bud before anything else happens.'

'The holding beams are on all of the ships.'

'Thank you, Dante. Athos, turn back to the United States of America. Find some nice forested area where they can't take off again. Dante, deposit these ships among the trees.'

'The Americans are planning to set off ten of their missiles.'

'Hurry up, Athos.' Athos found the right spot and Dante deposited them.

'Now, let's catch those missiles while they are in flight.'

Athos went up to 250,000 feet. It didn't take Dante long to find the rockets and ensnare them in the tractor beams. Athos went back to the dark side of the moon where Dante deposited them in the same crater along with the others.

Athos then swung the ship around and got back to earth as soon as possible. Soon they were over their original target in Russia. They found there were ten silo doors opened. Dante took the first missile out of the silo with such force that the umbilical cord snapped on its own. He then laid this missile down on the ground and then directed his beams to the others. One by one, the missiles were torn out of their silos until he had gotten all ten of them. He directed his tractor beams on all of them, and Athos raised both the ship and the missiles toward the moon. He went around to the dark side of the moon, and Dante deposited them along with the rest in the same crater. Athos went back to planet earth.

'Computer, where is that space platform?'

'Commander, during every time we were on earth and going to the moon, the space platform was out of range and couldn't see anything.'

'That was damned lucky.'

'Commander, Russia is now in touch with the United States. Both parties are claiming they had nothing to do with these incidents. The United States and Russia are telling each other that until they find out what has happened they are calling off any attack. China is now calling both Russia and the United States. They claim nothing has been done on their behalf.'

'Boy, am I happy about this! Athos, take us back to Peru and the Plain of Nazca. Porthos and Dante, as soon as we are back, rejuvenate our air tanks. I am beginning to think we are running low. Chris, look at this wound on my head. I have a headache that just won't quit. Computer, where is that space platform now?'

'Commander, the platform is out of range and should be back in another twenty minutes.'

'The Plain of Nazca is coming up. Those people you put down there certainly were busy.' Athos brought the ship right up against the force field.

A voice called out to them, 'Take the ship up to one thousand feet. Then go to the center and slowly ease the ship down. We can't see you but we know you are there.'

'All right, Porthos, drop the proton field and the invisibility screen.'

With all shields dropped, Athos raised the ship to one thousand feet, moved to the center of the complex, and slowly eased the ship down. Finally he had landed it.

The voice called out, 'Good job!'

Porthos depressurized the entire ship, opened the doors, and extended the ramp. Porthos and Dante immediately moved forward toward the elevator and went down to the third tier. They got the rejuvenation equipment out and started to hook up the hoses.

'Computer, what news have you received?'

'Commander, I have been scanning all frequencies as soon as you took the first missiles. At first the United States thought it was being attacked by Russia. They immediately launched their SAC planes. They found these planes had been diverted and forced down in a forested area in the state of Washington. This means the planes had been diverted almost one thousand miles from where they were. The United States knew Russia was incapable of doing this. They then immediately conferred with the Russians and laid it out on the line to them what had happened. At that point the Russians received a report that ten of their ICBMs had been stolen. The Russians and the United States agreed they would wait until they found out what was happening. China, to save its neck, made a statement that they had nothing to do with any of the funny business that had gone on. A report came in from the space platform saying that they had seen nothing and continued to see nothing. The United States advised the space platform that some thirty-five ICBMs had just been taken. At the present time, the whole world is worried about this theft. There are some doubts being expressed about the usefulness of the space platform to police all sections of the individual countries. The space platform has agreed to send down their ambassadors to Switzerland tomorrow morning to discuss this in greater detail. That is all so far.'

Bill thanked the computer for its recap and asked it to keep tuned in on all frequencies to keep him and Chris posted as to what was happening. The computer agreed to do this.

During this time Chris was tending to the wound on Bill's forehead. 'What I am still wondering about is what you were hit with.'

'Oh, beauteous one, I don't know. One thing I am sure about and that is that my head is pounding and I am very tired. How about you and I getting some sleep? Athos, go down to the ramp area and make sure no one tries to get on board for any reason.' Bill went around, making sure everything was turned off. Then he and Chris went down to the second tier, and Athos went to the third tier.

Both Chris and Bill slept for an entire day. They never realized they were so tired. Chris awoke feeling utterly refreshed. Bill woke up feeling pretty good himself, for his headache was gone. The swelling on his head had also gone down.

At his side were Porthos and Dante. Bill looked up and saw them hovering there.

Porthos thought, 'I hope the commander has enjoyed a pleasant rest.'

'Yes, I have, thank you. How are things? How long have I been out?'

Dante thought, 'It has been some sixteen hours.'

Porthos thought, 'Yes, we have finished our chores. The ship is now fully rejuvenated as far as the gases are concerned.'

'And what of Chris?'

Dante thought, 'She was as tired as you were. She has just waked up. Athos is still standing guard at the ramp area.'

'I will meet you both in the main control room. Send Athos back to the control room. Then seal off and close the doors, retract the ramp, then repressurize the entire ship. Tell the computer I will be right up and expecting a report as to what is happening in the world.'

Porthos thought, 'All right, Commander. We will see you in a few minutes.' With that, Dante and Porthos were gone.

Bill got up, showered, shaved, got dressed, and went to Chris's room. He was surprised to see her combing her hair. She had put on a new dress and looked ravishing. He realized she was a very beautiful woman. He stood in the doorway just admiring her.

Suddenly Chris realized she was being watched. She turned around to look at Bill. 'Come on in, you nut. I think the door will remain standing without your trying to support it.'

Bill came in, walked up to Chris, and kissed her behind the ear. 'Good morning, or whatever it is. I'm going to the control room and get us some coffee.'

'That is the best idea I've heard all day—or is it night? I'll see you in about five minutes.'

Bill left her and went to the control room. There waiting for him were Athos, Dante, and Porthos. He went to the dispenser and got two coffees and two sweet rolls. He took everything to the lounging chairs and sat down in one of them.

Porthos thought, 'Commander, everything is ready.'

Bill reached over and got the maps that showed installations with atomic devices. He started to study these very carefullly. He took a pencil and checked the area that was covered. He realized they could wipe out whatever potential China had. Bill asked the computer where the space platform was now.

'Commander, it is passing our quadrant and should lose any power to see us in the next two minutes.'

At that moment Chris came in and seated herself beside Bill. 'Thanks for the coffee and sweet roll.' She then examined his head wound. 'Yes, it is coming along quite nicely.'

Bill thanked her. 'Computer, fill us in with what is happening in the world.'

'Commander, in the last three hours there have been four reconnaissance craft which have made passes over this base. In the United States there has been the playing of the National Anthem every five minutes on the radio stations. There has been a general appeal to locate officers and recruited personnel in the southern states. There are two fleets of ships that have been redirected here. At the present time they are picking up personnel in the United States. A message has been sent to Russia by the United States, saying they think they have pinpointed the problem. Scouting planes have come back with disturbing information about Peru. An expeditionary force is being dispatched to find out about it. Russia has offered aid in this enterprise but has been turned down. Two fleets are supposed to rendezvous off the coast of California at San Diego.'

'Well, it looks like we are going to be attacked. Thank you, Computer. Hello, out there. Is anybody listening?'

A voice answered, 'Yes, Commander, what do you want us to do?'

'Do? Don't do a thing except stay underground and keep

your force field on at all times. I want to take off. This means your force field is to be interrupted for a few minutes. Can you do this?'

The voice answered, 'That should be no problem. Make sure you advise me before you take off.'

'That is an affirmative. Well, through the computer's advice, we now know what we have to do. Hello, out there. We are ready. Athos, take this ship straight up to a level of ten thousand feet. Porthos, once we get there, put on the invisibility screen and the proton field. Athos, proceed north until we encounter the two fleets. Dante, deposit these ships in the desert. Make a nice line.'

The ship proceeded northward until they spotted the fleets. The first ship Dante chose was an aircraft carrier. He locked on his tractor beams, and Athos rose, taking the carrier with him. They got to the northeastern sector of California, and Dante lowered the carrier into the sand. Athos repeated this fifteen times, and Dante made a nice neat row of battle cruisers in the sand.

Athos went after the other fleet, which was making its way through the Panama Canal. After some fifteen trips, this fleet found itself next to the first. After the last ship was deposited, Athos lifted the *Alpha Centauri* to an altitude of seventy-five thousand feet and held.

'Computer, what are you receiving? What is the feedback?'

'Commander, both fleets have advised the War Department where they are and how they got there. The space platform is verifying this. The Pentagon says a strike force is to be made up of helicopters and fighter planes. All of this is to be directed at the Plain of Nazca.'

The thought of this was unnerving to Bill. 'You know, there is a way to stop this whole thing. Computer, where is the platform now?'

'Commander, it is over the tip of Florida.'

'Computer, put us in touch with the platform.'

'Commander, voice transmission has been completed. You can talk at any time.'

'Thank you, Computer,' Bill picked up the communicator and spoke very slowly and deliberately. "This is the commander of the *Alpha Centauri*. Is there anyone who is listening?"

Bill got an immediate response. "That is an affirmative, *Alpha Centauri*. What can we do for you?"

"Put me through to the War Department of the U. S."

The platform answered, "It will take a few minutes."

"The longer the delay the fewer aircraft the U. S. will have."

"We understand, *Alpha Centauri*. Please hold on."

A voice broke in, "This is the War Department of the United States, *Alpha Centauri*. What is it we can do for you?"

"For starters, you have all kinds of fighter planes headed south. Divert these and send them back to their home bases. If you don't, you will find a lot of aircraft were forced to ditch in some cornfield. You already have to figure out a way of getting two fleets out of a sand trap. Do I make myself clear?"

"All aircraft are being diverted, *Alpha Centauri*."

"We are watching on our scopes. What about the helicopters?"

"All right. Those, too, are now being diverted."

"That is an affirmative with the exception of five aircraft."

"Of the five ships, two are domestic airlines. We are recalling the other three."

"That is a thank-you. You will be hearing from us again. Do you still have the United Nations in New York?"

"Yes, we do."

"When is the next meeting of the General Assembly?"

"I don't know, but I will find out and get back to you."

"Use the same frequency we are on now. Thank you for calling off the military procedure. Until such time as you get back to the so-called protection of the country, the *Alpha Centauri* will protect you. We have enough weaponry on board to level many cities."

"Thank you, *Alpha Centauri*."

"This is something we are not very proud of. This is an end of communication." 'Computer, what is happening now?'

'Commander, we have a difficulty with the countries of Colombia, Venezuela, Guyana, Ecuador, Bolivia, Peru, Chile, and Argentina. They are all amassing armies to march on the Plain of Nazca.'

Bill turned to Dante and then to Athos. 'Any plane, ship, or mechanized vehicle we come across will be considered fair game. We will take these things and deposit them in the forests of Brazil. Let's start from the southern tip of South America.'

Athos took the ship to the southern tip of South America and worked northward at an altitude of ten thousand feet. As he entered Chile, he saw tanks and trucks pulling cannons. Dante locked in and fired his tractor beams. He had picked up fifteen tanks and three trucks with cannon. Athos raised the ship to an elevation of thirty thousand feet and took these things to the forests in Brazil. As soon as Dante had deposited his catch, Athos turned the ship around and went back to Chile. They saw thirty jet fighters. Athos immediately raised the ship to forty-five thousand feet, and Dante caught them all in his tractor beams. Athos went directly to the Brazilian forest, and Dante deposited them there, one on top of the other, in the thick shrubbery. Athos went back, time and time again, as Dante collected planes, ships, tanks, and personnel carriers. They got as far as Guyana.

Finally Athos turned to Bill. 'The Brazilian forest is filled with a strike force that is very impressive. The only problem is that they have nowhere to move their equipment.'

'Yes, that is too bad. Let's go to our target in China.'

Athos immediately moved the ship across the Pacific Ocean and came upon his target. It was a fairly large double silo which housed two ICBMs.

Bill scanned the area. 'Computer, where is the platform now?'

'Commander, the platform is exactly three minutes gone. You won't have any trouble with it for another twenty minutes.'

'Porthos, make sure that proton field is on and working. I smell a big brown rat. This could be a trap.'

'Athos, get only as close as the tractor beams can be effective. Dante, make this a good shot. Athos, as soon as the tractor beams have secured the ICBMs, take the ship to within four million miles of the sun. Dante, as soon as we are there, turn the tractor beams off. Athos, take this ship to the dark side of the moon. Dante, pick up the thirty-five ICBMs. And

169

Athos, get rid of these missiles the same way. Then take this ship to the Plain of Nazca. Let's go, you guys.'

The extraction of the ICBMs, complete with umbilical cords, was done quite easily. Athos took the missiles to within the required distance from the sun, and Dante released them. They were just nearing the dark side of the moon when they heard the explosion of the two ICBMs.

'Those missiles went off before they entered the sun. It was a trap. The missiles were fused to go off.'

Dante picked up all thirty-five missiles, and Athos took them to the sun. Dante released them and Athos returned to the planet earth. As he was entering the atmosphere, he sighted the space platform.

'Athos, change course and pull up alongside the platform. Computer, use the ship-to-ship communicator.'

'Commander, contact has been made.'

"Hello, platform. This is the commander of the *Alpha Centauri*. How are things?"

This time it was a woman's voice that answered back. "Hello, *Alpha Centauri*. There is much that we want to learn about you."

"You flatter me. What is it you wish to know?"

"Our mission is to protect earth from its misbehavior and to make sure nothing happens to disturb this."

"Madam, we are quite aware of your job as a policing body to earth. We have not disturbed your role, in this regard. There are, however, some minor adjustments we have put into effect. Take into account the Plain of Nazca in Peru. We hold this land as ours. Our documentation of this goes back some two thousand years. It is ours, and we intend to keep it. Any force that tries to take it away will be dealt with. Do I make myself clear?"

A male voice got on in place of the woman's. "We are disturbed about the disappearance of thirty-five ICBMs. Do you have them?"

"Ah, a person who is direct and to the point. I like that. In the first place, your information is wrong. It isn't thirty-five, but rather thirty-seven ICBMs. In answer to your question, no, we do not have them. The sun has them."

170

There was a long pause and then another voice came on. "Do you expect us to believe you?"

Bill handed the communicator to Chris and told her to sock it to them. "This is cocommander Chris Spalding. What the commander has been saying is the truth. We have just come from a planet, which has devastated itself and the inhabitants on it in a nuclear war. The planet is now barren of life and vegetation. We don't want to see earth go that way. Last night there were ten ICBMs sent up by the United States. We grabbed onto them in time. We term this a dangerous situation. We realize we are dealing with inferior beings or intellects who now have the power of life or death with the pushing of a button. Something must be done. You see, you have been given the scientific advances but not the mentality to fathom what you have."

There was a long pause. "Please excuse me and the others here. You're right. It's good you have come back to Nazca. Perhaps between the two of us, we can do something about it."

"Yes, perhaps something can be done. We will be in touch with you. End of communication."

'Chris, you were great. You know, there must be some way in which we can use that nuclear power that is contained in those missiles. Do me a favor, Chris, and call the Elders.'

'Yes, Commander,' said a familiar voice. 'We have been listening to your conversation with Chris. We are wondering why it has taken you so long. There is a way to tap the power of uranium. On the table in the medical laboratory you will find ten black boxes with sheathed linings. When you are ready, take the sheaths off these boxes. It doesn't matter how far away you are or what the bombs are encased in. Just lay the box beside it. You will have to wear protective clothing to protect you from the alpha, beta, and gamma particles before you put the sheaths back on. This clothing can also be found near the black boxes. Once the sheaths are put on the black box, you will be safe from all rays. The absorbed power you derive can be beneficial in powering spacecraft, in electrical heating, and the like. Good luck, Commander. Make sure you handle these boxes very carefully.'

Bill thanked the Elders for their information and help.

'Computer, where in the world can the nuclear submarines be found?'

'Commander, a map showing the location of these submarines is being made. You should have it in a few moments.'

Bill thanked the computer and also Chris for her help.

Bill went over to the computer and very soon had his global map. He went over to Athos and showed him the map. There were six submarines off the coast of Peru. 'This map has greatly changed since the last report from the computer. Athos and Dante, deposit these six submarines on the wasteland of the South Pole. I will deposit the six boxes on the missile hatches.'

Athos responded by taking the ship down to water level. Dante came up with two of the submarines. Athos took the ships to the frozen tundra of the South Pole, and Dante deposited them there. Athos turned the ship and went back to the coastline of Peru. Dante came up with four of them this time. Athos went back to the South Pole. Dante deposited these next to the first two.

'Porthos, I will need your help. Take me down there with six of the boxes. Extend the ramp, open the ramp doors, and depressurize the third tier. Go down to the ramp with me and take me to the ships. Stay at a safe distance while I unsheathe each box. Athos, take the ship one mile away and land it. Wait for us to return.'

Chris went up to him, hugged him, and wished him good luck.

Porthos and Bill disappeared in the elevator. They went first to the second tier, hospital section. Bill got the black boxes and put on the antiradiation equipment. He made the comment that the boxes were smaller than he had thought they would be. Porthos and Bill went to the third tier, out through the ramp area, and to the first submarine. Bill asked Porthos to wait at the front of the ship. He unsheathed the first box and placed it in the center of the missile hatches. They went to all of the craft and did the same thing. Porthos took him back to the ship, with the help of Dante's signal. Bill was still clutching the six sheaths when they got back to the *Alpha Centauri*.

172

After all three of them were inside, Bill had Athos retract the ramp and close the doors. Dante, Porthos, and Bill went to the second tier, and Bill discarded the six sheaths on the table and took off his antiradiation gear.

Bill appeared with Dante and Porthos at the first tier. Chris was waiting for them with a nice cup of hot coffee for Bill. When Bill saw her, he smiled. 'Thank you, Chris. You want to know something? It's cold out there. Porthos and Dante, thank you both for your help.'

They waited around for an hour, and then Bill asked Porthos for the same help he had previously given. Porthos turned, opened the doors, and extended the ramp. He and Bill went down to the hospital section. Bill put on the antiradiation equipment and grabbed the sheaths. They went down to the third tier, out the ramp area, and to the six ships. They went from one ship to the other, gathering and sheathing the black boxes, with Porthos standing at a respectable distance each time. Bill had his boxes and Porthos took him back to the *Alpha Centauri*. Once again Bill had Athos retract the ramp and close all the doors. This time he had Dante and Porthos go to the first tier. He told Dante to stand by the tractor beams, and Porthos was to repressurize the entire ship. The two of them took the elevator. It returned, and Bill took it to the second tier. He went to the hospital section and put the six black boxes in a lead-lined container. He took off the antiradiation equipment, checked it out with a geiger counter, and went to the first tier. As before, there was Chris with a hot cup of coffee. Bill thanked her for her thoughtfulness and Porthos and Dante for their help. 'It was damned cold out there. Dante, can you lift all six craft so we won't have to come back here?'

Dante thought he could lift all six craft, and the computer confirmed it.

'Athos, take these ships to some rock quarry in the United States. Dante, deposit these ships very gently, side by side, in this quarry.'

Athos raised the ship and steadied it over the submarines. Dante fired his tractor beams and locked onto all six ships. Athos started to haul the ships and the *Alpha Centauri* forward and northward. He got to a level of seventy thousand feet.

'Commander, the six ships are being tracked by radar.'

'Athos, change that original course and take these ships to the same place in Brazil where we took the others. Also, lower your altitude to twenty-five thousand feet.'

Athos corrected his altitude and course. Soon they found themselves in Brazil over a highly forested area. Dante let the ships down among the underbrush. Dante released the tractor beams. Athos gained altitude and soon was over the Plain of Nazca. Porthos turned off the proton device and the invisibility screen. Athos went to the top of the force field and then let the ship down very slowly. Athos touched down on a landing pad that was now provided. Porthos depressurized the entire ship, opened up all of the doors, and extended the ramp.

'Chris, you and I are going to have to study this map, if you have the time.'

'Bill, I have all the time in the world for you. Now, what is so interesting about this map?'

'It's the deployment of these submarines around the United States that worries me. Would you like a cup of coffee?'

'Yes, I would love a cup with cream. Now, this map indicates that every city on the eastern seaboard is covered by these craft.'

Bill went over to the dispenser and got coffee for Chris and himself. He went over to Chris and handed her the cup of coffee. 'How do we stop twenty-seven ships with only four black boxes? Can you call the Elders again?'

'I'll try. These people might feel imposed upon.'

'Imposed upon?', said a voice in surprise. 'No, not at all. What do you wish, Commander?'

'I will need some thirty black boxes which are similar to the four I have left down on the second tier.'

'That would leave you with a spare of seven.'

'I also want some lead-lined boxes, in addition to the sheaths, to put these highly volatile power packs in, with the lids made of lead and rope handles on the sides for transporting. I will need six of these boxes. The spare seven black boxes and the spare tote box is so I won't have to disturb you again.'

'Disturb us as much as you wish. That is what we are here for.'

'Thank you very much. I appreciate your kindness. So far things have gone very smoothly in our favor. I only hope things will continue in this direction. Please tell us what these black boxes do.'

'It immediately transfers all radioactive particles to the black box. It not only drains all of the radioactive material from the missiles but also from the ship's propulsion itself. In one-half hour the black box will have all of this power.'

'Bill, were you aware of this?'

'I surmised it. When I went back to the six boxes, they seemed to be emitting a glow.'

'I think it is about time you made an appearance. You will also have to inspect your Nazca base.'

'Madam, if you will be so kind as to join me. You also play an important role in the scheme of things. Please, Chris, come and stand beside me.'

'I find it very hard to refuse an offer like that. Well, let's go and see these great works.'

'Athos and Porthos, come with us. Dante, stay on board near the ramp area. No one is to come on board except us. Is everything turned off? Okay, let's go.'

'Commander, the United States War Department has been on the last known frequency and is trying to get in touch with you.'

'All right, computer, patch us in.'

Bill picked up the communicator. "This is the commander of the *Alpha Centauri*. How can I help you?"

"This is Brig. Gen. Blackwell. Our information says you have been very busy today. How much more do you intend to do to earth?"

"Your question, General, was a blatant outcry. Please be more specific or clarify the point you have expressed."

"You have done some unbelievable things, i.e., completely

immobilized the armed forces of five countries, taken four nuclear submarines, and a host of other things. What do you want from us?"

"In the first instance, your count of nuclear submarines is off. There were six of them — not four, as you report. Now, as to my purpose. It is quite simple: I want total disarmament of all of the nuclear weaponry in the world. If you don't do this, I will. Have I answered your question, or would you rather like to think about that?"

"What you are asking is impossible."

"The only reason why it's impossible is that your mentality is inferior to the technological advancements which have been made."

"We will discuss your demands and get back to you."

"General, I'm not issuing demands. I'm only answering a question that has been put to me. The different countries will disarm. That is not a threat or a demand. It is only fact."

"We will get back to you on this. Over and out."

'Bill, let's get going. I want to see this paradise.'

'Okay, let's go. Computer, keep scanning the frequencies.'

The computer replied it would do so and wished Chris and Bill good luck on the planet's surface.

Bill thanked the computer, and then he, Chris, Athos, and Porthos took the elevator down to the third tier. Dante followed close behind and positioned himself in the middle section. Chris, Athos, Porthos, and Bill walked out to the ramp. Athos and Porthos carried Chris and Bill to the ground. 'Athos and Porthos, make sure you stick with us at all times,' Bill cautioned.

At that moment they were met by six people who seemed to be in charge.

The first one thought, 'Welcome, your Highness. We have been waiting for you. It is good you have waited until this day, for today we have completed the air vents to the Equator and to the South Pole. This complex breathes the air from these two regions.'

'How have you taken care of the immediate food requirement?'

The second thought, 'This was no simple problem. What we

176

did was use the vent to the Equator. There were forty of us. We confiscated a trawler and caught a sufficient amount of fish. We sold this trawler with its cargo of fish and purchased all of the supplies and staples we will need for four months. We sent this food back and then set out to take clippings of the different types of plants we wish to grow and harvest.'

'You are looking to harvest a crop in four months' time?'

The first one thought, 'No, the first crop should be ready in only three months' time. We want you to personally examine our underground fields.'

'That is why we are here. Let's go down and see them.'

Chris, Bill, Athos, and Porthos followed the six to a large elevator in a fairly large building and took it down to the farming area. This area was huge. Fields stretched as far as the eye could see. All of these fields were neatly cultivated. Above them, about three stories higher, were the ultraviolet and sun lamps. Some of the workers in the field stopped what they were doing and bowed to Chris and Bill. Chris waved at them and they turned their backs and continued doing whatever it was they were up to.

The complete tour took about four hours. Bill saw that these people did very good work. 'Now, about your energy source. I know one is required for heat, radiation, watering, ventilation, the force field, etc. Where is it?'

One of the party of six thought, 'We have driven down to the earth's core. Through electronics, we have tapped this great core. It has provided everything that you see here, including the force field. Our buildings are small but adequate. They are all lighted and can be this way for over one thousand years.'

'What happens after the one thousand years?'

The man thought, 'It's quite simple: we replace the bulbs.'

'I've been observing you. You are six people, three men and three women. Are you all paired up in a similar manner?'

The first person thought, 'Yes, we are. There is an odd man who does not have a mate. It is his job to make all of the mathematical computations, design all of the equipment, and test it out.'

'He sounds to be a very important individual. I would like to

177

meet him.'

The first person thought, 'We will arrange to have him meet you after we have dinner.'

'That is very kind of you to invite us to dinner with you, but we must decline. There are things we must do in the ship. You may not believe this, but Chris and I are very busy people. Please have this person beside our ramp within three hours. Thank you all for the guided tour. I'm sure that you have more important things to do. We will see you all in three hours.'

With that Chris and Bill, followed by the robots, went back to the ship. Porthos took Chris, and Athos took Bill, and soon they found themselves back on the ramp area of the *Alpha Centauri*. Bill assigned Porthos to keep guard and to remain there. He then asked Athos and Dante to go up to the first tier. When they got there Chris made a dash to the dispenser for a cold drink. Bill sat down in one of the lounging chairs.

'Bill, what can I get for you?'

'Coffee with cream.'

Chris came over to where Bill was and handed him his coffee. Then she, too, sat down in one of the lounging chairs.

'Chris, please summon the Elders.'

Chris looked at him questioningly. 'You have just spoken to them. However, I hereby summon them to have another conference with you.'

'Yes, Commander, what is it you require?'·

'Do you trust those six hundred people that you have placed here?'

'These people have put their trust in you. They would do anything that you commanded them to do. Your kingdom has been founded. Both Chris and you have assured your lifespans by five thousand years, without getting any older than you have already aged. Trust these people; for you have recreated them and therefore they owe you their lives. In answer to your question, yes, we, too, trust them. We did not mean it to be a shock to you. With the taking on the responsibility of rulers, your lifespans would also automatically increase.'

Chris looked a little bewildered. 'Never in my wildest dreams did I anticipate this.'

'Commander, it is the War Department of the U. S. again,

178

through the space platform.'

'All right, patch them into us.'

Bill picked up the communicator. "This is the commander of the *Alpha Centauri*. How can I be of assistance to you?"

"This is Brig. Gen. Blackwell. We have been unable to reach all of the interested parties at this time. We feel certain that your demands will not be met."

"General, for the last time, we are not issuing demands. This is not coercion, bribery, or blackmail. Quite simply, we are advising you what will be. You will either disarm or be disarmed."

Brig. Gen. Blackwell said, "In our quizzical way of thinking, this is nothing more than blackmail. We have established these missile bases as a form of protection. Now you are telling us this cannot be done and we must dismantle these bases. That, sir, is blackmail."

"Are all men like you?"

"They are all like me. They all believe as I do."

"All right, General, call it what you want. In a few days we hope to be invited to talk at the United Nations in New York. We wish to speak to the General Assembly. If you have anything further to say to us, it can be at this time."

"At the present time, the meeting of the General Assembly of the United Nations is an utter impossibility. They have adjourned for the next three months."

"Now listen, General, and listen well. I want that General Assembly reconvened. You have exactly two weeks to do this. In the meantime, I'm taking this obsession upon myself. Is there anything else you wish to talk about?"

"Any action you might take now would be considered a form of aggression, and you would be considered dangerous and be put on the most-wanted list."

"I would be most honored if you did that. End of communication."

Bill asked the computer if it had broken the tie lines.

The computer said it had and they were receiving only the broadcasts.

'Let me say this, Commander. There are three things you must accomplish: first, you must disarm all the political powers on earth; second, you must be faithful to your

179

followers; thirdly, you must find a suitable place for us to dwell.'

'All right, these things will come to pass.'

Chris looked at Bill. 'I'm sorry, Bill. It looks as if I got us into a pickle.'

'Now, look, beautiful, we both went into this with our eyes wide open. I don't mind telling you I will love you all my life.'

'And I feel the same way about you.'

'I didn't realize what the time has gotten to be. Do you realize that three hours have gone by?'

'Let's go and meet this person they've spoken of.'

Chris, Bill, Dante, and Athos went down to the third tier. There they met Porthos. Bill had Athos take Porthos's place, and then Dante and Porthos took Chris and Bill down to the ground. There were seven people waiting for them. Bill saw the seventh person was different from the rest of them in that his head was larger and his look was very penetrating. Bill seemed to feel an aura of intelligence surrounding him.

'You are truly the person whom we are seeking.'

'Your Highness, that is a thought-provoking and interesting statement you have made. How can I serve you?'

'We will need something similar to a spaceship, with the exception this ship should fly in the atmosphere. The seating capacity will be for Chris, me, and two of the robots. The speed it can attain will be five thousand miles per hour. It will be able to hover over any spot for more than four hours. The source of power will be nuclear. It must be able to act like a helicopter. Can you do this?'

'What will be its effective range?'

'Over ten thousand miles.'

'I will need a power pack. What kind of weaponry will you need?'

'A laser gun in the nose of the ship.'

'If you have a power pack, I can have it ready in three days.'

'Dante, go to the laboratory on the second tier and get one of those packets from the lead-lined box. Make sure that the packet is sheathed. Bring one of those packets down here with you.'

Dante disappeared and soon returned with one of the

packets.

'You must be careful with this packet. The alpha, beta, and gamma particles are very strong. Make sure you wear protective clothing before you open this.' He handed the man the packet.

'I'll be particularly careful. I am quite aware of what radiation can do.'

Bill thanked all of the people there. 'By now this place is ringed with guards. Is there some way we can use our invisibility screen and still land here?'

The second man thought, 'Yes, there is. As you make your approach, contact us telepathically. We will lift our force field. However, make sure you are over the pad first before advising us to lift the screen. Then, as you are fifty feet from the pad, tell us, and we will reactivate the force field.'

'I understand. We will be taking off in a few minutes. We will try this out.' He thanked them again and then he, Chris, and the robots left the area for the *Alpha Centauri*.

Before they left, the first man thought, 'Your Highness, can we be of any assistance to you in your endeavor?'

'Thank you very much, but the way I see it is that these are my people. I realize you started this whole thing. It is my contention it us up to Chris and me to stop it. If I do need help, you will be the first people I will ask. At any rate, thank you for your offer.'

Dante and Porthos lifted Chris and Bill to the ramp area. Bill then had Athos, Porthos, and Dante accompany Chris and him to the first tier. He had Athos take the helm and Porthos close off and seal the ramp area and retract the ramp. Dante pressurized the entire ship.

'Porthos, make sure the invisibility screen is on. Athos, take this ship to fifty feet and hold.'

Athos advised him the ship had been raised fifty feet and he was now holding.

'Hello, down there. We are now awaiting your turning off of the force field.'

A voice thought, 'The field is off. You can go now.'

'Athos, raise this ship to an elevation of ten thousand feet and hold.'

181

In seconds the ship had reached an elevation of ten thousand feet. 'Okay, we're clear now. Turn on the force field. Thank you for your help.'

Chris thought, 'Computer, please give us the latest locations of the nuclear submarines around the eastern seaboard of the United States.'

'Yes, cocommander. Here is the information on their locations. It varies only slightly to their previous positions.'

Chris got the revised map from the computer and immediately handed it to Bill, who scrutinized this new information.

'I thought we might use the North Pole region this time. We will fly these submarines under the radar networks by sixes. We will place our little boxes on them and then go back for more submarines. As soon as we have another load of subs, we will take the first ones back to where we found them, with the exception that these will be beached on the shoreline.'

'I can handle this little action. In the meantime, Bill, you can get those boxes and get suited up in the antiradiation gear.'

'Chris, thank you for putting your trust in me. I only hope we are doing the right thing.'

'There are many ways to skin a cat. I think you have chosen only one of the routes. At any rate, we are now committed and must see this thing through. We must reach a conclusion.'

'You make things sound so simple. I'll see you all in a little while.' He then went down to the hospital section.

'Athos, here is the map which pinpoints the locations of those twenty-seven submarines. What you and Dante are going to do is to take the first six that we come across to the North Pole.'

Athos had come up with the first submarine in a matter of seconds. Dante locked his tractor beam on, and Athos then went on to the next ship. Soon they were taking the six submarines to the North Pole.

Bill appeared in his costume with the six black boxes under his arm. Athos was in the process of setting the ships down. Dante was releasing the ships as they landed in the snow by turning off his tractor beams as the ships touched the ground.

Bill requested Athos to land about one mile away and in-

182

structed Porthos to accompany him to the submarines. Porthos opened the ramp area, extended the ramp, and depressurized the third tier. Porthos followed Bill to the third tier and then they went to the ships. Bill planted all six of the boxes and instructed Porthos to take him back to the ship. They got on board the ramp area. Then Bill and Porthos went to the first tier.

They made eight trips in all. All of the black boxes were charged, sheathed, and put away in their lead containers. The powerless submarines were deposited along the coastline. When Bill finally came up from the second tier, he stood and observed. 'That was a nice piece of work, you guys.' He instructed Porthos to make sure the ramp was retracted, the doors sealed and closed, and the third tier repressurized again. He also had Porthos check the invisibility screen and the proton device to make sure they were both on and operative. He told Athos to take the ship up to seventy-five thousand feet. 'Computer, I want all of the information possible on all of the ICBMs left in the world.'

'Yes, Commander, working. You should have your answers in a few moments.' Soon a map was made and processed through the computer.

Bill took the map from the computer and gave it to Chris who, in turn, gave it to Athos.

'Now comes the tough part. We have to rip out these ICBMs from their launch pads before they are fired. We won't have time to take these to the moon, but we'll have to deposit them about twenty-five miles away from the launch pads. Any missiles that are fired we have to track and capture before they are detonated on the ground. Computer, keep all frequencies open and report anything that you hear is pertinent. It looks as though both sides have approximately fifty missiles of the ICBM classification. Our job should be made easy because by now all of the silo doors are opened on both sides. Athos, let's take care of the United States first and then go on into Russia. Computer, where is the space platform?'

The computer replied that the platform was right overhead.

'All right, this is the plan. Take all of the missiles from their launch pads and then come back for them after all are lying on the ground. Then take them to the dark side of the moon.

183

Questions? Chris, you are in command. Let's go.'

In less than one hour they were through with the United States. Then they went into Russia. Within one hour's time they had gone through that country. They collected all the ICBMs and deposited them on the dark side of the moon.

'You guys are terrific, or did I say that already? Now we have six black boxes left. Let's go after the submarines that are ringing the coast of the U.S.S.R. and take these to the North Pole. Remember, I need only six of these vessels.'

Chris checked with the computer as to where the submarines could be found. Soon she had a map, which she showed to Bill. He checked off six submarines with his pencil and handed the map to Athos.

After they had gotten the six ships to the North Pole and put the black boxes on them, they waited for one-half hour. Bill went back for the boxes. When they had these, Athos took them back to their original locations and deposited them on the shoreline of the Russian coast.

'Let's go to the moon and send these missiles into the sun.'

Athos gained altitude and they were soon orbiting the moon. He then was hovering over the center of the crater with the missiles. By using his tractor beams, Dante pulled them out by sixes. After some sixteen trips to the sun and back, they were just returning from their seventeenth trip when the computer advised them of another danger.

'Four SAC planes have broken through the Russian defenses and are heading toward Moscow.'

'We have to intercept the four planes before they drop their payloads. Athos, get to Moscow immediately. Computer, keep your scanners on these craft.'

The *Alpha Centauri* got there just in time. Bill had Dante put the tractor beams on the ships and had Athos take them to two hundred thousand feet. Then, as before, he had Athos take them to a forested area in the state of Washington where Dante deposited them.

'My scanners indicate a counter move by the Russians in the direction of the United States. There are four craft going over Canada, heading for the United States.'

'Athos, intercept. Dante, get ready with those tractor beams.'

184

Soon Athos caught up with the craft, and Dante put his tractor beams on them.

'Now, let's deposit these ships in Russia.'

In less than one minute they were over Russia. Bill had Dante deposit these craft in Moscow. Then, with his disintegrater rays, Dante took off the wings of these ships. It was as if the craft had never had wings.

'Now let's go to the space platform. I want to say something to them. I would also like to find out what, if anything, they saw.'

Soon the *Alpha Centauri* was directly beneath the platform, and Chris made sure that Porthos had turned off the invisibility screen.

She made a fast comparison. 'You know, our ship is larger than the Space Platform.'

'Why, yes. It gives us more space to run around, trying to catch each other.' Then he looked at the computer and asked for a general tieline with the platform.

'Yes, Commander, the tieline is complete. You may talk whenever you wish.'

Bill picked up the communicator. "This is the *Alpha Centauri*. Is anyone picking up this conversation?"

A voice said, "What is it, Commander?"

"I would like a tieline to Washington, D.C., and a certain Brig. Gen. Blackwell, and I want you to listen in."

"All right, Commander, but this will take a few minutes. How are things in Peru?"

"Things are just fine. We should have our first harvest in three months."

"We are amazed. Where on the Plain of Nazca are you doing your cultivating and planting?"

"We have rich fields and good irrigation. We can grow anything."

"The War Department is ready with our call to Brig. Gen. Blackwell."

"Gen. Blackwell, this is the *Alpha Centauri*. How are things with you?"

Blackwell was furious. "Where are the fifty missiles that were taken from us tonight?"

"General, if you knew it was us, why did you send the

185

bombers to Moscow? It has occurred to me that you want to start a war under any pretext."

"You don't know what you are saying."

"General, you can find the remaining bombers, four of them which we snagged over Moscow, in a forested area in the state of Washington."

"Then you wouldn't know something about twenty-seven submarines we captured off the coast of the eastern seaboard tonight."

"General, how did you capture them? With sticks? We put those submarines there after we disabled them, rendering them helpless and the missiles they carried, duds. You cannot call the beaching of twenty-seven submarines an act of war. Unless, of course, you are looking for a reason for war."

Chris got on the communicator. "Gen. Blackwell, we did the same thing to your submarines. I would like to ask you, what power does not wish to accept our demands, as you call them? It is not demands, but one demand. And that is that you completely abolish all nuclear warfare. I am getting the distinct impression it is the United States who is opposing this. Is that true?"

The brigadier general tried to sidestep the question. Chris immediately pounced on him. "Then you are, in fact, confirming it is the United States."

Bill got on. "General, we are tired of this whole thing. Within two weeks, all nations will be entirely disarmed of their nuclear threat potential. I would have rather done it by the use of the United Nations. You, however, have given us no other choice. This ends our communication. Good luck to you and all sword rattlers like you."

A voice replied, "It appears there is a great problem looking us right in the eye. That problem is with a few individuals in power in the countries of the world. I hope you don't mind, but we have taped this whole conversation."

Chris got on the communicator. "Your taping of the conversation is all right as far as we're concerned. Yes, I think what you have said about a few individuals in power is correct. What the commander has said about ridding the world of nuclear weapons is also correct. This means you are going to

186

have to take a longer look at yourselves and your neighbors. All I can say to you is good luck. This is your problem and not ours."

A different voice came on this time. "What you have said is definitely true. This is our problem and not yours. Thank you for letting us have this other chance."

Bill then got on. "Use it well. God go with you. You will need his help."

During the next few days and with the acquisition of more black boxes and lead-lined tote boxes, the *Alpha Centauri* totally disarmed the whole earth of nuclear devices, including the smaller devices. There wasn't any more need for the ship to hunt down nuclear weapons. Sixteen boxes were given to the odd man. He immediately took these and made sixteen spacecraft. Bill had his so-called helicopter and went over the controls very studiously until he was sure he could operate it. Time, although it seemed to weigh heavily, slipped by very quickly. Soon the Plain of Nazca was to have its first harvest. Everything seemed to be going well. They had not heard from anyone during this time. It was very calm and peaceful. Chris liked her new home very much. She started to show that she was carrying a child.

One day the computer aboard the *Alpha Centauri* summoned Bill to the main control room. Bill came up with Porthos and asked the computer why it had summoned him.

'Yes, Commander, you are getting a call from the space platform advising us that the War Department of the United States wishes to talk with you.'

Bill picked up the communicator. "This is the *Alpha Centauri*. Whom am I speaking with and how can I be of assistance?"

"Hello, *Alpha Centauri*. This is the War Department in Washington, D. C., calling. My name is Brig. Gen. Adams."

"I'm a bit surprised. Where is Gen. Blackwell?"

"Brig. Gen. Blackwell has retired. I have been assigned to take his place. What we are calling about is your request to convene the General Assembly of the United Nations. I am calling to report that the General Assembly will be in session in another week. You are cordially invited to attend."

187

"I'm honored. However, there's been a change in my original request. Things have already been taken care of."

"We are quite aware of the changes that have been effected. We are asking that you attend in our honor."

"I will get back to you concerning this." 'Porthos, I hope you have been reading this person's mind.' "I will contact you in four hours."

"I will be looking forward to hearing from you. End of communication."

'All right, Porthos and computer, what did you pick up?'

The computer went first. 'Within one week's time they are going to send in two companies of Marines. They will wait until the *Alpha Centauri* is about to take off. They will use missiles and all of their fire power to bring down the ship. They are then to take over the Plain of Nazca and demolish everything in sight. There is also a trap being set for you at the United Nations.'

Porthos thought, 'That's what I got out of it too.'

'That makes three of us. Let's go consult Chris on this.'

Porthos took Bill down to the ground. 'Porthos, get with Athos and Dante. Load that smaller craft on board in the ramp area.'

Bill walked up to Chris. 'You heard?'

'Yes, I did. What are we going to do?'

'I never thought I would do this but, with your condition, I have to ask for help.'

Bill then went up to the odd man and the first man and asked them for help. Both of them agreed immediately. Bill then told them of his plan. Both agreed to this. Bill turned around and walked up to Chris.

'It's all settled; we're leaving tonight.'

The two men were ready and waiting for Chris and Bill at the ramp area. Bill then turned to the others.

'Remember, I am to turn the invisibility screen on, go up fifty feet, tell you people to let down the force field, raise the ship to one thousand feet plus, and then you are to turn on the force field again. I want this place to be impenetrable. You are going to have visitors. If they do get in, get out through the vents. I don't want you to fight them. Your lives are far too

188

important for that.' All five people nodded their heads in agreement.

Chris and Bill were lifted to the *Alpha Centauri* first. Dante stayed on board to greet them. Athos and Porthos went down after the other two people. 'I see no reason not to give them the freedom of the ship.'

Chris was in full agreement. 'It will be nice seeing others in this ship, aside from the robots and ourselves. You know, we do have a large ship.'

'I have to agree with you. Now I can let someone else chase you around the ship. I was getting tired anyway.'

Almost immediately the two people came up to Chris and Bill.

'Commander, we will defer this conversation to a later time. I have yet to give you my two cents on this matter.'

'Where do you want us to stay?' thought one of the two.

'Let's all go upstairs to the first tier, take off, and then we can worry about accommodations.' They seemed to be in agreement to this. Porthos, Athos, and Dante went up first. They were followed by Chris, Bill, and the two men.

When they got to the first tier, Bill instructed Athos to take over the helm and Porthos to retract the ramp, close and seal all doors, and to repressurize the ship. Dante was instructed to put on the invisibility screen and activate the gravity device. Bill turned to the computer.

'Please advise me when I am to contact Washington, D.C. Also, keep your channels open. We are looking for an attack.'

The computer agreed to do this. Porthos and Dante reported that their work was finished. Bill instructed Athos to take the ship up to fifty feet and hold. Athos advised that this had been done.

Bill advised the people on the ground to lift the force field. Athos was to raise the craft ten thousand feet. The ship went up ten thousand feet in a matter of seconds. Bill had Dante activate the proton device and told the people on the ground to reactivate their force field.

'Commander, it's the space platform. They have Washington, D.C., on the radio. They are asking to talk with you.'

Bill told the computer to instruct the space platform it was trying to locate the commander and to please hold. The computer advised Bill it was looking for him. The space platform was holding.

'Let's all have a cup of coffee. Then I'll contact Washington.' They all had some coffee.

Bill went over to the computer and advised it that it had found the commander. He picked up the communicator. "This is the *Alpha Centauri*. How can we help you out?"

"This is Brig. Gen. George Michelin. How are things with you?"

"Very fine, thank you. What has become of Gen. Adams? I seem to be talking to a different person each time."

"Brig. Gen. Adams has been called away. Until his return, I am taking his place."

"What has become of all those ships in the desert?"

"I believe they are still there in the sand trap. That was a very nasty thing you did."

"Sorry about that. If you would be so kind as to send token crews to Los Angeles, they will soon be having their ships in the water."

"That's great. You're not pulling my leg, are you?"

"No, I wouldn't do that. Get your crews ready, and I will get the ships. Now, is it true the General Assembly of the United Nations will be in session one week from today?"

"Yes, it's true."

"What time should we be there?"

"About 10:00 A.M."

"We'll be there."

"That's good. We will advise them of your intent."

"Fine. Unless there is something else, this will be the end of our conversation."

"End of communication. Thank you for the ships."

Bill turned to the computer. 'Computer, an evaluation of the conversation, please.'

'Yes, Commander. Brig. Gen. Adams is at the head of the two companies of Marines.'

'Thank you for your evaluation. That is what I picked up too.'

He turned to Athos and Dante. He instructed Athos to go

190

where the ships were and for Dante to retrieve them and put them in the Pacific Ocean.

'Commander, it's the space platform. They would like to speak to you.'

"*Alpha Centauri* here. How might we help you out?"

"This is the commander of the space platform. We are calling to warn you not to try to go to that meeting next week at the General Assembly. It's a trap."

"We are in your debt. That is one we owe you."

Athos soon had them over the desert area and the ships Dante had left. Athos got Dante within range, and Dante fired the tractor beams. He got two of the ships, and then Athos took them over the coastline of the Pacific Ocean. Athos swooped down low and Dante deposited them in the water. Athos went back for more ships and he repeated this until the desert was void of them.

'Athos, take us to Alpha Centauri at the speed of seven parsecs per hour. Go to planet three. Make sure you don't enter the atmosphere, but orbit the planet.'

'Chris, how good are you at taking pictures?'

'Not bad, but I think you'll need a bear rug.'

'Very funny. Will you please call the Elders?'

She called for the Elders. Soon a voice answered, 'Yes, you called?'

'It was not for me but for the commander that I have summoned you. I also have been reading his thoughts. He needs a 8 mm. camera that will process the film as the picture is taken. He will need fifty feet of film. We will also need a projector and a portable screen. The film is to be sensitive enough to be used with the viewing screen.'

'Hello, Commander. Let me see. You have the impression that if people at the General Assembly see these pictures, they might believe your emissaries.'

'Why did I think I had to say something? You're both right. Can this be done?' Bill asked.

'You'll find all you require in the hospital section.'

'Thank you for your help.'

'You are entirely welcome, Chris, and you, too, Commander. Good luck to you both.'

191

The two people that had come along were listening to this whole thing. They glanced at one another in amazement. Then the odd man said to the other, 'These two people really are the king and queen.'

13

The Filming of Planet Ohg, a Visit to Planet Four, and the Space Platform ───────

THE FIRST MAN THOUGHT, 'I must agree with you. It is my belief he set those ships free knowing full well they would be used against our base on planet earth. What he is doing is testing how invulnerable we have built the force field.'

The odd man thought, 'I think that he is showing us he has a degree of confidence in us.'

Both men became silent as Bill came over to where they were sitting and went to the dispenser for some more coffee. Bill turned to them and thought, 'You thought I couldn't hear you. Let me say this, I have more than a degree of confidence in you. I am putting this whole thing on the line. We, gentlemen, either have it or we don't.'

Both men looked at Bill and then at Chris. The first man thought, 'Please excuse us. We didn't know how extensive your powers were. Even we do not communicate with the Elders the way you do. This makes us very humble. You really are the king and queen. You see, we weren't sure.'

The odd man thought, 'What he says is true. We don't even have the power to communicate and hear as well as you do.'

Chris came over to them. 'Is he showing off again?'

They all laughed.

Athos thought, 'We are approaching planet three and should be in orbit within the next two minutes.'

Chris communicated to one of the two men, 'Would you be

so kind as to go down to the second tier, hospital section, and get the camera? In the meanwhile, we will adjust the screen.'

The person thought, 'I would be most happy to.' He left on the elevator down to the second tier.

Chris then asked Porthos to adjust the screen downward and give her six power.

Porthos adjusted the screen and magnified to six power.

They orbited the planet twice and then Bill asked her what she thought.

'This would make a fine picture. The whole thing is gruesome. The way those buildings have twisted and buckled makes one sit back and wonder.'

'I want you to save fifteen feet of film. Computer, please give us a readout on the atmosphere of this planet. Make sure it is printed in your best and biggest type.'

'Yes, Commander, my readout is finished, in my biggest and boldest type.' The readout read as follows: Nitrogen, 78%; oxygen, 21%; argon, 1%; water vapor, .01 - 4%; carbon dioxide, .03%; cobalt, 10%.

'I want you to take a picture of this readout card first.'

At that moment the man returned with the camera. He gave it to Chris, who was also holding the readout card. She placed the card on one of the lounges. She lined it up with the camera and shot her pictures. Then she lined up the viewing screen and photographed everything she saw. She was careful to leave fifteen feet of unexposed film. It took about an hour to do this.

'How would you people like to see your new home?' He asked Athos to land at planet four in the same spot as before.

Athos acknowledged his commander's request. He swung the ship out of orbit around planet three and increased his speed to six parsecs. This increase in acceleration threw everyone back. 'I want to apologize to everyone. I just wanted to get out of there.'

'Porthos, turn the invisibility screen off and adjust our viewing screen to straight ahead at two power.'

Porthos effectuated all that was ordered of him and then went back to his station.

Athos was now in orbit around the fourth planet. Suddenly

Bill received a telepathic communication from Gurkha and Aryana.

Gurkha was thinking, 'Put your invisibility screen up. We have been attacked and enslaved by the same ones you helped out.'

'Porthos, put the invisibility screen on and change the power of the viewing screen to a magnification of six. Athos, don't land, but keep orbiting the planet. Chris, look out for bogies.'

'Bill, what is it?'

'It's that darned ship we thought we saved. It has returned bringing more of its kind. They've captured and enslaved all of the people we left here.'

'How do you know that?'

'Aryana and Gurkha just told me.'

'I didn't hear a thing.'

The two passengers thought, 'We heard nothing too.'

'I'd feel as confident as you, if it weren't that we had four bogies at twelve o'clock on the viewing screen. Dante, use your tractor beams at the farthest distance possible. Athos, after Dante has the tractor beams in place, take them to planet three. Dante, deposit them in the atmosphere. Let's go, guys.'

Athos inverted the ship. Dante fired and locked on to the four vessels. Athos went immediately to planet three. At the speed of four parsecs per hour, these craft were moving quite swiftly as the tractor beams put the craft well within the atmosphere. Dante then released the tractor beams. The ships tried but couldn't escape the gravitational pull of the planet. Bill and the others watched as the spacecraft crashed on the surface of the planet.

'That guy said they had only twelve ships. We have just eliminated one third of their fleet. Athos, take us back to planet four and hover in orbit around the planet.'

Athos put the ship in orbit around the fourth planet. Porthos made sure the invisibility screen as well as the proton field were in place and working. Bill tried to communicate with Aryana and Gurkha. Finally they came in loud and clear.

Gurkha thought, 'We saw what you did and want to thank you.'

'How many people are holding you captive?'

195

Gurkha thought, 'I'd estimate there are one hundred of them. It wouldn't mean anything, except that these people have weapons and we don't.'

'What we intend to do is free both you and Aryana. In order to do this, you will have to keep your minds open and keep thinking *Alpha Centauri.*'

Just then they picked up two more ships in orbit around the planet. Bill instructed Athos to land in the same spot they used before. As soon as he, Porthos, and Athos were on the ground, Chris would raise the ship ten thousand feet and hold.

'Computer, are you picking up any signals from Gurkha and Aryana?'

The computer replied it was and had given the coordinates to Athos.

As soon as Athos had landed the ship, Chris took his place. Porthos extended the ramp, opened the ramp doors, and depressurized the entire ship. Bill went over to where Chris was and gave her a kiss—for luck, he said. Then he, Athos, and Porthos went down to the third tier and out the ramp area. As soon as they were safely on the ground, Chris raised the ship ten thousand feet and held.

'Hold it, Chris. Land the ship where it was. Dante, as soon as Chris gets to within five feet of the ground, turn off the proton shield.'

'Sorry about the inconvenience.'

'It's okay, Chris. The fault was mine.'

After the three were safely on the ground, she raised the ship to ten thousand feet and held. She instructed Dante to put on the proton shield again.

In the meantime, Athos, Porthos, and Bill proceeded to where Gurkha and Aryana were. They found a rather large fortification with many guards on duty around it. Athos, Porthos, and Bill took care of the guards quite efficiently. Then Bill went into the fortification quite easily and quickly found Aryana and Gurkha. In their place they put all the guards, without their weapons, behind the cell doors.

'It's good to see you again, Aryana and Gurkha.'

Gurkha thought, 'It's doubly good to see you again.'

'Where to now?'

Gurkha thought, 'Follow me.' With that he moved out with

great speed. They soon came upon another fortification. There were guards all around it. Gurkha thought, 'This is where they are keeping the women.'

They caught many of the guards unaware. Soon they had rounded up the women and replaced both the guards they had subdued on the outside and those they had found on the inside in the cells that were intended for the women. Each woman took a weapon.

'We are now thirty-one strong.' Bill cautioned the women about using the weapons. He and the robots would take care of that. Only if he didn't return, he told them, were they even to consider using them. The women agreed to this.

Gurkha thought, 'Let's go to the men's prison.' Soon they found yet another fortification. Once again Bill, Athos, and Porthos took care of the guards on the outside, which was double the force they had found at the other two prisons. They made short work of these guards and went inside. They found a radio and an operator at the controls. They knocked him out and proceeded to the cell section. A little while later all of the guards had replaced the prisoners.

'One thing I am worried about is the two girls we brought here.' He asked one of the guards where he might find them. The guard said the two girls were in the interrogation room at the end of the hall. Bill, Athos, and Porthos rushed down to the end of the corridor. They opened the door, and there, upside down with metal helmets on their heads, completely naked, were the two girls. Beside them were the four captains of the ships that Bill had just destroyed. Bill immediately knocked these men out and rushed over to the two girls. He uprighted them and took off the helmets. It was then that he realized their heads had been completely shaven. Bill was furious but contained himself. He told Athos and Porthos to take these fine gentlemen to the cells with their friends.

Bill revived the two girls and unbound them from the tables they were on. Both threw their arms around him, saying that they were glad he had come when he did. They told him about the mind machine. Apparently, the machine was capable of consuming a person's mind, leaving that person completely devoid of a brain.

Afterward, Bill joined Aryana and Gurkha outside and

197

immediately asked how their food supply was. Aryana came up to Bill and kissed him, then she told him their food supply was adequate.

'You know that you are welcome to anything we might have.'

Aryana looked at him and smiled. 'I will have to remember that.'

'Gurkha, you have a very beautiful and sexy woman here. I trust you can do something about that.'

Gurkha looked at Bill and smiled.

Bill looked at Athos and Porthos. 'Come on, guys, we have to get going.' He looked at Aryana and Gurkha and smiled. 'Good luck to you both. I will be back in three days.'

The three of them had gotten to the meadow upon which the ship was to land. Porthos advised Dante that they were ready to come on board. Almost immediately the ship landed. Although they couldn't see it, they received Dante's call that they were there. Dante directed Athos and Porthos with Bill to the ramp area of the ship. Bill went immediately to the elevator with the robots. When he got in the elevator he instructed Porthos to retract the ramp, close off and seal all doors, and to repressurize the ship. 'Dante, after we are airborne, give us our own gravitation and turn on the proton field. Athos, take Chris's spot and take the ship up to five hundred thousand feet. Dante, after you are finished with your chores, stand by the disintegration rays.'

When he had reached the first tier, the first thing he thought was, 'Nice job, Chris. Computer, put us in touch with the two alien spacecraft.'

Bill picked up the intercommunicator. "This is the commander of the *Alpha Centauri*. Is there anything or anyone there who can understand us?"

"Yes, Commander. We are receiving you loud and clear."

"Then I will say this only once. Get the hell off of my planet and don't ever try to come back again. Today you have lost four craft and your prisoners have traded places with their captors. You will beam them on board your two vessels immediately or else they will starve or die."

"You have a very warm and friendly way of putting things, Commander. We will beam our men on board as well as the

198

ones from the other craft. After this is done, we will prepare to leave."

"There is one more thing that I forgot to mention. You have exactly two minutes to do this or else I am going to do to you what I did to your sister ships. End of communication."

The next voice they heard was Gurkha's. 'They are evacuating their men from the prisons. Now all of the men have been evacuated.'

'Commander, the two ships are preparing to go.'

'Computer, listen to their conversation with their home base. Pinpoint their location and put it on a map. Athos, follow these ships to the end of this solar system. Find out and track where these communications are coming from.'

The two people who were riding with Chris and Bill thought, 'We have never, in all of our lives, felt like so much extra baggage as we do now.'

Bill came over to them. 'You have your jobs to do. No one on this vessel need feel like excess baggage or anything else like that. What we are trying to do is first, to save a race from self-destruction, and, second, to set up a base—a permanent base—for 3.5 million people. This makes everyone an integral part of the whole. I don't know what else to say except that we need you both.'

The first man thought, 'Thank you for those words. I believe both you and your words are sincere. All I can say is that we are with you 100 percent. Just tell us what you want done, and we'll do it.'

'Thank you for your vote of confidence. It's not taken lightly. When I bark, it will be because I am not kidding.'

The odd man thought, 'We'll listen when you bark.'

They all laughed.

'There is another person whom you will also heed and that person is Chris. She is as important to this whole thing as anybody or anything concerning our efforts.'

Chris looked up from what she was doing and smiled.

The first man thought, 'Together you make a good team.'

'Commander, you scared the pants off those aliens. They have no wish to fight with you. They have contacted their base and are hightailing it for home. I have the coordinates. Do you want them?'

'No, I don't need them right now. Keep them handy, though. We'll need them in the future. Porthos, you can turn the invisibility screen off now. Athos, proceed back to planet earth at a speed of seven parsecs per hour. Notify us before you enter the solar system.'

Athos proceeded to the planet earth at a speed of seven parsecs per hour, and Porthos turned off the invisibility screen. Bill changed the viewing screen to the second power and adjusted it to straight ahead with the flight of the ship. He went to the dispenser for a cup of coffee. Chris joined them with her cup in hand. Both Chris and Bill seemed so perfectly calm that they made their guests feel the same way. Within approximately one-half hour, Athos announced they were now about to enter the solar system.

'Chris, take ten feet of film of this and the last five feet on the space platform.'

Chris took ten feet of film on the solar system and then told Athos to go to planet earth. 'Orbit around it and catch up with the space platform.'

Athos performed this little maneuver in a matter of seconds. Chris took the remaining five feet on the space platform with the earth in the background.

'All right, let's see what we have on film.' She asked one of the men to get the projector and the screen. When the man returned, he had the screen, projector, and cutters.

He thought, 'We have to halve the film before we show it.' He took the film, cut it in half, fed it into the projector, and set up the screen. For the next fifteen minutes they all viewed the film. It was good. Everything had come out in the fullest detail.

'Commander, the space platform is calling. They would like to know what we are doing here.'

'Computer, ask them what day it is on earth.'

'Commander, today is Thursday in the United States.'

'Computer, ask them if they have done anything to damage the base on the Plain of Nazca.'

'Commander, all efforts to gain entrance to the city have been in vain.'

'Computer, ask them if we might come on board the platform.'

200

'Commander, Chris and you can come on board. They have many questions to ask you both.'

'Computer, advise them we will systematically destroy the platform if anything happens to Chris or me.'

'Commander, they are fully aware you are not alone on the ship, and they promise no harm will come to Chris or you.'

'Computer, tell them we are bringing a projector with us. There is a film we would like to show them.'

'Commander, they would be very interested in seeing this film.'

'Okay, gal, let's suit up in pressurized gear and take the small ship over there. Porthos, come along with us.'

Porthos instructed Dante to depressurize the third tier, to turn off the proton shield, to extend the ramp, and to open all doors to the outside.

Chris looked at their two guests. 'Would you mind if we took a short trip? We will be right back.'

The two men looked up. One of them thought, 'You two go on. We have some sleep to catch up on.'

Chris, Bill, and Porthos went down to the second tier where both dressed in astronautical gear. After putting on their helmets and pressurizing their suits, all three of them went down to the third tier. They climbed into the confiscated spaceship, and Porthos took them over to the space platform. Porthos went right into the platform's opened ramp area. Chris and Bill got out. Bill instructed Porthos to stay with the ship and not to let anyone come around snooping. Porthos agreed to this.

Chris and Bill were very ceremoniously treated. They were greeted by Dr. Hapsberg, who was designated the head of the complex. He ushered them into a room that was filled with people. These people were of all races and nationalities. They were all introduced as scientists, each with his or her field of specialization.

Bill found a screen and placed the loaded projector several feet away from it. He looked at the group and telepathically said, 'You will have no need for interpreters. I will speak to each of you individually and you will understand what I say.' The people were amazed and startled. They looked at one another and sat down.

Bill showed his film and explained why Chris had taken it. He stopped during his dissertation and looked at a Japanese person. 'No, Mr. Matsumura, stay seated. You do not wish to see my craft.' Then he continued addressing the group. In a closing comment he advised he would be gone from this solar system within forty-eight hours. It was not his intent to dominate the earth. All he wanted to do was to warn them that they were going in the wrong direction.

He received a terrific round of applause. He thanked them very much and asked if they had any questions. The questions he got were voluminous. He took them one at a time and answered them very cordially. Finally, he came to the most critical group of questions. He put the projector under his arm. 'My purpose for coming here tonight was not to discuss my ship, how many hulls it has, the type of drive it uses, how fast it can go, how many there are in my crew, how the invisibility screen works, the type of force field we employ, the antigravity device and how it works, or, for that matter, what weapons the *Alpha Centauri* has. You never ask this of an alien. I originally came on board to see human beings again. Well, I have seen them. Thank you for your cordial behavior. I'm glad you think the film is effective. All I can say to you now is good luck. Come, Chris, let's go.'

Chris got up from where she was sitting and addressed the whole group. 'Never have I been so wrong about anything as I have about you. I seriously wonder if we have done the right thing about trying to save your race. You are truly sponges. Little children with big ideas. We will return to you every five hundred years to see how you are doing. Good luck to you and go with God. You will always need his help.' With that, Chris followed Bill out.

Porthos, Chris, and Bill got back on board their ship. The ramp doors of the space platform were opened, and they left to go back to the *Alpha Centauri*. When they got on board, Porthos advised Dante, who immediately retracted the ramp, closed the doors, and repressurized the third tier. Nothing was said all the way up in the elevator. Just as they reached the first tier, Chris broke the silence. 'How about some coffee?'

Bill looked at Chris. 'I am sorry, gal. I didn't mean to put you through that. Some of those questions were real headaches, weren't they?'

'You know, Bill, seeing them and watching you tonight really gave me a different perspective on you.'

'With a statement like that one, I don't know whether to be complimented or struck down. How did you mean that last remark?'

'Oh, I'm just glad you're you. You know, a person could learn to like you very much.'

Bill thanked her and gave her a big kiss. 'Chris, would you call the Elders?'

Chris did, and soon a voice answered, 'Yes, Commander. Hello, Chris.'

'I want our passengers to speak English. Can this be done?'

'It already has been done.'

'Thank you very much.'

'Why, you're welcome, Chris, You, too Commander.'

Bill walked up to the two passengers. "My name is Bill. How do you two want to be called?"

The two men looked up and the first one replied, "My name is Mark; my friend's name is Peter."

Chris said, "Very good. You can call me Chris."

"Chris, would you like to tell these people what to say at the General Assembly of the United Nations tomorrow?"

'Commander, it is the space platform. They are calling to apologize for their actions. They are also sending a detailed report of their encounter with you to planet earth. Nothing is left out. You must have made a startling appearance to them. They report they have no fear of you at all. It is not your intent to conquer them at all.'

'Computer, scan the entire globe and pick up where they are making nuclear bombs.'

'Yes, Commander, working.'

'Computer, after you finish, make a map showing the exact locations of these manufacturing points.'

Chris looked at Peter and Mark. "This is what we want you to say at tomorrow's meeting. Show them the film and tell them that this is what they can expect to happen to them if they persist in making nuclear weapons. This is all firsthand information. Extract the film from the projector and give it to the chairman of the assembly. Tell them we took all of their nuclear weapons and exploded them on the sun's surface. It is our opinion they should amalgamate into one power to stem the tide of building any more weapons. Tell them, as an alien, you have already interfered too much and can do no more. It is up to them how they are going to handle their own lives. We have warned them, and that is all we can do. Show them the map the computer is now putting together. Tell them that within forty-eight hours, earth time, we will be leaving them to whatever fate destiny holds for them. Make sure to stress their fate is now in God's hands. We will periodically check on them every five hundred years to see what has happened to them. Make your excuses and leave. We will have Porthos pick you up, and he will take you to the Plain of Nazca. Are there any questions?"

Peter said, "Yes, will we meet you at Nazca?"

Bill answered, "Yes, you will."

Mark said, "How does this speaking English affect our regular language?"

"Why don't you try this out yourselves?"

Both Mark and Peter spoke in their own tongue and then telepathically. Peter said, "It looks as though we have picked up another language."

Chris said, "We should make a good team."

'Computer, would you please put me through to the space platform?'

'Yes, Commander, working. Here is the map you have requested.'

Bill tore the map from the carriage and handed it to Chris.

'Commander, I have made contact with the space platform. You can communicate with them whenever you want.'

Bill picked up the communicator and thanked the computer. "This is the commander of the star ship *Alpha Centauri* calling the space platform. Are you receiving? Over."

"This is professor Hogan. Your cocommander said you would visit us again in five hundred years. Was she kidding us?"

"No, professor, we weren't kidding. What I am calling you

people about is that I wish to apologize for my behavior. I was too impetuous and expected more from you than you could give. For this I am sorry. It will never happen again."

Yet another voice came over the radio. "We, too, wish to apologize to you and your lovely cocommander, Chris. We hope you will not be gone as long as you say. It is mainly because our life-span is only about seventy-five years."

"We shall see. In the meantime, go with God."

Then another voice came on. "Your cocommander said the same thing about God. Do you really mean there is a God?"

"Of all of the people of earth, you are the only ones who have seen God's works. There is a God who is familiar to air breathers as well as those who are anaerobic. Don't ever discount God. We are composed of very miniscule elements. Someone had to put them all together. Yes, there is a God. He is just not akin to your planet. He is universal. In your travels through space, don't ever forget this. End of communication."

The space platform replied, "Thank you. We won't ever forget what you have said. End of communication."

'Athos, take the ship to the United Nations Building in New York City, New York, the United States of America. Hover over the building at approximately five hundred feet above the building. Porthos, put the invisibility screen on.' He turned to the two passengers.

"You will need some sleep. There are cots in the main section of the third tier. We will be right overhead at all times. It will be Porthos who will take you down in your own craft. When you are through, we will bring the craft down to you. You will then board the craft, which will take you to the Plain of Nazca."

'Porthos, after you let these people off, raise the craft to fifty feet and hold. After you pick Peter and Mark up, go to Nazca. Hover over the base at Nazca and do not land until we say it is all right to do so.'

The two men left to go to the third tier.

'Bill, let's check out the Plain of Nazca.'

'Chris, that's a good idea. But let's do it telepathically.'

205

14

The United Nations, the Fifteen Grain Ships, and the Epidemic on Planet Four

CHRIS SENT A TELEPATHIC message to the Plain of Nazca. Immediately she got a response. All was well at the Plain of Nazca. They had just gotten their crop in and were in the process of replanting their fields. Chris asked them if they were hit hard. The comment she received was amazing. Apparently the forces had thrown everything at them, but the force field was strong and holding. Chris advised them they were due at the United Nations tomorrow and that they then planned to return that afternoon. Chris was strongly advised not to return, in that their force field was ringed by the army. If they were to put the force field down, they could not guarantee someone in the party or the ship itself wouldn't be hurt or damaged. Chris advised them they were not to use force themselves. They would think of a way of getting around the military. They advised it was good hearing from Chris again and asked if everything was all right. Chris reported that everything was fine. Everyone was in good health and they were waiting it out for tomorrow. They would be in touch again. In the meantime, they could package up all of the grain they wouldn't be using into fifteen of the sixteen ships that were just built. The grain was badly needed at Alpha Centauri. Chris was advised this would be done.

'Never again will I question you, Chris. You are indeed beautiful. Why, you know my thoughts before I even have time to utter them. Now, how about you and I getting some shut-eye?'

'Why, Bill, that's the best suggestion I've heard all day.'

Bill went around and checked everything out. He asked Porthos, Dante, and Athos to hold the craft where it was and to call him if anything unusual happened.

Both Chris and Bill went down to the second tier and to their respective rooms. They both slept well that night.

Before they were aware of it, it was already nine o'clock in the morning. It was almost time for Mark and Peter to make their debut. Both Chris and Bill woke up at the same instant. Quickly they got dressed and both popped out of their rooms together.

'You go to the control room, and I'll get our two guests.'

When Bill got down to the third tier, both Peter and Mark were all set. Bill called for Porthos, and he walked both Peter and Mark to their ship. Mark had the film, projector and the map the computer had made. Porthos soon met them. Bill had Chris take the *Alpha Centauri* up to one thousand additional feet, and Dante depressurized the third tier, extended the ramp, opened all the doors to the outside, and turned off the force field. Porthos warmed up the engines, and Peter and Mark got on board. The ship cleared the ramp area and went down to the entrance of the United Nations Building. Porthos let Mark and Peter off, and then immediately rose to fifty feet and held. Bill went upstairs to the first tier. He immediately had Dante put the viewing screen down on the area where the ship was and increase the magnification to six. It wasn't until shortly thereafter that Bill spotted six of the armies' helicopters approaching Porthos's ship.

'Dante, get back to your station. Use the tractor beams and put those six ships on the ground approximately three feet apart from one another. We will let them destroy themselves with their own rotor blades.' Dante did this and it worked.

'Bill, there are six more helicopters coming on fast. This place is really swarming with soldiers. This really was a trap.'

Dante took care of these new arrivals as he had done with the first ones. He put all twelve helicopters together on the ground.

'Well, Chris, this time we had help. That's why I told the space platform we owed them one. I intend to keep this promise. Computer, open all channels to make a direct communication to the entire group of people on the ground.' Bill picked up the communicator.

"This is the *Alpha Centauri*. You are being scrutinized very closely. Let me say that if you even wrinkle my men's clothing or fire one shot, I personally will demolish you and then take New York City apart. This is no threat; it is fact. The ship under my direction is capable of doing this. Put your weapons down. The first ones to go will be those who are still holding onto their weapons. You have exactly three minutes, at the end of which time I will begin to destroy you. You will form sort of an honor guard to the landing site. I hope I have made myself clear."

The soldiers on the ground immediately laid their weapons down. The ones on the roof of the building thought they were relatively safe and held onto their weapons. Bill picked up the communicator.

"You people on the roof are still holding onto your weapons. Is it you wish to die so soon? Would you people in the tanks get out of them? You people manning those field pieces, stand back away from them."

There was a rush on the ground as all of the people left their tanks and those that manned the field artillery moved back. The commander of the troops on the roof told his men to stay as they were.

Bill then told Dante to use his destructor beams on the tanks and field pieces.

Dante did this and they all vanished from sight as if they had never really been there. The men on the roof saw this and they, too, threw down their weapons. The commander held onto his piece.

Bill directed Dante to use the destructor beam on this individual. Dante did this, and the commander — he was a captain — disappeared before the eyes of his men. The men on the roof immediately quit their positions on the roof and joined the others on the ground.

"Human life is very precious to me. I am sorry to have had to get rid of your captain that way."

Soon Peter and Mark came outside. They were quickly able to surmise what had happened. Bill had Porthos lower his ship to the ground, and both Peter and Mark got in. The ship moved upward and then forward. It disappeared in the distance.

"Thank you one and all for the courtesy afforded to my men." 'Athos, let's go home at all possible speed.'

Chris thought, 'Mark and Peter, how did your talk go?'

Peter thought, 'The audience was composed of ringers. Even the ringers were on our side.'

Chris thought, 'Well, that's a step in the right direction.'

'Chris, you saw the map as well as I did. What we have done is stop an immediate disaster. We cannot stop these people from killing each other. As soon as we could get rid of one impending danger, there would be another one. One thing we can't have happen is to let these people be dependent on us. They must be able to work things out for themselves. We cannot interfere any more than we have. Let them work it out somehow.'

'Okay, but I think we should have worked harder. These people are our responsibility, since we emanate from them.'

By this time the *Alpha Centauri* had caught up with the shuttle craft and was shielding it with the proton ray they had just remembered to turn on. Just then they were hit by two missiles. Both of these missiles had nuclear warheads. They hit the proton field and exploded. The *Alpha Centauri* took itself and the shuttle craft up to sixty thousand feet and then headed for Peru. Dante went down to the third tier and the ramp area. He then steered the shuttle craft into the ship. He then told Athos to close the doors, to retract the ramp, and to repressurize the third tier. Athos gave the helm over to Chris and did what Dante had requested. In the meantime, Chris was hovering over the Plain of Nazca.

Dante, Porthos, Mark, and Peter came up to the first tier. They were greeted with a round of applause by Chris and Bill. Peter went into a long dissertation as to what had happened in

209

the United Nations Building.

'Thank you for the time you have expended. You shall soon be home.'

Chris said, "Yes, your efforts on our behalf will not be forgotten. We owe you much."

Both Peter and Mark looked at Chris. Mark said, "No, it is we who should be thanking you. You and the commander have extended yourselves, and for this we are grateful."

"Our major problem now is how to break through the lines of troops that have been established around your force field."

Peter said, "That is no problem. We have enlarged the vents to the extent that our shuttle craft can easily fit through the duct at the South Pole. We can bring the spacecraft out the same way."

"We bow to your ingenuity and to your ears. You heard Chris talking to Nazca last night."

'Athos, head for the South Pole. We can bring the spacecraft out the same way.'

Mark said, "It isn't easily found. We must be very careful in our search."

Athos reached the South Pole. Mark had them make a small circle. Suddenly Mark had them hold it right there. The duct was camouflaged so well it was difficult to see. Peter and Mark went down to the third tier and got into the shuttle craft. Bill told Porthos to extend the ramp, to open the doors, to turn off the proton device, and to depressurize the third tier. He had Dante turn off the invisibility screen.

Soon Chris and Bill saw the craft circling down to the ground. It disappeared in what looked like the mouth of an extinct volcano. Then they were gone. Bill contacted them through telepathy.

'Are you two all right?'

The answer he got back was very precise. 'Yes, your Highness, we are, thank you. It is our job to keep producing food until such time as the planet at Alpha Centauri is proficient enough to produce its own food.'

'Then you know your own job.'

Peter thought, 'The first fifteen ships will be coming out the same way we got in. There is one small favor we would like to ask of you. You promised to show us the new planet at Alpha Centauri. Can you take us there?'

'All right, bring out fifteen grain ships and one shuttle craft.'

Mark thought, 'Thank you, your Highness.'

'Put the shuttle craft in the ship. How fast will the grain ships travel?'

Peter thought, 'They have been designed to go four parsecs per hour in open space.'

'That's good. They will stay in a V formation and will be easy to keep up with.'

He looked at Chris and asked her to rejuvenate the gas supply. 'Take Athos and Porthos with you.'

Chris, Athos, and Porthos went down to the third tier. Chris immediately came back up to the first tier. Bill had a cup of coffee waiting for her. She took the coffee. 'You forgot to mention how cold it was down there.'

'Sorry about that. I only realized it myself when you disappeared. How is the rejuvenation coming along?'

'Athos and Porthos are taking care of it.'

'That's good. I thought we were running low. It is the opening and closing of that ramp door that does it.'

'The space platform is too far north to see anything we are doing.'

Just at that moment, the fifteen ships appeared and the shuttle craft followed close behind. The fifteen ships stayed below and the shuttle craft moved into position for docking. Dante hurried down to the third tier to guide the ship into the *Alpha Centauri*. Soon Dante informed Bill that everything was all right now. He could close the doors, retract the ramp, and repressurize the third tier. Bill did this, in addition to turning on the proton field. The repressurization took them a little while.

Finally they were ready to go. Athos started out and the fifteen ships fell in behind him. The formation was in the form of a perfect V, with the *Alpha Centauri* at the apex. They flew in a straight line toward the stars Alpha Centauri. Peter and

Mark appeared on the first tier with Dante.

Peter said, "I hope you won't mind, but I brought my girl with me."

Bill said, "What's your girl's name?"

Peter said, "This is Lana."

"How much of our conversation is Lana picking up?"

Peter said, "Why, none of it. Why do you ask?"

"If we are to be talking about them, they ought to be included in our conversation. Don't you think that is only right?"

Peter thought, 'Is it all right that Lana comes with us?'

'We have no choice, unless we were to turn around and let her off. Lana, on behalf of all present, I would like to welcome you on board the *Alpha Centauri*. Please sit down and make yourself comfortable. We will reach our destination in about one hour.'

Chris immediately came over with a cup of coffee and gave it to Lana.

Bill excused himself, saying that he would be gone for about a half hour. He asked Chris to take over until he got back. She nodded that she would.

Bill told Athos to maintain a speed of four parsecs per hour. He then told everyone on board he was giving the helm to Chris. He left and went to the second tier. Immediately he went to Chris's room and started to tune the harpsichord.

Although time had elapsed quite quickly, the notes on the harpsichord had retained their fine tuning. Then Bill noticed something unusual about one of the strings in the base register. Rather than striking the string with a plectrum, he removed it entirely and replaced it with a new one. The string started to give off a strange glow. Bill immediately summoned Porthos, but before leaving his post, he was to depressurize the third tier, to extend the ramp, and to open all of the doors. Porthos soon came down to where Bill was, holding a box that was smoldering. 'Porthos, take this box down to the third tier and heave it out the ramp area.'

Porthos took the box and was gone. Soon he was back again. 'I thought we had checked everything about this instrument. It is fortunate you know so much about harpsichords.'

'We were lucky. We should be happy Chris didn't start

playing this thing. I wonder what would have happened if that note was struck by one of the plectrums while we were all gathered around it. As it was, it was some sort of poisonous gas. Porthos, go over this entire instrument again, looking for any more booby traps.'

Porthos went over every inch of the instrument and found nothing.

'I believe you. That string, or whatever it was, would have finished us all off. Let's go to the first tier and see how everybody is doing.'

When they got to the first tier, Chris came up to Bill. Porthos retracted the ramp, closed and sealed all the doors, and repressurized the third tier.

'Well, your harpsichord is all tuned. How about playing a little Bach or Handel?'

'I'm glad you found that little booby trap. I was listening to your talk with Porthos. The others have no idea what has gone on. Their powers are limited, which is good to know. Yes, I will play anything you would like to hear.'

'No, Chris. You play whatever it is you want to. You see, we have an audience.'

He walked up to the three guests and asked them to join him in hearing Chris play. Bill told Athos to take control of the ship and to report anything unusual to him at once. The three very eagerly said they would be more than happy to hear Chris play the harpsichord. Bill turned around, and all five went to Chris's room.

Chris sat down at the harpsichord and started to play, first Bach, and then Handel. The three passengers couldn't believe their ears. Chris was good, very good. The harpsichord resounded in melody. Chris played for one-half hour without a break. No one was timing her.

Just then Bill heard from Porthos. Athos and the fifteen ships were in orbit around planet four.

Bill excused himself and asked Chris to continue playing. It sounded so good he hated to interrupt her.

'All right, I'll keep on playing. Advise me if I might be needed.'

'You're on.' Then he left to go to the first tier. As soon as he

213

got there, he tried contacting Gurkha. Instead, Aryana contacted him.

'Something is wrong. I'm glad you have come when you have. Gurkha and thirty-one others have become ill. They all show the same symptoms. Before you land, please check out our atmosphere. This has me puzzled. Can you help us out?'

Bill contacted the other fifteen ships and told them to hold in orbit around the planet. Then he contacted Aryana again and told her not to worry. He would be down as soon as a check on the atmosphere was made.

Then Chris appeared and immediately summoned the Elders. A voice came seemingly from nowhere and thought, 'Yes, Chris. What is it?'

'We have just heard from planet four. Over half of the population is stricken with some sort of ailment. Do I have physicians in the necklaces? If so, which necklace or necklaces are they on?'

'On the fifth necklace, or the bottom one on your neck, are five physicians. They will be the first five people on the necklace.'

'Thank you for your help.'

'Thank you for considering this possibility.'

'Computer, give us a readout on the atmosphere of the planet.'

'Yes, Commander, working.' Just then a readout appeared on the teleprinter. Bill studied this very closely.

'The atmosphere is the same as when we left it. There are no pollutants. Spore activity is at a minimum.

'Chris, you will have to let those five physicians free yourself. Take Dante with you. In the meantime, I will contact Aryana and tell her of our findings. I also want to explore every avenue so that these people will have something to work on.'

'All right, I understand. Dante, come with me. I'll need your help. Bill, keep me posted on anything you might find.' Chris and Dante left the control room and went to the medical section.

Bill tried to reach Aryana. When he did, he told her they had checked the atmosphere and found nothing wrong with it. He told her to gather all the foods that these people might

214

have consumed. That included all food and drink. It might be more than one thing they are looking for. He would be down in about one-half hour with five very knowledgeable people. They would need these things to make a proper diagnosis.

Aryana said she would have these things ready by the time he set down. She had only thought it might be the atmosphere because so many people were stricken by this ailment.

Bill told her to hang on. There was help on the way. Bill told the fifteen ships to maintain their orbit. He would advise them when he knew everything was all right.

'Computer, take another atmospheric check at ten thousand feet. Chris, how are you doing with those five doctors?'

'All I can say is I have had a very sexy experience. All of them are dressed and ready to go.'

'H'mm! Make sure that all of the equipment is turned off and that you have extricated the necklace from the machine.'

'That's already been done. Dante and I are bringing the five to the first tier. See you then.'

Athos reported that he was now at ten thousand feet and holding. The computer had just finished its second readout on the atmosphere.

Bill looked at the computer's findings and immediately saw it was the same as before.

15

Planet Four ——————————————

JUST THEN CHRIS CAME in with the five doctors. Then the other guests appeared. All three immediately bowed to the five physicians. Mark thought, 'We had no idea we are among the most dedicated doctors of our time.'

'It looks like we have a problem on the planet that calls for good doctors. Until it is taken care of, we must ask you three to stay on board.'

He turned to the doctors and told them about the atmospheric checks he had made. Also, he told them a girl named Aryana was gathering all the food substances, including the liquids consumed, and should have them ready for inspection by the time they set down.

One of the doctors asked for all the drugs and facilities of the medical laboratory.

'Our house is yours. We have all of the known ailments cataloged on tape for your perusal. This is an adjunct to the main computer.

'Athos, land the ship at the main complex. Porthos, turn off the proton device.'

As soon as Athos landed the ship, Porthos depressurized it, extended the ramp, and opened all the doors.

Bill told the three people to get thirty-one cots from the third tier and put them in the hospital section. He said he wanted three of the doctors to stay in the medical section. 'Porthos will bring you everything he finds. Two of you doctors are to come with me for a firsthand look at the matter. Athos and Dante, you will come along with us.'

One of the doctors thought, 'Your Highness, please permit

us to introduce ourselves. My name is Tiahuanaco, this is Dr. Sacsahusman, and the three over here are Drs. Kuyunjik, Sumeri, and Akkadian.'

Bill looked a little flustered. 'My apologies are extended to you all. I didn't realize I was addressing people of such eminence. If I can be of any assistance, please don't hesitate to ask.'

'Bill, do you know these people?'

'Only through what we call ancient history. All of these people figured into our past development. All of them were revered and honored in their day. Chris, you are looking at the development of our planet earth when you look at these men.'

'I didn't know.'

'Unfortunately, there aren't many who do. Christian zealots have seen to it that all of the past was the work of nonbelievers, and nationalism says their glorious ancestors did these things.

'One more thing you could do, Chris, is to take that small geiger counter with you.'

Chris left the control room followed by three of the doctors and went to the medical section. She showed the doctors how they could use the tie-in to the computer. She picked up the small geiger counter and left to go to the third tier. The robots were ready to take them down to the ground.

When they did get down, they found a very concerned Aryana waiting for them. Chris introduced the two doctors Tiahuanaco and Akkadian to Aryana, who acted a little surprised. Aryana advised them she didn't ask for doctors of such high rank. Akkadian advised her everything possible would be done to curb the ailment.

Akkadian thought, 'How is that old warhorse Gurkha?'

Aryana thought, 'He still lives. He'll be happy to see you again. And Tiahuanaco, too. It has been such a long time. I know I am glad and honored to see you both again. Over there is the drink and the foodstuffs Bill had requested.'

Porthos gathered up all he could carry and immediately went back to the ship and the medical section. He came back for a second load and disappeared again.

Tiahuanaco, Akkadian, Aryana, Chris, and Bill made the

217

rounds of all those that were stricken. As they were making their rounds, they passed a woman who was grinding grain. Bill asked Chris to go over the grain with her geiger counter. It showed an unusually high degree of radioactivity. Bill asked Aryana where the grain originally came from. Aryana advised that kernels of the grain were taken from the other planet. Bill then brought Tiahuanaco and Akkadian over to where they were and showed them the abnormal reading they were getting on the geiger counter. The doctors asked Aryana if everyone was consuming the same grain. Aryana replied everyone was using the same grain. It was a part of their daily consumption. The doctors turned to Bill and asked him to get those ships down as soon as possible. Bill knew what they meant and told Aryana to burn the fields of grain.

Aryana looked at Bill. 'You can't do that.'

Bill looked at her and thought, 'There are fifteen ships up there waiting to come down and land that are loaded with grain.'

Aryana gave the order to her people to immediately burn the fields.

In the meantime, Bill told the ships to land beside his craft. He had the computer set up a homing signal to guide the grain ships to land beside the *Alpha Centauri*.

The computer acknowledged Bill's request and advised him that would be done.

The doctors said they wished to go to the medical laboratory. Bill summoned the robots and told them to convey the doctors and Chris back to the ship. He advised them he would stay there to make sure the grain was distributed correctly. Aside from that, he wanted to stay with Aryana because of her love for Gurkha. Chris and the two doctors were transported to the ship by the robots and then disappeared from the ramp area.

Bill turned to Aryana and told her to assemble all her people in the spot where they were standing, for immediate inoculations, and to bring all of the tools they used to grind their grain with them. They were too radioactively contaminated to keep around. Those implements had to be buried. After that was done, they would have to make new grinding tools.

Aryana gathered all her people together and told them what had to be done.

Bill thought, 'Aryana, you are a very beautiful woman. I have one question for you. In all that I have read—which was termed ancient history on earth—the Aryana that was depicted was a girl with only four fingers on each hand, not six. Can you tell me why this was?'

'The only reason I can think of was the space gloves I wore. It was in these gloves that there were only four digits. At the time, it was thought only four digits were required to operate the spacecraft.'

Bill looked at her and thanked her for her patience with him. He thought that every now and then stupid questions would pop out of him and that she could easily handle them with the care and patience she was exhibiting now.

Aryana laughed at this. 'Bill, with the help Chris and you have given to us, you can ask anything you want to. I will be more than happy to answer one question at a time.' Bill thanked her.

Bill turned to the ship and asked Chris how she was coming.

Chris thought, 'Everything is going quite smoothly. It has been determined the entire population has been consuming small amounts of radiation with every bite of food they've been eating. An antidote has just been made up for the entire population of the planet. It seems the birds and animals have also fed on the grain. These birds and animals can't be treated and will soon die off. All five doctors are ready now and will be transporting down. I'll see you in a few minutes.'

At that moment the ships started to land close to the *Alpha Centauri*. They made a perfect circle around it. The pilots, with their copilots, deplaned and came up to Bill and deeply bowed before him and Aryana. Bill was quick to notice the copilots were women. He pointed to a clearing and told them to pile the grain their ships held in the clearing. After they were finished, they were to report to him. They all started to work as Bill had directed.

Then Athos, Porthos, and Dante came down from the ramp with three doctors under tow. They deposited these three close to Aryana and Bill. Then they went up again for Chris and the other two doctors.

219

Bill thought, 'Aryana, you have already met doctors Tiahuanaco and Akkadian. Now let me introduce doctors Sumeri, Kuyunjik, and Sacsahusman.' Aryana bowed deeply, as did the three doctors.

Aryana looked at Bill and thought, 'You really don't horse around when you ask for help. This is the greatest honor that I have had. Do you have any idea as to who these people are?'

'Yes, each of the five were very prominent figures on earth.'

'Please tell me whom I have been addressing as Bill. Who or what are you really?'

Bill asked her if it really mattered.

'Yes, it does matter. No one but one of the highest rank could have gathered these five doctors here in one time and one place, except a king.'

Sacsahusman thought, 'His Highness is a little shy. He is also a little backward about titles.'

Aryana bowed to Bill and thought, 'I'm sorry I have treated you as an ordinary person.' She had no way of knowing, but she and Gurkha had surmised that such was the case.

Bill looked at all of them and thought, 'You people all have a job to do. We can talk about titles and other things later. At the present time there is a planet that needs our help.'

Just then Athos, Porthos, and Dante appeared with Chris, Tiahuanaco, and Akkadian. Bill thought, 'Chris, help to inoculate the people.' Chris moved over to where Aryana was, who immediately bowed to Chris. Chris looked a little bewildered and puzzled.

Sacsahusman told Chris, 'Please forgive me, your Highness, but it was I who told Aryana who you really were.'

Chris told Aryana she should rise and not stand on formality. There was a job to be done. Until that job was accomplished, both she and Bill would be known by their first names. Nothing else.

The five doctors and Aryana bowed to both Chris and Bill and thought, 'By your leave, we will go and attend to these people.'

Bill thought, 'By all means, go with our blessings.'

Chris went with Aryana, but before going, she looked at Bill and thought, 'Maybe it is a good thing the cat is out of the bag. I will see you later.' Then she, too, was gone.

220

Bill turned to the robots and told them to get the three people who were left on the ship and to bring them down to where he was. The robots left immediately.

Soon all thirty people reported to Bill, saying they were finished with the unloading of grain. Bill looked over their heads and saw a large mound of grain. Bill told them that he needed a hospital built that would accommodate seventy-five people. They said they would get working on it immediately.

Aryana came running up to Bill and thought, 'One of the pilots of the small craft has come up to me and asked where he might find a rock quarry. After I gave him the directions, he was gone as quickly as he had appeared.'

'Aryana, don't worry. I asked that a hospital be constructed. With the help of the lasers and holding beams on those small ships, the job will be accomplished. Why have you left your people?'

'With the help we received, the inoculation of all the people, including me, has been accomplished. Chris and the doctors immediately went to help those who were already stricken.'

As she was talking to Bill, the first of the ships had returned with a large block of stone, very neatly cut.

'Aryana, get your people together and take the grain away. Half of it is to be planted and half is to be ground up.'

'It will be done now.'

'Thank you, Aryana. The time has come for some hard work.'

As he was saying this, five more slabs of rock had been delivered and some fifty beds were lined up. Bill told her that what he said was not in jest. Aryana disappeared to get her workers.

The three passengers were deposited next to Bill by the robots. Bill told the engineer he thought the fifteen ships and the thirty people should remain here on this planet. He wondered how soon the engineer could have fifty such craft ready and set to go.

The engineer thought that fifty ships could be ready to go by the time it took them to get back, but they would need power packs.

Bill told him that the power packs were ready to go. Bill

221

then asked the engineer if he would be needed for the final assembly of these ships.

The engineer thought he would be needed.

'That settles it. You're going back with us. You other two people are free to remain here with your friends on this planet.'

The other two looked at Bill, and the man said, 'Begging your pardon, your Highness, but we have talked a long time about this, and we also would like to be with you on your return to the planet earth. We, too, think we can be of some assistance.'

'Well, it looks as though we have some permanent passengers. On behalf of Chris and me, I can only say welcome aboard. Now, if you people don't mind, I need some help over there. I'm having a hospital built and need your expert handiwork.' The three left and went over to the construction site, once again leaving Bill alone.

Bill told Porthos to take him up to the ship, and he had Athos and Dante check out the gas supply. All four of them went up to the ship. Porthos followed Bill to the control room. Athos and Dante broke out the rejuvenation equipment.

Bill sat down after he had gotten a cup of coffee. He lay his head back and, through telepathy, he concentrated on the earth base. Soon he reached them and asked how they were doing. The answer he received was that everyone was fine. The military had stopped trying to get into the base. They had a large supply of grain to be picked up and shipped. Bill told them that he needed fifty more spacecraft built such as the one they had there. He would supply the power packs when he got back. Also, the seating would be for four people, rather than for two. These ships were to come to the fourth planet of Alpha Centauri. He asked them how much grain they'd be able to haul with four people on board.

A person answered, 'That means fifty ships times four, or two hundred people. That would leave the base with 370 people. By increasing the size of the ship, we could easily carry the same amount of grain as the original fifteen ships did without much difficulty—or a reduction in speed, for that matter.'

'All right, get busy on those ships. We'll discuss who goes

and who stays upon my return to planet earth. I am thinking there will be a constant rotation of people. Is everything clear? I should be back in another four or five days. It was nice talking with you.'

At that moment Chris came into the control room with Dante.

Dante faced Bill and thought, 'The gases are all right now. Athos is putting the equipment away. Chris wanted to come on board, so I went and got her.'

'I overheard your conversations with the three passengers and also with the station on planet earth. Why are you leaving fifteen spacecraft here? Do you think it is wise to abandon our station on planet earth? What do you have in the back of your mind?'

'I believe these people will need the fifteen ships to construct the city that is needed and to provide transportation from one continent to another. It is not my intention to abandon our established base on planet earth. But I see no reason to have a large contingent of people at the station when they are not needed there. Back in the recesses of my mind there are 3.5 million people. There is much that this planet offers. I think we should establish this planet for our base of operations. Do you disagree? If so, give me a better plan.'

Chris was silent for a while, then she summoned the Elders. A voice came through loud and clear. 'Yes, Chris, you called?'

Chris then told them what had transpired.

'Yes, we have been listening also. We think the commander is correct in his action. This is indeed a fine place to live. But remember, Commander, when you free these people, it does not mean you will get rid of us. You are stuck with us until you die.'

'Can you extend our lives by another five thousand years? That would make a total of ten thousand years.'

'All right, ten thousand years it is.'

'Thank you very much.'

'Bill, that's a long time.'

'All the more time to love you. That thought appeals to me.'

'You're just a horny old man. But when you put it that way, I like the thought very much.'

Dante interrupted their conversation and told them that the

people had finished the hospital and needed a power pack for lighting. Bill advised Dante one power pack was coming up and that he would be down with it directly. He also wanted to see the hospital.

Dante disappeared, and Bill went to the second tier. He went into the hospital section and drew out one power pack. He went down to the third tier and the ramp section. Porthos had been following him all this time. When Bill was ready, Porthos took him down to the ground, where he was met by some very enthusiastic people.

One of the men thought, 'Your Highness, the hospital is almost ready for your inspection. All we need is a power pack to supply the lighting, which has already been put in place. We would like to have you inspect it.'

Bill advised them that he was carrying the pack and was anxious to see their endeavors. He said whoever handled the power pack had to be careful with it. There was deadly radiation in it.

The engineer made his appearance, 'Your Highness, you should have nothing to worry about, since it will be I who will be handling this pack. If your Highness would be so kind, I would like to borrow your antiradiation gear.'

'Porthos, go up to the medical section and bring down the antiradiation gear.'

Porthos was gone and back in an instant. He gave Bill the gear. Bill handed it over to the engineer, who took it and was gone.

Just at that moment, the five doctors made their appearance with Aryana and Gurkha.

'Ah, Gurkha, it is good to see you up and around again. You look far better now than you did when I last saw you.'

'It is you again. Why is it you come when I need you the most? Once again, it is doubly good to see you.'

Bill called for Chris to join them, for they had guests.

Gurkha told Bill he wasn't certain why he and Chris always seemed to show up when they were needed the most. He said he had a long discussion with Aryana about this. Then he had the great honor to meet with the esteemed doctors. Never before had he been so honored. They, too, had a long discussion about him and Chris. He wanted Bill to know that whatever they could do to help him get started, he and his people would be pleased to do. As far as he and his people were concerned, Chris was their queen and Bill was their king. Anything he asked them to do would be done without question.

'Gurkha, I am overwhelmed. Thank you for your vote of confidence.'

At that moment Chris appeared, and everyone bowed to her.

Then Bill resumed his talk with Gurkha and informed him that within a few weeks there would be 3.5 million people there. They would need a city built and beds to sleep in. They would need all the accoutrer, and, above all, food. It was their job, along with the thirty people who had come with him along with their machinery, to get this job done. In addition to the thirty people were another two hundred who would be coming soon. They would be carrying grain also. They would need a landing strip constructed.

Gurkha asked if there was someone he could work these plans out with.

Bill looked around, and his glance came upon a pleasant sort of man. 'What, sir, are you called?'

The man thought, 'Your Highness, I am called Forest Swanson.'

Bill seemed to be a little taken back. 'Sir, you are the first one I have met who has two names. Henceforth, you shall be the liaison between Gurkha and his people and yourself and your people. We are all working toward a common cause here. That cause is the establishment of 3.5 million people on this planet.'

Forest Swanson told Bill he could count on him. 'Your Highness, does this mean you are going to leave the fifteen ships here?'

'Your assumption is correct.'

Just then the lights went on in the hospital. Bill invited Swanson, Gurkha, the five doctors, and Chris to go with him to inspect the building. Out of respect he also asked Aryana to come along, and he took her hand. The tour lasted only a few minutes.

'Swanson, is there anyone here who can make a computer?'

Swanson said he didn't know, but he would find out. He was gone. Soon he was back saying that there was a man who was very proficient in that regard.

Bill asked him to have this person report to him immediately. He then turned to the five doctors and asked them how they liked it.

Akkadian thought, 'As a shell it is excellent.'

'I understand what you are saying, and all I can say is: it's a start. We had to begin somewhere.'

At that moment Swanson came running up to Bill with his computer expert.

'Can you build a computer?'

The man said that he could.

'Henceforth, you will be working with Dr. Sumeri.'

Bill told the doctors it would not be easy, but they were going to do it. The doctors told Bill they had no doubt of it.

'Swanson, I want to see the person who can tap the core of this planet.' Swanson soon arrived with this individual.

'I want you to tap the core of this planet. I want you to tap the core in such a way to generate enough electricity to provide enough heat and light for an entire city.'

The person said he would do this.

Bill said he would be away for about two weeks. When he returned, he wanted everything ready. Both Swanson and Gurkha assured him that would be done, in addition to the housing.

Bill thanked them very much and motioned to Chris and the others. It was time they got going.

16

The Encounter with the Aliens, the Rescue and the Space Platform, the Plain of Nazca

BILL WISHED EVERYONE the best of luck. Then he turned to Porthos and told him to take him up to the ship. He told Athos to take Chris up. When both he and Chris were on the ship, in the ramp area, he had Porthos and Athos go down again for the others. Once there, they all went to the control room.

Chris immediately went to the dispenser and got some coffee for Bill and herself.

The engineer thought, 'Aryana, Gurkha, the five doctors, and the entire population of the planet wish to thank you very much. They all wish you Godspeed and a safe return.'

Bill thanked him very much for the message. He told Dante to get some chairs for their guests. Dante disappeared and soon came back with the chairs.

'Athos, close the doors to the ramp, retract the ramp, and repressurize the ship. Dante, effectuate our own gravity. Porthos, take the controls and link in with the computer for navigation.'

Then he asked the passengers if they wanted any refreshment. They thought that would be a nice idea. Bill told them to go to the dispenser and get whatever they wanted. He also told them where the washroom was. The entire ship was repressurized, and Bill asked the computer if it was all right to take off.

The computer replied everything was operational.

Bill asked the computer to give a flight plan to Porthos for their trip back to planet earth. Then, turning to Porthos, he thought, 'Do not land, but maintain an orbit around the planet until the gases are checked out. Rise above the atmosphere of this planet, and then head for earth at seven parsecs per hour.'

The ship rose straight up beyond the atmosphere. After a course correction, Porthos kept on increasing the speed until he was traveling at seven parsecs per hour.

'Dante, turn on the proton field.' Dante confirmed that it had already been done.

'Chris, monitor the radio.'

'Bill, what am I monitoring for?'

'I don't know why, but I have the feeling we are being watched. I don't know why I feel this way. I hope I'm wrong.'

'Unfortunately, these hunches you have have always been right ones.' She went over to the radio and very slowly started to listen to all of the frequencies. Suddenly she stopped turning the frequency gauge and started to listen.

'Damn your intuition, Bill. They've picked up our craft and are in pursuit. They are to track this craft down and blast it from the universe. There are two of them.'

'Dante, turn on the invisibility screen. Porthos, bring this ship to a dead stop. Athos, adjust the screen to the rear and increase the magnification to six. Dante, get back to the panel and man the holding and disintegration beams. Athos, increase the inside temperature to seventy-five degrees Fahrenheit.'

'Those ships are getting closer. The communication is becoming louder. They say they have not lost us in that they know where we are going. Their tracking devices have lost us. They are maintaining their present course.'

'Okay, we have a visual. We are right in their path. Porthos, raise the ship fifty thousand feet and hold.'

Bill asked the computer how fast these ships were going. The computer replied it estimated the speed to be four parsecs per hour.

They watched the ships go directly beneath them.

'Porthos, pursue and catch up to these craft. Dante, get ready on the disintegration beams.'

By this time Porthos was directly above his targets. Bill adjusted the viewing screen down on the two ships and told Dante to fire at will. Dante fired and they looked down on where the craft had been. There was no debris; they had just vanished from sight.

'Porthos, drop down by fifty thousand feet and resume a course to planet earth at a speed of seven parsecs per hour.' He adjusted the viewing screen forward and changed the magnification to two. 'Athos, turn off the invisibility screen.'

'It's the home base. They are wondering why they haven't heard from the two ships.'

'And we won't tell them, either.'

The passengers were overawed. They saw it, but they couldn't believe it.

The engineer thought, 'We weren't aware of your power. Where did those ships go?'

'They were vaporized; they no longer exist.'

Bill told his guests they need not be concerned, since these people had been warned. The two ships were destroyed because they had been given the order to wipe out the *Alpha Centauri*.

Chris got up from where she was sitting and went to the dispenser. Bill saw this and asked her for a cup of coffee.

'Coming right up, sir. The alien has declared a state of emergency. All of their available craft have been directed to the Alpha Centauri system. They are to wait for you there.'

Bill thanked her for the coffee and the information she had just given.

Porthos advised them he was entering the galaxy and was starting to decrease his speed. Then he announced he was in orbit around planet earth.

'Computer, give us a readout on the atmosphere.'

The computer responded by giving him a complete printed readout. Bill tore off the results from the carriage and studied them. Nothing had changed.

Porthos advised they were fast approaching the space platform.

'Porthos, hold it, and park the ship just a little above the platform. Computer, open all hailing frequencies.'

The computer advised that that had been done already and that Bill could talk at his leisure. Bill picked up the communicator.

"This is the star ship *Alpha Centauri*. Does anyone copy?"

A voice said, "Just one minute, *Alpha Centauri*. We couldn't be happier."

This was broken up by yet another voice. "Hello, *Alpha Centauri*! We desperately need your help. Would you help us out?"

"That all depends on your problem. What is it? How can we be of assistance?"

Bill asked the computer and Dante to listen into this conversation.

The voice continued, "About two weeks ago we sent out one of our ships on a scouting mission. Since then, one of the rocket banks went out on them on the portside. They are stuck out there and cannot get back to base. We need your help to bring them back. Our recovery craft will not be ready for another two weeks. Even then, we are afraid the ship has gone so far out that by the time help arrives, it will have been too late for the crew. Can you help us out by retrieving this craft?"

"Do they have a transmitter? Are you still in communication with them?"

"That is an affirmative, *Alpha Centauri*."

"Have them send out a distress call. Then have them keep their key open for five minutes."

"*Alpha Centauri*, we are in touch with them right now. They are sending out a distress call and will keep their transmitter on for five minutes."

'Computer, have you picked up the coordinates yet?'

The computer replied that it had and was giving them to Porthos. As far as the computer was concerned, the request was a sincere one. Dante confirmed this opinion.

"All right, we have locked onto the coordinates and will pursue. Tell your ship that help is on the way. In the meantime, open up your ramp doors for receipt of the craft."

"Thank you, *Alpha Centauri*. We will open up the ramp doors immediately. End of communication."

The *Alpha Centauri* headed to the coordinates at seven parsecs per hour and arrived at its destination within minutes after its communication with the space platform.

Bill had the computer run a complete scan on the damaged vessel and asked for conclusions.

The computer replied there were six persons on board, all very healthy, and that the rocket assembly on the portside had meteor damage.

'Dante, put the tractor beams on the ship. Porthos, take the ship back to the space platform at six parsecs per hour.'

Within minutes after the request had been made, the *Alpha Centauri* reappeared at the space platform. It deposited the craft gently on the opened ramp.

'Dante, put the invisibility screen on. Porthos, take us to the Plain of Nazca.'

When they got there, he had Dante turn off the invisibility screen and had Porthos take the ship up to one thousand feet above the force field and center it. Then he had the people of the base turn off their force field. He got to within fifty feet of landing and advised them to reactivate the field again. He had Porthos land the ship.

'Athos, turn the temperature down to sixty-five degrees Fahrenheit. Dante, open the doors, extend the ramp, and depressurize the ship. Porthos, turn off all the instruments and equipment.'

Chris stayed by the communication gear for a while. Then she turned off the radio and moved directly to Bill's side. She looked at him. 'You are going to see these people who wanted to exterminate us, aren't you?'

'You know, it's been a long time since I told you that you are beautiful. Well, you are beautiful. I think I love you very much. In answer to your question, yes. Nothing will harm either you or these people again.'

The computer thought, 'Well, that was very well put, Commander. I think I am a little jealous.'

'Hold on, Computer. I love you too.'

'I believe you. You are sincere. Have a good time ashore, folks'

Bill then asked Athos, Porthos, and Dante to accompany him to the hospital section. He told Chris to take their three

231

guests to the ramp area and said he would meet them all in a little while. Then Bill and the robots left the control room.

Chris turned to the three guests and asked them to follow her. All four went to the ramp area and waited. The crowd of people began to thicken and the roar of tumultuous praise lifted high in the air.

Bill soon made his appearance with the robots. They were all heavily laden with the power packs. Bill instructed the robots to take him down first with the power packs and then to go up for Chris and then the passengers. They took Bill down, unloaded the power packs, and all three of them went up again for Chris. After this was done, they went up a third time and brought the passengers down. When the robots came down with the passengers, both Chris and Bill got a hearty round of applause.

Bill suddenly looked at Chris. 'There isn't any force field. Did I turn it off? I can't remember.'

Athos thought, 'I turned it off, Commander, as we were making our way to this place. I am sorry to have usurped your authority, but I thought it was best.'

Bill thanked Athos very much.

'Well, that proves we are not perfect. I want to thank you, Bill, for everything you said up there. It wasn't taken for granted. I do appreciate it very much. I think though, that I've had it.'

The engineer came up to Bill. 'The ships are all ready, your Highness. All they need are the power packs. We should be ready to take off in the morning.'

'I would like to lie down somewhere and sleep,' thought Bill.

The first man and his woman came up to Chris and Bill. 'Your sleeping quarters are ready. If you will follow us, we will show you where they are.'

'That's the best offer I've heard all day. What do you think, Chris?'

'Lead on, MacDuff. I, too, can't wait to hit the sack.'

Instead, they were interrupted by the computer. 'Sorry to interrupt you, Commander, but there is an urgent call from the White House. It seems that the president wishes to talk with you.'

'I wonder what he wants. Computer, tell the White House that his Highness is indisposed and will contact him eighteen hours from now. Right now, he is going to have a long rest.'

The computer acknowledged the commander and said it would be more than happy to do so. The computer then wished Chris and Bill a pleasant and relaxing rest.

Chris and Bill followed their friends into a great hall and then to the bedrooms. Bill didn't even bother getting undressed. The moment he saw the bed, he lay down on it and was out like a light. Chris was more fastidious. She took off all her clothes, found a nightshirt to put on, lay down, and immediately fell fast asleep.

All was quiet for the next sixteen hours. Both Chris and Bill slept that long. All during this time the people were working feverishly to get the ships ready. Among themselves they had determined who would go and who would remain. The process they used was very democratic. No favorites were distinguished among the others. Chris and Bill would have been proud at the way this was handled. The decision was made with the whole idea that these people would have to observe the planets and the galaxy, and they would have to grow as much grain as possible.

When Bill got out of bed, he was very groggy. He went over to the wash basin and cleaned himself as best as he could. Almost immediately Athos, Porthos, and Dante were there.

Athos asked if his commander had a good rest.

'I had more than enough. I wish I remembered to bring my razor and the other shaving gear with me.'

Dante thought, 'That's all taken care of. Some people will be in to shave you.'

Bill looked a little puzzled and perplexed.

Porthos thought, 'These people just want to please you. It is a simple gesture on their part, for all that has been done for them.'

At that moment three young women appeared. One with a basin, the other with towels, and the third with a straight-edged razor.

The first one, the one with the towels thought, 'If your Highness is ready, we will wash and shave you.'

233

Chris awoke under similar circumstances. As soon as she was out of bed, there appeared three women. They gave her a thorough bath and fixed her hair. At first she didn't know what to make of it, but finally she decided to go along with them. After a while she found it extremely enjoyable to be fondled.

When Chris and Bill met again, they were dressed in long flowing robes. Chris looked at Bill. 'I see they got you, too.'

'Chris, you couldn't look more lovely.'

Chris only laughed. 'Down, Rover.'

Suddenly they realized they were not alone. They looked around them and realized they were both in the great hall, and this hall was packed with people.

Bill asked them all to sit down. He knew there was some urgent business to attend to.

Just then the engineer came up to him. 'The ships are all ready to go. The grain has been loaded and the crews picked. This was accomplished while you were still sleeping.'

Bill looked at him, 'By gosh, you all seem to have everything under control. As far as the three hundred people are concerned, it is not our intent to leave you here too long. We will be back for you. Or, if you think you can grow more grain there, since you are growing under artificial conditions, you are all welcome to go back with me. One thing I want you to realize is that my ship makes you three hours away. Under no condition are you to consider yourselves abandoned. If for some reason you feel pressured from the outside, give me a call by using mental telepathy and I will be there. The main reasons that I am asking you to remain are for the grain and your astronomical abilities. We must have a third base, which I haven't situated yet, to keep watch on the movement of bodies within the heavens.'

They all stood up and applauded Bill. He was deeply touched by their response to his thoughts. These people were solidly behind him, and he appreciated it very much. It didn't make him feel so alone.

'Don't ever feel you are alone again. I never knew you felt this way. Please forgive me, Bill.'

'Beautiful, there is nothing you have or haven't done that needs forgiveness.'

234

Bill held his hands up to the people. 'There is one more thing I would like to say to those who will be returning in the fifty ships that I will be escorting back with me. I want you to divide into groups of five. That means you will have ten groups. The ten groups should be separated by about fifty miles in a straight line. The five ships in each group should be twenty-five miles apart, starting from the leader, and twenty-five miles back. In essence you will be creating ten stacks of five and these should all fly in a wedge with my ship as the apex. Each ship in the stack will be making a wedge also, so that we will have five wedges. This will make us all look like military men with our ships equipped with weaponry. It is essential that we mislead those people who are still fighting us. Well, that is all I wanted to say. Except good luck to you.'

'You are still expecting trouble, aren't you?'

'Yes, Chris, I am.'

There was more applause and then Chris and Bill were treated to a feast in their honor. After he was filled, Bill excused himself and, with Porthos, left the party, saying he would be right back.

Bill and Porthos made their way to the ship. Porthos got Bill on board, and then the two of them made their way to the control room. When they got there, Bill asked the computer to patch him in with the White House. After a while the computer advised everything was in readiness. Bill picked up the communicator.

"This is the *Alpha Centauri*. Is anyone receiving this communication?"

"*Alpha Centauri*, this is the president of the United States of America talking. I don't know what to call you. Commander or your Highness. Which title do you prefer?"

"Mr. President, I am also known as Bill. I think this fits me best of all. How can we help you out?"

"I have heard from the space platform that you have saved the lives of ten people. I wanted to personally thank you and say we appreciated your action in this regard."

"Hold on, Mr. President. My scanners only showed six people and four caged animals. Not ten, as you have said. One thing that we do not do is destroy life — any life. It is only after warnings we even consider taking a life or lives, as the case may be. We have destroyed many people, but only because they wanted to destroy us. We also have saved many more people than we have destroyed. Your planet was one that was saved. It is through these people that I wish to convey this thought. There is a God. He does exist. Not only for this tiny speck of dust you call earth, but for the entire universe. That includes many galaxies and many planets that have life on them, just as you have life on planet earth."

"I must caution you. Your every word is being transmitted on radio as well as television."

"Were my last words conveyed to the people?"

"Yes, they were."

"I hope so. Nothing is more important to me."

"Then there is nothing you would care to retract?"

"I wish to add to this and not to retract anything. I would like to say that when you visit other planets, and some day I believe you will, you remember these people, whom you are visiting, will also have a God. Keep this in mind and respect him as you do your own God. Tomorrow I will be leaving you. It is imperative that I do so. I will come back to observe your progress. Your very puny efforts to dominate one another is of great interest to me. It is very stupid when you consider there is a whole universe out there to explore and protect."

"This conversation is a little strange. You tell us there is a God and then you tell us you have destroyed many people. This God you refer to must sanction the taking of lives."

"Only if there is no other way. The people we disposed of were trying to play the part of gods. It is very similar to your trying to impart that the love of country is one and the same with the loving of God. Well, these people took it one step further. They literally and figuratively dominated whole planets under the guise of eternal brotherhood. We eliminated these people and thereby set the planets free. This freedom is necessary in order to find the true meaning of God. I had better get off my soapbox."

"What, may I ask, do you have in store for us here on earth?"

"At the present time, you are less than insignificant. I am sorry. I do not wish to demean your people in any way. I have gotten rid of two peoples that were about to dominate you.

You are free to develop or kill yourselves off. But this will be your decision. Your people have yet to reach maturity. At the present time you have nothing to offer. Your sciences are still in the realm of growing. Take your time. I will see it all happen, but you will not. As I see it, you have the choice of either blowing yourself up with your childish weapons or learning more about the sciences and loving your fellowman. Our time has come to a close. Is there anything further you wish to say?"

"I wish to thank you for the time which you have spent with me. It's hard to accept the fact we are so insignificant and have yet to reach maturity beyond that which we have already obtained. We hope your trip will be a good one."

"Thank you. End of communication." 'Computer, tape and monitor the rebuttals on radio and television. I only hope I didn't make a complete ass of myself.'

The computer agreed to put everything on tape.

Bill and Porthos went back to the party. They really had not been missed, for there was too much merrymaking.

Chris found Bill. 'I have heard what you said to the president and how you were trying to give him a message. I wonder what the effect will be. Do you really think you can tell them that they are not the kingpins they have always considered themselves to be and that they will have to grow up and mature?'

'It would be hard for anyone to accept. I don't think people will believe that, but at least it might make them stop and ponder. Their role on this planet would have been absolute and unequivocal power and domination. All we can do now is sit back and watch.'

'Well, there is one thing we have done. It was to show them there is another race of people who are more advanced and stronger than they are.'

'Perhaps you're right. We will see everything when the wash is hung out to dry. In the meantime, let's go to bed. We both have a busy day tomorrow.'

'Your Highness, are you suggesting that we go to bed together?'

'Unfortunately, no. Although the thought has occurred to me many times.'

'All right, I am giving you fair warning. Watch out, brother. I am going to attack you when that day finally comes.'

'Beautiful, you have a deal.'

They both went to their bedrooms and got ready for bed. When he had finally put his head down on the pillow, he kept on thinking what he could do on earth. There must be something he had overlooked. Whatever he had forgotten or overlooked was gone now. He had his chance, and he thought he had blown it. There was no more time left for him. He was about to embark on a new and exciting life that didn't include the world's problems. He also thought about Chris and how much he loved her. He rolled over on his side and soon was fast asleep.

During all of this time Chris had Bill's wavelength tuned in and followed his thoughts with interest. Finally she thought to herself, 'Bill, you didn't fail as you think you might have. I too, love you with all my heart. Our life together is going to be enriched and full. Try to sleep, my darling.'

The morning came fast. It seemed as though there wouldn't be enough time. Bill had coordinated everything through the engineer. They were to meet the fifty ships at the South Pole where they had picked up the other fifteen ships. Everything was ready.

17

The Elimination of the Alien Vessels, the Establishment of Life in the Alpha Centauri System

CHRIS AND BILL HELD A final meeting with the people who were to remain at Nazca.

'You have all heard what the commander has said to you. We are indeed three hours away from you. You can reach us at any time telepathically. The main things that we are interested in are the planets and planetoids that may crash into earth and/or planet four of the Alpha Centauri system. We want this culture to survive, above all costs. We appreciate your readiness to help by staying here, both keeping tabs on the terrestrial bodies and growing the grain that is so urgently needed on planet four. On behalf of the commander and myself, we wish to thank you very much.'

There was another round of applause by those who would be staying.

Chris, Bill, the engineer, the first man and his woman, and the robots went to the ship. Athos, Porthos, and Dante carried them all to the ramp area. Then they all went to the control room where Chris and Bill took their places on the lounges and the other three sat down on the chairs that were provided.

'Computer, were you able to document all of the radio and television coverage and rebuttals?'

'I have all of the information. They used the whole conversation. They didn't delete anything. You sound good.'

'Thank you, Computer. Athos, take the helm. Porthos, turn

on the invisibility screen, retract the ramp, close and reseal all of the doors. Dante repressurize the ship, turn on our own gravity, and raise the temperature to seventy-two degrees Fahrenheit. Athos, bring the ship up to fifty feet and hold.'

Bill notified the people on the ground to turn off the force field.

Soon he got confirmation from the ground. Athos ascended to ten thousand feet and held.

'Porthos, turn on the proton field.' Bill then notified the people on the ground to activate their force field again. He thanked the people for their hospitality. 'Athos, go to the South Pole.'

At the South Pole they found all fifty ships waiting for them. Bill had them arrange their ships into a wedge that was six hundred miles long and twenty-five miles deep.

'Chris, as soon as we leave the gravitational pull of earth, I want you to man the radio on or about the same frequency that you picked up those other communications.'

'I hope you will let me finish my coffee first.'

'Okay, beautiful. Take your time. Computer, where is the space platform?'

The computer replied that it was directly overhead.

'Athos, deviate your course and fly right by the space platform at a level of one hundred thousand feet above it. Dante, turn off the invisibility screen.'

They continued to orbit around planet earth until Athos found the right window for the Alpha Centauri system. The ships broke off toward Alpha Centauri at a speed of four parsecs per hour.

Chris already manned the radio. 'You have really gotten those people on earth talking. The space platform says it has taken pictures of you and your fleet. They have never seen anything like it. They have estimated you had a wedge that measures seven hundred miles long by about twenty-five miles deep. All of the ships looked very formidable. The pictures have turned out well.'

'Let's hope we can fake these other people out also.'

'You were right, Bill. There are six ships waiting for us. Their commander is with them. Their lead ship has spotted

240

our formation and has advised the other ships of our coming.'

'Do you have the coordinates of this lead ship?'

'Yes, I have given them to the computer.'

Bill picked up the communicator. "This is the *Alpha Centauri*. I am going to disappear for a little while. Maintain your course, positions, and speed. You are on a direct course for the Alpha Centauri system. If I don't return, keep going and you should reach your objective. Remember you are looking for the fourth planet. Good luck to you all. End of communication." 'Porthos, turn on the invisibility screen. Athos, take the new coordinates from the computer and increase your speed to seven parsecs per hour. Dante, get ready with the disintegration rays.'

Bill went over to the viewing screen and adjusted it forward at a magnification of six power. Then he went over to the dispenser and got himself a cup of coffee. He sat down in one of the lounging chairs and watched. Soon he spotted the ship.

'Athos, start slowing this ship down to three parsecs per hour. Chris, do you have the coordinates of the main body of ships? Is this lead ship of theirs still broadcasting?'

'The data on the main body of ships has been given to the computer. Yes, the ship in sight is broadcasting.'

'Athos, bring our ship within range of Dante's rays. Dante, disintegrate that ship.'

Athos got within range. Dante fired his rays, and the ship disappeared.

'Athos, proceed to the next coordinates at seven parsecs per hour. Get your navigation from the computer.'

Within fifteen minutes Athos had reached the next coordinates. Bill spotted the five ships, which were also in a wedge formation.

'Athos, slow it down to two parsecs per hour. Chris, can you pinpoint the main ship?'

'That should be an easy thing to do. The vessel having the most communications emanating from it is the center ship.'

'Athos, enter within range of the ships from the side. Dante, disintegrate all of the ships but the center one.'

Soon Athos got within range of the first two ships. Dante fired his disintegration rays and eliminated these two ships.

Athos then bypassed the center ship and got within range of the other two ships. Dante fired, and those vessels also disappeared.

'Athos, stop the ship and turn off the engines. Computer, set up a communication between our ship and theirs.'

The computer replied that it was ready for Bill to speak. Bill picked up the communicator.

"This is the *Alpha Centauri*. Does anyone pick up this communication?"

"Yes, Commander. What is it?"

"If you will look to the right or left of you, you will find that your vessel is the only one left. If you count how many lives have been lost—four hundred people per ship—you will see that forty-four hundred people have lost their lives. What, may I ask, are you trying to accomplish?"

"Now that you put it in those terms, I really don't know. Are any of these ships or people returnable?"

"You jest at a time like this! All of my weaponry is trained on you. And all you do is make light of it. I will come to your home base and we can talk further about you and what you are attempting to do. Right now you have exactly ten seconds to get out of there before I change my mind." 'Athos, reverse your direction and raise the craft five thousand feet.'

The commander of the alien ship started his vessel up and advanced it by ten thousand feet. Then he held his craft still at this point.

'Dante, blast the ship out of existence.'

Dante fired and the ship vanished from sight.

'Porthos and Dante, check out the tiers. Any unexpected visitors you see, knock them out and bring them to the control room. Athos, return to the ships. It will be good to talk to some sane people again.'

Athos started to move the vessel out at a speed of seven parsecs per hour. Soon Bill found himself at the apex of a very somber wedge of ships.

A voice called to Chris and Bill. 'Welcome back, you two. We can't see you, but we know you are there. We were starting to worry about you.'

'Porthos, turn off the invisibility screen. From now on we are going to be escorted.'

In a little while they were in the Alpha Centauri system and in orbit around planet four. Bill had the smaller craft land first.

'Porthos, turn off the proton field. Athos, land just a little ahead of the incoming craft.'

He looked around for Dante but didn't see him.

'Porthos, extend the ramp, open the ramp doors, and depressurize the ship.'

After they had landed, Bill ordered Athos and Porthos to go hunting for Dante. He advised everyone to stay where they were. He knew that something was wrong. Soon Athos and Porthos returned with two stowaways. Their weapons and communication gear had been taken away from them, and they were both unconscious. Porthos and Athos went out again and soon came back with two more stowaways, unconscious and weaponless. They found Dante on the third tier. He had captured six of them and was keeping a tight surveillance on them. These six were unconscious, deprived of their communication gear and their weaponry.

'So that stinker had placed ten people on board by molecular transference to sabotage and wreck this ship. That is why he was so bland in his comments to me. He was trying to buy time. He didn't realize that we would be ready for him.'

Then they bound their captives. Bill had Athos, Porthos, and Dante go through the ship, looking for more stowaways. After a few moments all three robots came back and said the ten were all that there were. Bill ordered the robots to take the stowaways off the ship first, then the three passengers, and then Chris and him. He asked Gurkha to lock these ten people up.

Gurkha thought, 'It will be my pleasure.' He and two other people took these ten away.

'Aryana, what progress, if any, has been made by you, Gurkha, and Swanson?'

'You wouldn't believe your eyes. We have accommodations for 3.5 million people. The tap to the core has been made, and hot and cold running water has been supplied. The electrical and heating facilities are miraculous.'

'Where can we find these accommodations?'

'You will find these buildings directly to the north of us.'

243

Bill then asked Aryana, Gurkha, Swanson, the engineer, the first man, and his woman to take a trip with him to the north. Aryana became excited and told Bill to hold on. She would get all the people together. Bill also told her to get the five doctors. Aryana told him he would have these too.

'Dante, get eleven chairs for our guests in the control room.' Dante disappeared.

Aryana soon came back with the five doctors, Swanson, and Gurkha.

'Now that we are all here, we should get going, except for one small detail. Aryana, how is that grain doing in the soil?'

'The grain is doing well. We just had our first harvest from it.'

Bill pointed to the fifty ships that had landed with him. He told Aryana all fifty ships were loaded with grain and that she should make provision for it.

Aryana stopped a few people and told them of the stored grain. They told her it would be taken care of.

Just at that moment the squadron leaders came up to Bill and asked him what they should do with their craft. They requested additional orders as well.

'There will be some people who will help you with the unloading of the grain. Hold out twenty-five ships with grain to travel north on my order. I am going north with Chris and these other people to see a city. I have to check this out. As for the rest of you, I will be back shortly. And I will have a job for you.'

The squadron leaders saluted and left.

By this time Dante had returned. Bill asked the robots to convey all their passengers, including Chris and him, to the ramp area. This done, they all went to the control room. Chris showed them the dispenser and invited them to try it.

'Athos, take the helm. Porthos, retract the ramp, close and seal off all doors. Dante, repressurize the ship. The proton field and the invisibility screen are to remain off.'

The robots did their jobs.

'Dante, put the viewing screen down by ninety degrees and increase the power to six. Athos, take this ship up to ten thousand feet and proceed north at a speed of four hundred miles per hour.'

244

All the passengers tried out the dispenser and were really enjoying themselves. The ship seemed to be passing over high mountainous terrain. It was a spectacle of beauty to behold. Bill asked how far away this city was.

Aryana thought, 'It is some six hundred miles due north of our complex.'

Bill immediately advised the group leaders to unload everything but the twenty-five ships. He wanted twenty-five ships loaded with grain to come immediately due north about six hundred miles away. He got an immediate response from the commanders that twenty-five ships were in flight and that they would meet them there.

'Porthos, put the proton field on. Watch out for any sign of burnout of the outer hull. Athos, increase our speed to five parsecs per hour. Gurkha, why has this spot been chosen?'

Gurkha thought, 'It was the easiest place for them to tap the core.'

Quickly they passed a city. 'Athos, stop. Go back over the city, and hover above it.'

Bill studied the structure closely. 'It looks as if you have done a good job here. What do you think, Chris?'

'I can't help thinking I have seen this somewhere before.'

'Good girl. What you are looking at is an ancient Mayan civilization — circa two thousand earth years ago.'

Bill then asked Athos to land the ship. Athos chose a plain that was as flat as a pancake. After Porthos had turned off the proton field and Athos had landed the ship, Porthos extended the ramp, opened the doors, and depressurized the ship. Bill then asked the robots to go down to the third tier and rejuvenate the gases.

'If you people will come with me and rejuvenate some people, I would appreciate it.' All the guests followed Bill to the medical laboratory.

The doctors were amazed at this laboratory. Akkadian thought, 'Do you mean medicine has advanced so far?'

'That's the trouble. It really hasn't. You, among all your colleagues, should know this laboratory best, doctor. And yet you express wonderment. I don't understand this. Please explain.'

Dr. Akkadian cleared his throat as if he had some obstruction in it. 'It must have been the light, or, maybe I was too concerned about the illness that had befallen the planet. The fact is that I didn't see, until now, all of the things you have.'

Bill asked the engineer if he might be able to duplicate all that he saw.

The engineer thought, 'Yes, I think this can be done. Can I take some notes?'

Bill told him to go ahead. Then he asked Porthos how they were doing.

Porthos replied that they had just finished and were in the process of putting the bottles and equipment away.

'Athos, how far from the ground is the ramp?'

'Commander, it is forty-two feet.'

'When we were coming in to land, I noticed a small group of round hills to the west of us. Porthos, retract the ramp. Athos, take the ship over to one of those hills, so that the ship's back end is facing the mound.'

Athos thought, 'It is certainly worth the try.'

'I don't want anyone down here experiencing motion.'

Athos thought, 'That is understood, Commander.'

'Computer, are you there and listening?'

The computer replied, 'Yes, Commander, I am.'

'I will need some help from you. On the necklaces Chris is wearing are 3,499,394 people. Please keep a count on those that do appear.'

The computer replied it would keep a close count.

'Thank you, Computer, very much.'

Chris thought, 'Well, I guess we are all ready.' She slid in the first necklace and the people started to pop out of the machine. All of the doctors and the others helped each person get out safely and to get dressed. Bill showed them out of the medical laboratory, down to the third tier, and out through the ramp area. Chris started another necklace as soon as the first was finished and emptied of people. As soon as she was through with the fifth necklace, everyone that was coming out had made his or her appearance.

'Computer, what is the count?'

The computer replied it had counted 3,499,393 souls.

'Chris, we are minus one person.'

246

Excitedly, they ran all of the necklaces through the machine. They didn't go in any order because they hadn't arranged the necklaces in any order. Finally, they were about ready to give up. The fifth necklace was almost through when out of the machine popped the missing link.

'You don't know how relieved we are that you were found,' they told the new arrival.

Chris thought, 'Welcome aboard the *Alpha Centauri*.'

It was a woman, who was as glad as Chris and Bill were. She thought, 'I'm sorry to have caused you so much trouble.'

Chris thought, 'Don't give it another thought. I don't know how we might have missed you in the first place. But that is over with now. Go and live a very useful and exciting life.'

Bill then ushered her out the ramp area and came back for Chris. He held her for a long time, and then he lifted her face. 'You know something? That could give me ulcers.'

'One thing's for sure. You wouldn't be alone.'

The computer thought, 'Commander, the twenty-five grain ships are about ready to land.'

'Tell Athos, Porthos, and Dante we will meet them at the ramp area.'

Chris and Bill appeared at the ramp area. The round of applause that met them was deafening. Bill told Athos and Porthos to take him down to the ground, and he asked Dante to follow them.

The handshakes and the pats on the back were strange to Bill, but he knew what they meant. These people, Chris, the robots, and he had been through a lot together. Now they could rejoice and be happy for the first time. Bill had become one of them, and he knew Chris had also. It was only from some divine power that they had come so far. Bill would never forget this. Certainly he had become a father to 3.5 million people, but he had also reinforced his ideals. Bill walked toward the grain ships, which had just landed, and he knew Chris was scanning his mind. She knew everything he was thinking, and why shouldn't she? Her life and his were one and the same. They both had the same goals, desires, and values. He also knew it wouldn't end this way. There was too much for him to do.

The commander of the lead ship came up to him. He bowed

low and thought, 'Your Highness, where would you like the ships deployed?'

'Make a circle around my ship and tell the people to help themselves.'

Bill wanted to get back to the *Alpha Centauri,* but he knew he couldn't do this just yet. Bill helped the pilots and the people unload the vessels and helped to pile the grain into one tremendous mound. Chris stayed in the background and watched Bill work. She knew Bill was troubled, and finally she took it upon herself to do something about it.

She had Porthos take her back to the ship. Porthos carried her up to the ramp area. She and Porthos then went to the control room. Chris got a cup of coffee from the dispenser. Then she sat down on one of the lounging chairs, leaned back, took a couple of sips of coffee, and then summoned the Elders.

There was a long pause. Then a voice answered, 'Yes, Chris, what is it?'

'Bill is worried that you might have forsaken him.'

'No, we haven't forsaken him or you.'

'Thank you very much for replying to my request to speak with you.'

'That's all right, girl, we understand. Feel free to call us anytime.'

Chris was relieved and contacted Bill. 'Bill, they are still with us. I just contacted them.'

Bill stood up straight from what he was doing. 'Thank you, Chris. I was sure you would try. I feel much better now.'

The work went very rapidly. A group of men went out and hunted some wild game. When they returned, they had enough fresh meat to last them awhile. The women took some of the grain and made patties and loaves of bread. Bill supplied the teabags and they all had some hot tea.

Chris rounded up the first man, his woman, the engineer, the five doctors, Gurkha, Aryana, the robots, and Bill. 'We should get back to base before it gets any darker.' They all agreed with her, except that they advised her not to leave Swanson out. Chris agreed not to.

Bill told the commander of the twenty-five ships that he and his men could stay until morning, but that he had to go back now. The commander thanked him and said he and the twenty-five ships would be back in the morning.

Chris and Bill were put on board first, then the passengers. They all met in the control room, followed by the robots.

'Wait a minute. I'm sorry, but I don't see Aryana.'

Dante said he would go look for her. He soon came back with her.

Aryana thought, 'I was just admiring the medical section.'

Bill told her the engineer had memorized the room and that soon they would have their own room.

Aryana was very humble. 'I am sorry if I caused you any undue anxieties.'

'Don't trouble yourself worrying. Chris and I have enough ulcers for the entire population.

'Porthos, retract the ramp, close and seal the doors, and repressurize the ship. Dante, put on the proton field after we are above ten thousand feet. Athos, take this ship up to thirty-five thousand feet, and proceed south to the base at seven parsecs per hour.'

Athos's next comment was that they were there.

'Dante, turn off the proton field. Athos, land the ship.' He then informed the people that they were at the base. They looked at each other in disbelief. Athos landed the ship. Porthos depressurized the ship, extended the ramp, and opened the doors.

Bill told the people it was all right to follow the robots to the ramp area, where they would disembark. They all looked at Chris and Bill. Chris thought, 'We have much to do before we get off. We will see you all in a little while.'

They left with the robots, and Chris and Bill finally found themselves alone. Chris and Bill walked up to each other. They embraced for a long time.

'Bill, how would you like some coffee with cream?'

'That's the best offer I've had all day.'

Chris went to the dispenser and got two cups of coffee.

Bill reclined on one of the lounging chairs. Chris went to the other one. 'Don't you think it's about time we found out what we have to do?' With that, he called for the Elders.

A voice answered immediately, 'Yes, Commander, what is it that you want?'

'We have been through a lot. What else do you want from us?'

'After your takeover of the alien base, which is something I know you are going to do, you will make sure that these people have nothing but peaceful intentions. You will make sure of this all the days of your life. You will also make sure that these people believe in God and follow the Ten Commandments. Let the Bible be your guide. It will be your job to prevent any alien from subjugating these people. You are to play father, protector, and brother to these people. In your case, Chris, it is mother, protector, and sister.'

'What you are asking of Chris and me will be very difficult to accomplish. Are you aware of that?'

'I don't think it will be difficult at all.'

Chris thought, 'Thank you for the time you have spent with us. We really do appreciate it.'

After this conversation, Bill told Chris they really had a job cut out for them.

'Yes, we do. Shall we go out and prove it to ourselves?'